PRAISE FOR *FRIENDS IN NAPA*

"Smart and wildly entertaining . . . like drinking a glass of wine with an endlessly witty, scandalous friend."

—Mindy Kaling

"A perfect dose of suspense and deliciously complex friendships . . . Come for the mystery and friend drama; stay for the unbelievable lifestyle details. Marikar knows the best of the best from her years of writing about luxury travel, and it sparkles on every page. You'll be packing your bags for Napa. The vineyards, the food, the fashion, every chapter is a dreamy escape—with a dark edge. It's a Liane Moriarty set in gorgeous wine country."

—Kate Myers, author of *Excavations*

FRIENDS IN NAPA

ALSO BY SHEILA YASMIN MARIKAR

The Goddess Effect

FRIENDS IN NAPA

A NOVEL

SHEILA YASMIN MARIKAR

MINDY'S BOOK STUDIO

This is a work of fiction. Names, characters, organizations, places, events, and incidents are either products of the author's imagination or are used fictitiously. Otherwise, any resemblance to actual persons, living or dead, is purely coincidental.

Published by Mindy's Book Studio, New York

www.apub.com

ISBN-13: 9781662513152 (hardcover)
ISBN-13: 9781662513176 (paperback)
ISBN-13: 9781662513169 (digital)

Cover design by Tree Abraham
Cover image: © Benito Martin

Printed in the United States of America

First edition

For Nikhil Lal

A NOTE FROM MINDY KALING

A weekend getaway with your besties from college in beautiful Napa Valley? What could go wrong? If you are a fan of shows like *The White Lotus* or films like *Knives Out* and *Glass Onion*, then you know a lot can go wrong. Very wrong.

In Sheila Yasmin Marikar's *Friends in Napa*, a group of friends from college is invited to celebrate the opening of a friend's fancy new winery. It's not long before someone ends up dead, and we see that behind the perfectly aged wine, expensive wineglasses, and designer clothes, the characters are simmering with jealousy and greed. Luckily for this gang, there is someone who is willing to take a stand when things turn especially sour.

Friends in Napa is smart and wildly entertaining. Reading this book was like drinking a glass of wine with an endlessly witty, scandalous friend. I knew right away it had to be part of Mindy's Book Studio.

PROLOGUE

Saturday night
Kismet Cellars, Napa

The first thing anyone would notice, upon entering the winery, would be the puddle, dark red on the brink of black. The dim track lighting bounced off it like glints of sun on the surface of a river, and despite the drainage slats that ran down the center of the slate-gray cement floor, the amount of liquid refused to decrease. Or maybe it just appeared that way, because there was so much of it and it was staining everything: the Valentino heels, the Tom Ford tie, the Purple Label that, irony of ironies, was now practically purple.

It was a dry cleaner's nightmare. Correction: it was a nightmare, period, the type of scene from which you wanted to wake up immediately, clutching your sheets, thanking God that it hadn't actually happened.

But it had. It had, and now it was time to deal with the aftermath. No one was here—yet. This mess could be cleaned up. Because that was what had to be done, right? There were reasons, valid ones, ones that a judge—or at least the court of public opinion—would get behind, but they had to be presented in the right way, and that required the cleaning up of this mess. Alone. Because this, right now, was impossible to explain. The party would be ruined. Kismet Cellars would never recover—well, it *definitely* wouldn't have recovered had this *not* happened, but that was beside the point.

Arrests would be made. Charges would be filed. Press, mug shots, a body bag—no. It couldn't come to that.

Paper towels. There had to be paper towels in the winery. Or a regular towel? A mop? A rag? Wouldn't it make sense to keep the cleaning supplies here, where the wine was actually made? This floor had to be on some sort of mopping schedule. Monthly, if not weekly. Bottles had to break. Things had to happen.

Probably never things like this.

Something, anything, even a bunch of paper would help. Did people keep paper anymore? Was Xerox still a company? There had to be something, a binder of wine labels, a collection of wine lists, some coffee-table book about Burgundy or Bordeaux or some other far-flung region, something with pages as big as blankets and as smooth as silk. Well, one of those books wouldn't do much good; the mess would slide right off, and it took a certain type of skill to tear a page from that sort of binding, rigid as . . . *a dead body*, how awfully apt—to do it cleanly, and what a pity that would be, another thing ruined, another casualty, and it didn't matter anyway because there were no books in this godforsaken cellar and—

What things to think. Mopping schedules, Xerox, *books*, at a time like this. A sure sign of panic, psychosis, maybe both.

Every step produced a sickening sloshing sound and the sinking realization that the winery contained nothing but wine, tanks and barrels and bottle upon bottle, stacked in cedar racks that stretched up to its domed ceiling. The door to the cellar, where the supposedly priceless bottles were kept, creaked open, swinging on its hinges, wrought iron key still in its lock. It had bars, like a jail cell.

Time. There was time. It would drain. And then the body. *The body.* What to do with the body? Could wine dissolve a body? How long would it take? Could it be sped up? Would heat help? Or more alcohol? Or acid—didn't they use acid in movies? Could you make acid out of wine?

The motion-sensor lights clicked on. The staccato of stilettos bounced off the walls. Time evaporated. Someone else was in here. Someone else who had seen and heard it all.

1

Thursday morning
American Airlines flight 179, JFK to SFO

Anjali glanced up from the papers in her lap and thanked the beverage cart for its divine intervention. *Finally.* She had told herself that she would spend the time between takeoff and the appearance of the beverage cart editing James Moran's six-thousand-word screed on the ramifications of artificial intelligence on food production in southern Italy, but, good God, it was so boring it was a miracle she hadn't fallen asleep.

All she had wanted when she assigned this piece was a roving, romantic, sign-of-the-times-type story about twelfth-generation farmers butting heads with the tech company that had deployed tomato-picking robots across their rolling hills. It was a dream assignment, one a million journalists would kill for (not least for the per diem), a story meant to make you yearn for an afternoon in the Puglian sun, for a tomato sauce that lights up the inside of your mouth and leaves it begging for more.

Moran had decided to focus on the robots. The bland, steel robots. No one yearned for robots.

"I think he's lost it," she murmured, half to herself, half to David, although a cursory glance in David's direction confirmed that he was asleep, open-mouthed, head lolling on a C-shaped travel pillow in a way that she knew would make him complain about his neck for the rest of the day.

Well, she thought, as she stuffed the draft into the seat-back pocket, she'd tried. The robots would be waiting for her on Monday. Today was, technically, a vacation day, the first she'd taken since becoming a senior editor at *Highbrow*. She'd fastidiously set up an out-of-office reply before leaving Rockefeller Center the afternoon before.

> Thank you for your message. I will be out of the office until Monday, July 17, with no access to email.

What a farce. She'd refreshed her inbox even more obsessively than usual since turning on that autoresponder. Did anyone ever have "no access" to email? An OOO just gave you license to not reply, and even then, not all the time. (A photo editor had frantically emailed her prior to takeoff, and while Anjali had already listed the email addresses of not one but two people to contact in her stead, she had replied, because it was easier, and it was a thing to do, a box to check, a way to affirm her enduring role at the magazine and in the working world writ large, to underline the fact that, despite her age and dependents and clear misalignment with Gen Z, Zillennials, or whatever the pretty young things were called these days, no one could do her job better than her. You let down your guard, someone fifteen years younger and several thousand dollars cheaper swooped in. It was a fact.)

Yes, this was her and David's first vacation without the kids in years. ("Vacationing" with young children was just parenting with a better view, if you were lucky.) Yes, these four days were supposed to be about reconnecting—with David, with her college friends, whom she hadn't seen since the last wedding, eight years ago. But she couldn't just give up her responsibilities. She was a professional. She was important. She had things to achieve.

She'd sprung for the in-flight Wi-Fi "just in case," she'd told David, who'd shrugged as if twenty-nine dollars was of no consequence to them even though Anjali knew it was, and sure, she wanted to be reachable in case Lucie or Ryan needed her—she could hardly trust her sister to manage the basics of childcare, let alone a special case like Lucie—but she knew the real reason she wanted, *needed*, internet access was that she didn't want to be left out. Of work, of the news cycle, of whatever was trending online. And yet, every time she picked up her phone, she scolded herself. You should be reading. You should be writing. You should be editing that Moran draft.

She wondered if a condition of being an adult was that you always thought you should be doing something other than what you were doing.

The beverage cart had reached the last row of Economy Plus, which was the row in front of Anjali. She had, upon boarding, felt a pang of longing for those magical years, pre-Lucie, pre-Ryan, when she had a job like James Moran's at another magazine, reporter at large, and roamed the world chasing stories, racking up airline miles, achieving Executive Platinum status, which meant she got upgraded more often than not. It had been almost a decade since she'd flown first-class, two years since she'd flown at all, and her and David's combined loyalty miles or advantage points or whatever terminology airlines now used to make you think that you were playing a game when you were simply getting played had dwindled to 634. They were in seats 19E and F. Middle and aisle, which Anjali had claimed on account of her bladder, which had the capacity of a ziplock snack bag. (The smallest size. The inordinately tiny size. The size in which even an apple slice had to squeeze.)

David owed her the aisle seat. Oh, the things he owed her. She sometimes liked to make a list in her head, balancing grievance with remuneration.

She wished she was the sort of woman who'd accept a tennis bracelet as an apology. Well, she wouldn't *turn down* a tennis bracelet; she wasn't made of stone, but it wouldn't even occur to David to make a grand gesture like that, even if they could afford it. The problem with joint credit cards: if he spent $7,000 at Tiffany's, she'd get a fraud alert. As if she didn't already know.

Charitable thoughts. She was supposed to be thinking charitable thoughts—about her partner, about her marriage, about their life.

A club soda. She'd have a club soda and read the *New York Times* opinion piece that everyone in media was posting about and then get back to the Moran draft, use her trusty red Sharpie to X out fat, bloated paragraphs. It would be more virtuous to order plain water, no ice, for sure—better for hydration, better for tooth enamel—but she was allowed to live a little. Balance, it was all about balance. She got to have a treat because she was being virtuous, because she had earned it.

She was about to embark on a long weekend in wine country. How good would that first sip of bubbles taste if she knew she'd gotten this draft out of the way? How righteous would that feel? And maybe, if she churned through the Moran draft, she could go over that content marketing firm's pitch about how they could boost *Highbrow*'s social media engagement, add her two cents—after all, she had brought her laptop and paid for the Wi-Fi, she ought to make the most of it. If she wanted to keep moving up the ladder, she had to make the most of every hour, day off or not.

Or was she just afraid of what would happen if she let her mind wander?

The beverage cart inched closer. She watched as two women in the row diagonal to hers ordered mimosas, "hold the OJ," and giggled with the flight attendant, who did exactly that. One had on fur-lined Gucci mules, the other, open-toed Ugg slides. Did travel footwear get less practical? she wondered, as Ugg Slides wiggled her bare, purple-pedicured toes. Stilettos. Stilettos would be less practical. But only whores flew in those. Although, who knew, it had been so long since she'd traveled, maybe the whores also wore open-toed Ugg slides now.

God. She was so judgmental. Anjali's toes curled inside her Skechers (the kind that supposedly toned your butt, though she'd seen no evidence to that effect). When had she become this person? This boring, basic, working mom, forever refreshing her feeds?

The spirit of fun wafting off the two women was palpable, like that sickly sweet Victoria's Secret perfume that seeped out of the store and into the mall. They looked about the same age as her. Highlights, blowouts undone enough to demonstrate that they didn't *really* care. Childless women toasting their freedom with plastic cups of champagne. Childless and jobless, they had to be. Who else would be that brazen, this early in the morning?

"MILFs without borders?" The flight attendant cackled, peering down at what must've been a logo on a chest. "Okay, those are the best sweatshirts I've ever seen."

"We made them," Gucci Mules said. "Nordstrom just ordered thirty-six hundred."

So not only were they mothers, they were working mothers, working mothers that other people, presumably, given the acronym across their chests, would like to fuck. And buy sweatshirts from.

"Anything to drink?" The flight attendant, still glowing from his interaction with the borderless MILFs, had reached Anjali. He looked down at her, his smile fading like the sky after sunset.

"You know, I think I'll do a white wine," she said. "Actually, make it two."

~

She couldn't remember the last time she day-drank. Maybe half a flute of champagne in the conference room after a big issue closed, but that didn't count—that was just for show, solidarity, not for the genuine thrill, for the hell of it.

She unscrewed the cap of the second mini bottle of Robert Mondavi chardonnay. Some of her best memories could be linked back to that loose, lawless feeling that came with getting certifiably buzzed while the sun was still bright. Maybe it was the lack of food in your system, the absence of a base to soak up the alcohol. Drinking after dark always felt appropriate, social. Drinking during the day: subversive, naughty, borderline negligent. Bad.

She was with Rachel the first time she discovered the joy of day-drinking. Freshman year, Slope Day, the campus-wide bacchanal that capped off Cornell's spring semester. Things between them had recently gotten weird. Well, they'd been weird for a while in Anjali's book; she didn't know if Rachel felt it, too. They'd met up in Raj's suite in High Rise Five (the Four Seasons of freshmen dormitories) to pregame before heading down to the slope, where they'd technically not be allowed to drink on account of being under twenty-one. They had planned to fill Poland Spring bottles with vodka and Sprite; Raj had said his newly acquired frat brothers at Sigma Phi would "totally hook it up" when their supply ran dry. "I've got a case of Goose at the house," he said. The house was at the bottom of the slope that connected West Campus to the clock tower and the library with the good chairs, the cushy ones that Anjali liked to sink into when she had reading to plow through.

She had spent a lot of time in that library. She had no idea what Goose was. She watched as Raj reached beneath his desk for a frosted glass bottle, filched, presumably, from the stash at Sigma Phi, and glugged several shots into her and Rachel's red Solo cups. She thought vodka only came in plastic jugs with built-in handles, like gallons of milk. That's how she'd know what to get, she figured, in the distant future, in the off chance that she grew to actually enjoy the taste of vodka.

"What if it's not there?" Anjali asked, forcing herself not to wince as a splash of Grey Goose and Sunny Delight hit her tongue. "What if someone steals it?" In her mind, fraternity houses were havens of lawlessness, places where men lurched into walls and women ran around with their tops off. She had never been inside a fraternity house.

"Such an auntie," Raj said, pinching her cheek. She savored the touch of his fingertips on her skin and felt their absence when he drew back. She took another sip, a real one, hoping that he'd notice, see how tough she was.

He slung his arm around Rachel, who was standing between them in a ruffled, cropped Forever 21 tank top. Anjali was wearing a T-shirt. A regular, non-cropped Cornell T-shirt.

"Has your friend always been such an auntie?" Raj asked Rachel, who reprimanded him with a high-pitched utterance of his name and a playful shove. "That's gonna be my new nickname for you," Raj said to Anjali. "Auntie-ji." He ruffled her hair and walked off to find Hari, who was controlling the music, and who'd let Coldplay interrupt a streak of 112.

"Sorry," Rachel had said, in that exaggerated way of someone who doesn't want you to feel bad but also doesn't want to be responsible for whatever upset you. "He can be a dick when he's drunk."

Anjali had resisted the urge to tell Rachel that she knew quite a few varieties of drunk Raj and didn't need to be educated about their nuances; that, in the semester prior to Rachel's arrival on campus, she had gotten to know Raj quite well. She knew what Raj looked like when he was sleeping. She knew the soft skin in the crook of his neck. She had not gone "all the way" with him yet; no, she had needed to work up to that, but she had left campus, prior to winter break, with the smug satisfaction of the newly coupled. So what if they didn't call each other boyfriend and girlfriend? So what if every time she reached for his hand in public, his fingers slipped away? She knew what they had, and what they had was special.

Or so she thought.

Instead of elucidating any of this to Rachel—she never had, never would—she'd taken another gulp and suggested they chug their drinks and run down to the convenience store for sour worms. Really, Anjali had just wanted to get outside, and once they were on the sun-dappled quad, the scent of freshly mowed grass making a memory of Raj and Hari's suite, all Acqua di Giò and late-stage teenage testosterone, the

Goose kicked in, and Anjali felt this was what she had been waiting for, this was it: these were the best years of her life.

She grabbed Rachel's hand and they spun in a circle until they fell down in a heap, laughing. Who gave a fuck about Raj? Anjali thought then. She and Rachel had known each other since they were three days old. They were best friends, practically sisters. Chicks before dicks, and all that jazz.

She couldn't remember what they talked about during that brief interlude before they went back to High Rise Five and then down to the slope, but she remembered a feeling, a warmth, a pervasive sort of happiness, a sense that she was making a core memory, something that her subconscious would reference for years to come.

~

Now, as she rifled through her carryall for her cardigan—her nubby beige defense against the assault of airplane AC (feminism's final frontier)—she scoffed at herself. Oh, to be young and naive. She wondered if Rachel ever thought about that day. They hardly kept in touch now, beyond the obligatory HBD! and How are you? It's been forever. After those text messages came the propositions for a proper catch-up call, then the sharing of schedules, then the calendar invite, but inevitably the date would get postponed or forgotten about, and after some exclamatory sorries, their thread would go dormant again until the next birthday rolled around. You could set your watch by it.

Had Anjali dropped the ball more often than Rachel? Maybe. But Anjali had the hardest job of all—she was a mother who worked. What did Rachel do? Rachel had all the time in the world.

Anjali had thought about calling Rachel, when the invitation arrived. It was extravagant, over-the-top, something fit for the wedding of a Bollywood star or child of an oligarch: a cardboard box that contained a map, two logo-emblazoned baseball caps, embossed cards detailing the weekend's proceedings, and several handfuls of those crinkly-paper packing scraps that never fail to fall all over the floor.

There would be wine tastings, tasting menus, tours of vineyards so exclusive they had waiting lists to get on their actual waiting list. The main event: the grand opening of a Napa Valley winery recently acquired by Raj and Rachel Ranjani. A winery newly christened Kismet.

"No way," Anjali had murmured to herself. She flashed back to that moment, on the quad, with Raj, a seeming eternity ago. The run-in after their first kiss. Her calling it kismet, him screwing up his face. "You mean, because we kissed and then we met?" Her laughing and not quite believing that this man—boy, really—actually thought that's what the word meant, but also relishing the fact that she could teach him something, that maybe this . . . she couldn't call it a relationship yet, but whatever it was—maybe it had legs.

That couldn't have had anything to do with this, could it? Surely, this name had to have been decided upon after hiring a branding firm and doing competitive analysis and weighing the opinions of at least a dozen different well-paid professionals. You couldn't just name a multimillion-dollar winery—Anjali did not know much about wine, but she had heard a lot about Bay Area property values, and five seconds on Google revealed that Kismet was not a dilapidated-barn type of place—after some moment you had freshman year of college?

Right?

She swept that to the corner of her mind as she picked up a gold-rimmed card:

We can think of nothing better than marking this momentous occasion with our ride or dies, our college crew. Just get yourselves here, everything else is on us.

The itinerary unspooled over several more gold-rimmed cards: three nights in a Restoration Hardware–furnished vineyard estate. A dedicated Mercedes Sprinter to pick them up from the airport and ferry them about. An opening night gala—dress code: "Napa nice"—with a special performance. Meals to whet the appetite of foodies and skeptics alike, including a dinner by Sammi Ali, formerly of the three-Michelin-starred San Francisco restaurant Ali—"Halal cart by way of Noma," according to the *Times*—who would come to the estate and cook for them. Anjali had never been to a three-Michelin-starred restaurant. She couldn't remember the last time she'd been to a restaurant that didn't dole out crayons and coloring-book place mats when you sat down.

"We haven't been anywhere besides the shore in forever," she'd told David when he emerged from his "office" (which also functioned as the guest bedroom, gym, and Ryan's playroom) and joined her in the kitchen. She could think like an Upper West Side elitist—she and David had lived there for years—but her suburban New Jersey split-level told the truth: the prodigal son. Or daughter. Whatever—the girl who thought she was too good for the "dirty Jerz," all grown up and back to where she started.

He turned over the cards. "Don't you hate these people?"

"I don't *hate* them," Anjali said. She couldn't blame David for thinking so. Anjali used to have a habit of sending him Rachel's latest social media post with a comment along the lines of "Can you believe this bitch?" (Owing to "the incident," as their couples counselor called it, Anjali no longer sent David anything on social media.) David would reply with a thumbs-down or eye-roll emoji, or something anodyne like "oof." He only knew Rachel and Raj through Anjali. She came to realize that he probably *could* believe this bitch, because the entire time he'd known Rachel, she'd been the type to pose on a balcony overlooking an azure body of water, her back to the camera, translucent dress fluttering in the wind, never mind that it was the dead of January and a not insignificant number of her followers were huddled around space heaters. That bitch was nothing if not consistent.

"They're just very"—Anjali unfurled her fingers, searching for the right words—"new money. But if they want to spend some of that money on us . . ." She shrugged while trailing off. She thought of how much she'd spent to attend Raj and Rachel's wedding. Three grand, at least, if she counted Rachel's bachelorette in Cabo and wedding in Bel-Air. Anjali had gotten married at the Sheraton in Mahwah.

David considered this. "You think Lucie will be okay?"

Anjali bit her bottom lip. Lucie. Poor Lucie. Their darling nine-year-old daughter. Her new anxiety medication seemed to be working, though, and perhaps a few days apart would be good for her, too.

"It's only four days," Anjali had said. "She's doing better. Maybe a change of scenery will help. Priya's always offering to take the kids for the weekend." Anjali's older sister had been smart; she hadn't had kids. She had, instead, a loft in the city and a home on Shelter Island and the rarest gem of them all, an artist husband who actually made money selling his work. Significant money. He'd just done a mural for the Nike store in SoHo.

There was also something else compelling her to make this trip, and the more she thought about it, the more it felt like someone had turned a knob within her, winding her up like the Curious George jack-in-the-box that made Ryan cackle with glee. She wanted to go. Badly. She needed to see, with her own eyes, what Raj and Rachel Ranjani had built. She had last seen them at their wedding at the Hotel Bel-Air, eight years before. She had last communicated with Raj, in any meaningful way, two years before that, after the tragedy that befell his family, that had left him in pieces. Uncanny, how pieces could reassemble themselves. She needed to see what they looked like. What resemblance they held to what she saw on her screen, to her memories.

Anjali crushed her now-empty cup in the seat-back pocket and tapped at her phone. Nothing urgent at work. No texts from Priya. That op-ed everyone was posting about was clickbait that she couldn't bring herself to finish. The Moran draft—would it read any better now that she was buzzed? Probably not. She'd do it later, or tomorrow; surely, there'd be plenty of downtime at the vineyard estate. Maybe the fixtures and furnishings and quality of light would inspire her to work on her novel, that twenty-thousand-word document she'd started five years ago that was gathering dust in her Google Drive. (She liked to think that if her home looked like something out of a Nancy Meyers movie, if she had "a room of one's own," the manuscript would pour right out of her, as if that was what was holding her back, as if cream-colored seating and picture windows could cure what ailed her. Well, it probably wouldn't *hurt*.)

To Instagram, then; she needed visual candy: oh look, a new post from Rachel, a car-fie, a caption about the golden hour, a Louis Vuitton duffel in the background. God, she was so self-obsessed; had she aged even a day since they'd graduated? Had she done something to her lips, or was it just a filter? Anjali scrolled back through Rachel's older posts, even though she had seen and summarily judged them all before, shifting in her seat, attempting to ignore the sensation in her bladder.

Oh no—had she accidentally liked one? She tapped again. The heart disappeared, then reappeared. Had she tapped twice? Thrice? Was the Wi-Fi even working? Had she ever responded to that text from Rachel? She had to have, right? The things you did, the places your mind went, when you needed to pee. She swore her brain worked at 0.01 percent capacity when she needed to pee.

All four restroom signs in the economy cabin glowed red. She craned her neck into the aisle and squinted at the gauzy curtain shielding economy from first, the have-nots from the haves. Green. She saw green. Fuck it, what were they going to do if she blazed through that curtain—throw her off the plane?

She unbuckled her seat belt, stood up, and forged ahead, batting away the curtain like an errant housefly. While the two first-class restrooms closest to her were occupied, the two at the front of the cabin appeared to be empty. She zeroed in on the one at the left, for no reason other than she didn't have to cross through the galley to get to it, which meant faster entry, which meant less of a chance of getting caught, which meant—

"Ma'am? *Ma'am*. You can't be in here."

Out of nowhere, a flight attendant with a blonde chignon had materialized, blocking her path. Well, not out of nowhere. Out of the galley, where it seemed Anjali had interrupted her preparation of chocolate chip cookies. Jesus, first class got warm Mrs. Fields now? While her people had to pay thirteen dollars for a cold turkey sandwich that was mostly white bread and mayonnaise *if* they were lucky and the plane even offered food for sale? Airlines really knew how to fuck with you, how to turn otherwise well-adjusted adults into needy brats.

"It's an emergency," Anjali said. The flight attendant looked unmoved. She tried another tactic: "It's not *fair*."

~

Hari had been on the verge of falling asleep when the scent of melting chocolate and butter filled the air. There was nothing like it, nothing more American, in his opinion, apple pie and movie-theater popcorn and hamburgers on the grill be damned. He would allow himself one. He could afford to eat one. Truly, he could afford to eat, like, a dozen before even a hint of evidence would show on his abs, thanks to the personal trainer that he paid $300 a session, but he wanted to save his splurges for the weekend. Wine was full of sugar, a total carb bomb.

He refocused his eyes on his pod's seventeen-inch screen, which was playing *House of Homicide: The Family in the Cul-de-sac*, the latest true crime sensation on Netflix. True crime was his guilty pleasure. Well, not even guilty; it was absolutely fine now, on trend even, to talk about your obsession with grisly killers, cold cases, criminal masterminds—the gorier, the more psychologically unsettling, the better. It sometimes helped him break the ice with clients, made them think that he was one of them and not a hired gun to whom they were paying upward of six figures so that he could tell them how to run their businesses more efficiently. (Reducing redundancies. It generally boiled down to reducing redundancies.)

But he couldn't concentrate on his screen because of some commotion by the restrooms that was rapidly commandeering his field of vision. Thanks to the noise-canceling headphones doled out in first class, he couldn't hear what the woman wearing some dingy hybrid of a cardigan and a coat was arguing about with the flight attendant, but it was probably another plebe from the back trying to take advantage of what wasn't hers. You couldn't help but feel bad for them, really. To be stuck in economy, at this woman's age—he couldn't see her face, but judging by her pilling cardigan/coat, her skinny jeans, and her Skechers, he guessed around forty—was just sad. A mismanagement of miles, points, money, maybe life.

Was she Indian? He took in her hair, her skin tone, the way she waved her arm and flapped her hand. Yeah, she was almost definitely Indian. Such a bad look for his people. He sank deeper into the seat of his pod, as if its gray fabric walls and faux mahogany paneling could distance him from *that* type of Indian, from the stereotypes she was reinforcing: unruly, cheap.

She turned her cheek.

"Anjali?" Hari said, taking off his headphones. He'd known she'd be coming to Napa; he hadn't realized they'd be on the same flight. (EWR was closer to her home in New Jersey, although given that he took pains to avoid EWR, maybe she did, too.)

Anjali whipped around. The look on her face was like the one he'd seen on the intern he'd found the other day in the break room, shoving free bottles of Harmless Harvest from the fridge into the maw of an Ikea bag.

"She's with me," Hari said to the flight attendant, flashing an apologetic smile. "I know it's against the rules, but if you wouldn't mind, just this once . . ."

The flight attendant threw up her hands and turned away. (What was worse, one lone interloper or a batch of overbaked Mrs. Fields? First class would revolt if it didn't get its Mrs. Fields.) Anjali mouthed Hari a thank-you and sequestered herself in the restroom.

He had two piping-hot chocolate chip cookies in front of him when she came out. "I sprinkled Xanax on this one," he said, lifting the plate toward Anjali. "Let's try to get on the ground without you getting arrested, 'kay?" On the footrest, his toes, cozy in their long amenity-kit socks, wiggled happily.

Anjali rolled her eyes and snatched the plate. "It's practically a human rights violation, making 90 percent of the plane share one set of bathrooms and 10 percent share the rest."

"More like 1 percent."

Anjali punched his arm. "Great to know that you haven't changed, Hari—oh, I'm sorry, *Harry V*, wouldn't want to blow your cover. Does everyone at MCG still think that you just have a good tan?"

It was true, Hari—technically pronounced *Har-EE*, short for Harish—generally introduced himself as Harry. If a surname seemed necessary, he added, after a beat, "V." The "V" was short for Venkataraman, and the cringe quality of his chosen moniker had not escaped him—had in fact been made the subject of mirth, many a time—but one had to play the hand one was dealt. He'd adopted this abbreviation in the fourth grade (public school, Cleveland suburbs), and it had served him well through Cornell (BA in econ for his dad, minor in English for himself), Columbia (MBA for the opportunities born out of beer-soaked "networking"), and nearly a decade at the Manhattan Consulting Group, where he was now a managing partner. He wanted to be easy. He wanted to be liked. He wanted to be innocuous. Initially, anyway.

"Best to keep them guessing, you never know what the diversity and inclusion folks will want next," he said. "Speaking of names, has anyone ever told you that you look like a Karen? Or should I say, *Kareen*?"

She punched his arm again and called him a dick, and they both laughed. This was the dynamic he knew and loved; this was what he came for: the joking, the joshing, the insults that held within them little bursting hearts. The stuff he couldn't get away with saying to anyone else.

He recognized in Anjali a version of himself: a first-generation kid who had grown up with privilege, sure, but without a silver spoon, with no connected father or uncle who could call in an internship or grease the path into the right school. He and Anjali built what they had with their bare hands (even if what they built was mostly stored in the cloud). Unlike other people they knew.

They chatted until the chignoned flight attendant shot them a look. Anjali took that as her cue to leave. "Have you talked to Rachel, by the way?" Hari asked, before she stepped away.

"I haven't."

Hari saw a shadow pass over Anjali's face. Guilt?

"Why?"

"Just curious."

He hadn't reached out to Rachel, either. It didn't seem right. Raj was his primary target, anyway. Raj was the guy who could give his side hustle the help it needed, an infusion of cold, hard cash that would transform it from a clunky prototype into a must-have app for people who took pride in what they swilled. Raj would get it. Raj would want in, Hari was sure. He just had to figure out how to bring it up. For all his braggadocio, Raj could be surprisingly sensitive about certain subjects. Money, parents. Mostly money.

"Catch you later," he said to Anjali. "Try not to go viral back there."

"Bhenchod." She slapped him lovingly on the cheek and walked away.

Hari turned back to his screen and *The Family in the Cul-de-sac.* He kept having to rewind. Another scene had splayed across his mind: a woman and a bed and dawn on the verge of breaking, time running out when he wanted it to last and last and last.

He turned up the volume of his headset. Murder. Murder would take his mind off things. Murder would set him on the right track.

2

Thursday morning
Jet Edge flight 2, Van Nuys to Napa

Rachel shifted in her seat, trying to keep the fabric between her legs from bunching up. A romper had been a bad idea. A romper with a back zip, to make matters worse—what was she going to do when she ultimately had to go to the bathroom, let it pool at her feet? Gross.

She had initially descended the stairs of their estate in the Trousdale neighborhood of Beverly Hills in an oversized taupe Fear of God hoodie (hood up), matching sweatpants, Ultra Mini Uggs, and Celine sunglasses. She did not have the wherewithal, after the previous night, to steam and *gua sha* and eye patch and curl and line and do all the other things that would make it look like she had not cried herself to sleep.

She didn't think she had it in her, at that early hour, to do a photo shoot. The Money Honeys ate up her travel posts and she loved to give them what they wanted, but the vim and vigor required to turn and pose and latch on to her angles felt far out of reach, a balloon that had escaped her grasp and gotten tangled in a tree.

But as she passed the floor-length mirror that separated their bathroom from their bedroom, she caught a glimpse of herself. If she kept the hood up and sunglasses on, it just might work. Why not try?

So before summoning Ahmad to grab the bags, she had taken seventeen mirror selfies with the carry-on suitcase that had arrived the previous week, edited the best (No. 11), and added a flurry of tags (#travel, #jetset, #privatejet, and #RollingDeep, the manufacturer of the suitcase that she had paid for, that she hoped would one day pay *her*) and a caption that felt equal parts off the cuff, authentic, and aspirational:

> when uve been up all nite but gotta stay fly [peace fingers emoji]

While debating between whether to put her hand on her waist or in the pocket of her pants or on the handle of her roller-board—seven thousand mirror selfies on her camera roll and she still could not figure out what to do with her hands—a wave of despair washed over her. Empty. She felt empty.

She imagined, as she often did, her Mini-Me, next to her, with her own Rolling Deep carry-on (they made a version for toddlers that was a little larger than an iPad Pro, which, from what Rachel understood, was all a toddler really needed), in her own Essentials set. In Uggs with soles the size of her palm.

Baby shoes. The thought of them made her want to cry, brought her back to the last time they were in that cursed waiting room, with the fake fig tree, waiting to see the fertility specialist who would be the bearer of more bad news.

Maybe that's why she reacted the way she did when Raj, at the foot of the stairs, had glanced at her sweatshirt and sweatpants with resignation and looked back down at his phone. She knew what that look meant; she didn't even have to ask. He hated this set. He thought it looked too "street," too trendy, too try-hard—well, he'd never *said* any of those things; she just assumed, based on his response to a similar set she'd worn on a flight to Maui. God forbid she look like anything other than a fifties housewife, cryogenically frozen and brought back to life. He was in slacks, a lightweight Loro Piana pullover, and John Lobb loafers.

Unsaid, in her mind: Why don't you look like the woman I thought I married? Why did you spend half an hour taking mirror selfies? Why are you not what I want anymore?

Such was the state of their marriage that one sideways glance from her husband made her think all her worst thoughts about herself.

She'd swallowed hard, turned around, and marched back up the stairs, down the hall, and into her walk-in closet, where she extracted a burst of fabric diametrically opposed to what she had on: a ruffled Zimmermann romper with a deep V of a neck and studded hot-pink Valentino stilettos.

Raj had said nothing when she came down the stairs again, striking the marble extra hard with her four-inch heels because she knew he hated when she did that.

"Well," he'd said matter-of-factly, "we should go. Jason's already in the lounge."

Because *Jason's* welfare mattered more than hers. How absolutely *awful* it would be for the owner of Cline's to *wait* in a soundproofed, window-walled private suite where breakfast was catered by République. Where the coffee came from some obscure part of Colombia where only individuals under four feet (read: children) could pick the beans. Where massage therapists previously employed by the Ritz-Carlton remained on hand and on call should anyone require a shoulder rub before boarding their private jet. People arrived at the Excelsior Lounge of the Van Nuys Airport hours before takeoff so that they could soak it all in. There were entire Reddit threads devoted to the best strategies for availing oneself of every amenity. Jason had probably slept on the sidewalk, that free-loading fuck.

The rational part of her knew she was being childish. That she was projecting her frustrations onto Jason. That this was not a healthy way to deal with conflict, to behave in a marriage, to get what she ultimately, in her heart of hearts, craved. That she ought to use her words. But her words had failed, thus far. It was time to be fiery. Time to be unpredictable. Time to throw a tantrum, at least, as much of a tantrum as one could get away with on a private jet. (The bathrooms were better than commercial, but the doors still lacked the heft to produce a satisfying slam. She blamed fake cherrywood. Fake cherrywood and the laws of physics that would presumably prevent a plane with cement bathroom doors from getting off the ground.)

Maybe she should've stuck with the Uggs, she thought now, adjusting the back strap of her right Valentino, which was already cutting into her flesh. She'd forgotten how the Valentinos tore up the backs of her ankles and necessitated Neosporin and Band-Aids after a couple hours of wear. If these things affected her ability to place in the top ten in Megan's live run this weekend, she would kill someone. Running would be necessary. Absolutely essential.

Megan. The mere thought of her made Rachel feel even more inadequate. Megan was a shape-shifting criminal defense attorney who'd represented drug dealers, tax evaders, and heads of state before deciding, at the age of forty—the age that Rachel would be in a matter of months—that her true passion was running. Now she was Peloton's head treadmill instructor and the woman who determined Rachel's schedule. Rachel never missed one of Megan's live runs, never missed an opportunity to put one foot in front of the other on a revolving belt of rubber, waiting for that blessed moment when Megan would bestow her with a shout-out, racking up miles while going nowhere at all.

On a whim, she had invited Megan to the opening. Megan had attended the weddings and baby showers of Peloton superfans in the past. Why not? What was the worst she could say? No?

Well, she could not respond. Not responding would be the worst, and as far as Rachel knew, she hadn't yet. Rachel made a mental note to ask the event planner if Megan had RSVP'd. Just in case the event planner had some kind of event management access that Rachel didn't. (Rachel had wanted to keep things simple and use Paperless Post; Raj had said that Paperless Post looked poor. Whether that was an indictment of Paperless Post's ubiquity, aesthetics, or both, she didn't know.)

The plane had turned west after taking off and now, at seven thousand feet and climbing, Rachel could see a ray of sun illuminating a rare patch of undeveloped land along the coast north of Los Angeles. Malibu, maybe, or Montecito. Fluffy green treetops and nary a road in sight. She felt an urge to parachute down to that place, to shed her skin and emerge as someone new.

"Anything to drink, love?" The flight attendant, Kimberly, beamed down at her from above.

She liked Kimberly. Kimberly with her British accent and low bun and kitten heels. Kimberly worked a lot of their flights, especially the LA-to-Napa jaunts. She had thought about inviting Kimberly out for drinks, or coffee, or over for lunch at one of the homes she and Raj owned, in Beverly Hills, Manhattan, or Napa. But then she would picture the two of them sitting across from each other, poking at a tray of sashimi, having absolutely nothing to say. What would Rachel do, tell Kimberly what her life was really like? Be vulnerable? Become a story that Kimberly would relay to her friends over Cadillac margaritas at Casa Vega? "You won't *believe* this client I had to go to lunch with, designer everything, doesn't have to lift a finger, three homes, still miserable."

No. She could not have lunch with Kimberly.

She smiled politely and looked over at Raj and Jason across the aisle, in creamy beige leather seats that faced each other. They were drinking coffee, black. Raj never drank black coffee; he liked enough milk and sugar that whatever ended up in his cup qualified as dessert. He was probably "leveling," a thing he did with people he wanted to impress. Rachel recalled that Kimberly had taken Jason's drink order first. Raj had probably planned it that way. He liked to leave nothing to chance.

He'd like it if she had coffee. Or water. But you could drink coffee and water anywhere.

"What Champagne do we have today?" she asked. Kimberly went to check. Dom. They had Dom Pérignon. Vintage, at that. To hell with Raj, if he got mad at her. She wasn't going to say no to vintage Dom.

Raj's mouth turned down as the cork popped.

"Getting the party started early, *all right*," said Jason, clapping his hands and addressing Rachel for the first time that morning. Wiry and compact, Jason reminded her of a dog that only perked up when it sensed you had a treat. So that's what it takes for a woman to get through to you, she thought. A perceived willingness to party, a signpost indicating lowered inhibitions ahead. Rachel wondered whether Jason had ever slipped something into the drink of one of Cline's many regulars, women who rotated through the doors of Beverly Hills plastic surgeons and Pilates studios, seeking validation that proved ever more elusive. Women like her. (She preferred to drown her sorrows at home while wearing a moisturizing mask. Multitasking.)

Jason's approval made Raj react in kind. "Great idea, babe," he said, flashing her a smile and motioning for Kimberly to pour two more glasses. See, Raj, Rachel thought, sinking back into her seat as they resumed their conversation, I do know things. I do understand how to do business. The previous night he'd said that she didn't live in the real world, but she knew exactly what was at stake.

An order from Cline's, Jason's high-end wine bar with outposts in Beverly Hills, TriBeCa, and Las Vegas, would put Kismet on the map. Instant street cred. Kismet would go from being a vanity project—Raj would never use those words, but that's what it would be, until it started turning a profit—to a respected wine house. Cline's could pave the way for a much-coveted spot on the wine lists of the French Laundry, Carbone, the Delta Sky Club, and everything in between. "Market saturation," he'd told the marketing team he hired when they asked what his goal was for the winery. "Penetrate the premium sector first, then launch a secondary brand, something for the sports bars, the discount liquor stores, Trader Joe's."

She'd heard him say "market saturation" a lot. He was compelled to do two things: make money and "build wealth," "to give us the life we deserve," which once meant over-the-top date nights, a helicopter to Santa Barbara for sea urchin, fresh off the boat. It once meant being present at home, indulging her by accompanying her to the Veuve Clicquot Polo Classic or the Fourth of July party at Nobu Malibu or another similar event that she had finagled an invitation to through her own connections, to an arena in which she was not just the woman on Raj Ranjani's arm.

She had never pushed for a role in one of his ventures because she didn't want to be a nepo-wife, a figurehead flattered to her face and bitched about behind her back. She'd been in enough of his meetings to know how much control he liked: all of it.

The last time she'd asked him to come to something—the opening of a West Hollywood steakhouse owned by that guy who was Instagram-famous for putting salt on things—he'd shaken his head, removed from her hand the glass of chardonnay she'd been sipping (which was the only thing that kept her from sticking her head in the oven sometimes, the taste of that first sip of chard, or tequila, or pinot noir, or really anything with a higher ABV than water), and held her at arm's length.

"Babe, I know things have been hard," he'd said, referring, presumably, to their last (failed) round of IVF and her last (failed) attempt at launching a product around which her career and identity could revolve, a carry-on suitcase wide enough to sit on that allowed you to scoot through the airport like you were on a skateboard (the prototype cost too much and was too big for any overhead compartment).

"But these events, your obsession with this Facebook group . . . what's the point? What are you getting out of it?"

She'd lost it then. Pushed him away, said he didn't understand, he didn't get what it was like, to just be someone's wife, arm candy, to not be taken seriously. He kept rubbing her shoulders and repeating, "Babe, it's okay," "You put too much pressure on yourself," other platitudes.

"What can I do? How can I help?"

He'd looked down at his phone then, albeit discreetly, but the gesture reminded Rachel that he was leaving on a flight to Hong Kong that night. Any illusion she might've had that he really cared evaporated like hot breath from a mirror.

"Stick around long enough to get over the jet lag and maybe we'll find out."

Oh, the fight that line had caused. She'd slammed the bathroom door enough times that she could still hear the sound, if she concentrated hard enough.

Since that outburst, it felt like Raj was distancing himself from her, getting more involved in his work, his companies, always having to go to dinner with this potential business partner or golfing with that maybe-investor. She wondered if he was cheating. They hadn't been intimate in months. The other day, she'd sent the house staff to their quarters early and met him at the door in a marabou-trimmed Kiki de Montparnasse set—garters, Louboutins, all the accoutrements it took to look like the reincarnation of an old-school centerfold, which meant an extra dose of filler in her lips. He'd given her a piteous smile and claimed exhaustion, requested a rain check.

Then he'd flopped onto the couch and turned on the Dodgers.

Now, sipping her Dom and gazing out the window at the clouds below, she wondered, not for the first time, whether their relationship had run its course. *Other* people liked her. The Money Honeys. People on Instagram. People who left smiley faces with tongues hanging out and stars for eyes under her posts. Could she start all over? Would she?

~

Raj winced at the sound of the cork popping, not because he didn't like vintage Dom (who didn't like vintage Dom?), not because he didn't want to have fun, but because he could not deal with Rachel going to the dark side. Not today. Not in front of Jason and the untold numbers of Napa Valley elitists he had to charm the pants off, from touchdown onward, if Kismet was to be a success.

He had hoped she'd stay sober until they got to the estate and met up with their friends. That had been his plan, unless Jason suggested otherwise. People in the alcohol industry, he'd learned, did not drink all the time—well, *some* did, but the moguls, the successful ones, the people like Jason, whose wine bars brought in hundreds of millions in annual revenue, they didn't muddle through the day in an alcohol-induced haze. They lifted weights, did HIIT workouts, intermittent fasted. They conducted themselves like Jack Dorsey or Jeff Bezos. Discipline. You had to have discipline.

"It's booming, dude, *crazy* returns. I don't know if you're looking to diversify beyond wine, but if you're curious, come down to Oaxaca with me next month."

Raj availed himself of the Dom interruption and the cheers with Rachel—maybe this time will be different, maybe she'll keep it together—to remember what he and Jason were talking about. Mezcal. That's right. Jason was going long on mezcal, producing an in-house brand for Cline's.

"How crazy are we talking?"

"Cost, all in, for one of our bottles—$8.50, including the hand-painted label. We're going to retail for $85."

"Sick, dude," Raj said, nodding in a way that conveyed game recognizing game. Rare, margins like that. Though, he could not stomach any alcohol harder than wine, which meant pretty much all alcohol. But you didn't have to love everything you sold, right? Look at all those Hollywood actors who did Hyundai commercials. Did any of them drive a Hyundai? Did any of them even know what a Hyundai was?

He let Jason go on about the food in Oaxaca and this mezcal resort in the highlands that was "like a goth Amangiri, like, bitches in black getting freaky with agave." (Cool?) He tried to picture himself in the Oaxacan highlands. What did they even look like? Mars? Would he have to wear a cowboy hat? Not his vibe.

In any case, he had enough irons in the fire. One of them would pay out, he knew; he just had to stay laser-focused on his existing investments. Rachel had no idea, the stress he was under, the amount that he did for them, the risks he was taking.

The call from the lawyer pinged into his mind, like a notification popping up even though you're sure you've turned on Do Not Disturb. He'd gotten it in the car on the way back from Oxnard, three days prior, during one of those kill-me-now bumper-to-bumper stretches of traffic on the 101, and the call had lasted until he'd pulled into the driveway of the Trousdale house, by which point all he could think about was what he possibly had on hand that could take the edge off. Did he still have any Xanax? Could Ahmad get some if he didn't? Ahmad was very by the book. Forever afraid of ICE.

Raj was scrolling through his contacts when the door flung open, revealing a *Playboy* centerfold in the shape of his wife. Like the girls who once lived under his bed, dog-eared and creased. Thirteen-year-old Raj wouldn't have been able to hold out past the landing. Thirty-nine-year-old Raj . . . would have traded her for a bottle of benzos. Figuratively speaking, of course.

He probably should've skipped that Dodgers game. Watched the highlights. But there was something uncouth about a woman, even your wife, throwing herself at you. He liked a fight. He liked a conquest. He knew he couldn't admit that.

Power of positive thinking, he reminded himself. His father had given him Norman Vincent Peale's seminal book on the subject, and it sat on Raj's desk at the Trousdale home, a constant reminder to reorient his thoughts when they veered into the dark. This weekend. This weekend would get them back on the same page. Surrounded by their college friends, the people who knew them best, he and Rachel would find their groove.

She loved a project, a party to host, a reason to get dressed up. He didn't quite understand what she was wearing today; she always complained about those Valentino heels—Uggs and sweats would've made more sense, even though she probably would've overheated because Fear of God made their stuff so damn thick and hello, Napa in July, global warming, ninety-eight in the shade, if they were lucky. But he hadn't had time to reason with her that morning, had been in the middle of drafting an email when she'd stomped down the steps and then stormed back up. What was done was done. This weekend, he would think positive and keep his mouth shut in all matters pertaining to Rachel. Happy wife, happy life.

Well, he knew one surefire way to make her happy. But he wasn't ready. *They* weren't ready. Their net worth, not nearly what was necessary to give a child the life it deserved while maintaining their standard of living. His father's words always rang in his mind, but never more clearly than when the subject of children came up: "Don't write a check with your mouth that your ass can't cash."

His father had been reviewing the bill at the Grand Velas Riviera Maya at the time, and Raj had been tall enough to peer up at the reception desk and see the total on the folio in boldface type: $19,754. His father had signed with a flourish, clapped him on the back, and said, "Luckily, this ass doesn't have to worry about that." He'd guffawed loudly and looked at the employees behind the reception desk, who offered ready smiles of approval. Raj couldn't put it into context back then, but now it seemed like a steal for seven days, for a family of four. Twenty grand hardly bought you anything anymore, when it came to raising children in Los Angeles. A semester of private school? Nope. A nanny for a year? No nanny you'd trust with your children. A week at one of those Disney-themed places in Hawaii where all the dads he knew found excuses to golf and cart girls to fuck? Not a chance, what with all the people you'd have to pay off to make sure the trysts with the cart girls never got back to your wife.

He'd inwardly sighed with relief after their last appointment with the fertility specialist. Someday, maybe, yes. But not yet. Not with who she was at the moment. Her Money Honeys obsession, the frivolity of it, high school stuff. Why did she care about the woes of a bunch of women she would never meet in real life? Why did she crave their approval?

Reorient, he reminded himself. Rachel is good. Rachel is pretty. Rachel can be the perfect wife when she wants to be. You want the perfect—

"Mind if I join you guys?"

He looked up as his wife perched on the armrest of his seat and swung her smooth legs over his lap. The Valentinos dangled from her toes. She was smiling at him like he was a god. *Jason* was smiling at him like he was a god.

Shit, he thought. Norman Vincent Peale knows what's up.

~

Rachel laughed and tossed her head back at all the right moments, asked the right questions, played the part of the perfect wife. She saw a light in her husband's eyes, when he looked up at her, that she hadn't seen in a while. As the first round of Champagne bubbles had coursed through her system, she took out her phone and pulled up the sole reason she still maintained a Facebook account: the Money Honeys Peloton group, the strangers for whom she performed a pantomime of her life. Nominally for women (and gay men) who owned a Peloton and self-identified as flush with cash (or lines of credit), it had little to nothing to do with working out and functioned as a forum for rich people who needed help.

> LV cross body zipper broke [crying emoji] [crying emoji] [crying emoji] Need it for high school reunion this weekend. Where can I get it repaired in Minneapolis????

> Just found out my husband is having an affair . . . with a stripper . . . and that they had sex in our bed while I was taking our youngest to a dance competition

> in Tucson. Have proof on the doorbell cam. Anyone know a great personal investigator & lawyer in the Phoenix area? (Is it too much to hope for someone who does both???) Thx in advance [heart emoji]

> Recently divorced. Finally felt confident enough to put myself out there. Went on a date with a guy I met on Bumble. Seemed so nice and normal online . . . . . . total weirdo in person. Good looking enough, good job in sales, but asked me to give him a hand job under the table at Mastro's AND THEN asked to split the check. Tell me this isn't normal????

(The top comment on the last post: "Is his name Jake? Does he live in Newport Beach? Same thing happened to me at Javier's!")

Reading these posts and seeing the comments and likes on her "stay fly" one from that morning—more than four hundred, she was basically the Kim Kardashian of this group—she decided that no, she could not start all over. (Even if Raj was cheating on her, he'd never do it in their home. They had the CCTV feed. They had an agreement. He had a moral opposition to strip clubs: "Why pay for a lap dance when you can pay for actual sex?")

She had everything she wanted, almost. Raj would come around. She would make him come around. She thought about what one of the Money Honeys had told a mother of two who had posted about her own, nonexistent sex life:

> Tie him down and gag him if you have to—he'll probably like it even more, LOL!

This was Raj's weekend—truly, *their* weekend to shine, and she would play her part, even if it killed her.

She could feel the plane descending, saw Kimberly motioning for her to return to her seat, all anxious and apologetic. (Another reason they could never be friends: the power dynamic would always be off.) Outside the window next to Raj, row after row of vines, neat and orderly, filled up the middle distance. They made her think of *Madeline*, "twelve little girls in two straight lines." One day, she would read that book to her daughter. *Their* daughter. She could prove herself, in this patchwork of plots. She could reap what she sowed.

She pulled her phone out of her romper pocket and squeezed Raj's shoulder. "One before we land, babe," she said. He threw up a peace sign and leaned into her side.

She scrolled through the Facebook group, feeling the bloom of self-satisfaction and doing nothing to hide it. Why should she? She and Raj were fine. Look at all these things that other people had to deal with: cheating spouses and hellish in-laws and game-changing inheritances that may or may not be coming their way. And these were people who self-identified as bougie. Imagine what regular people dealt with. Imagine what the Peloton Moms group was like!

She tapped her notifications and noticed one from @anjaliparker.

Anjali. Anjali was on Instagram?

She missed Anjali. Her former neighbor, her all but sister, her oldest friend. Anjali had declined Rachel's last two attempts at a girls' trip, citing work, Lucie, "too much going on at home, things fall apart without me."

Rachel had felt slighted, but what could she say? You couldn't criticize a mother for not making time. She had been elated to receive Anjali and David's RSVP, had texted her immediately, YAY, as well as several exclamations about how wonderful it would be to finally catch up. No reply. Now she had liked a thirst trap Rachel had posted in January from St. Barts?

She could ask Anjali about it soon enough, she figured, folding her hands in her lap. She sometimes wondered if Anjali was jealous. She wondered if Anjali wanted to be her. If only Anjali knew.

She closed her eyes and mentally repeated her mantra until she felt the wheels skid against the ground. *You have it all. You have it all. You have it all.*

3

Thursday morning
Baggage carousel 5, SFO

The photo-editing apps made it more difficult every day, V thought, scrolling through VSCO's array of textures. In the beginning, there were the default filters, the ones that came with Instagram, and they were easy enough to figure out: Clarendon was basic, but it really did make everything pop. Gingham was vintage by way of What Goes Around Comes Around (you didn't have the wherewithal to trawl the racks at the Pasadena Flea; you needed a consignment boutique to do the dirty work for you). Valencia was #vanlife, X-Pro II was what finance guys used when they wanted to seem artsy, and so on. Then VSCO came around with C9 and L7 and AL3 and dozens more filters made to mimic actual cameras, which was a misnomer, because the cameras inside today's smartphones were light-years more advanced than the Kodaks and Fujis of yore. And now there were textures. Did she want to overlay a grain on the photo she took of the sun rising over Costa Cara that morning? Or make it look like a Polaroid? Or animate it, throw a video filter on it, have a cavalcade of bulbous pink hearts rain improbably from the sky?

A text message interrupted her process.

Carl Actor Lindoviento: You = magic. Mykonos?

Poor Carl, she thought. You have no idea how far back in the queue you are. Carl was one of many men—well, people, or "conscious beings," which was the term the organizers preferred—she had met at Lindoviento, a five-day festival at Costa Cara, a luxury resort community on Mexico's Pacific coast. She had gone, officially, to teach a master class in "Conscious Confidence" (a term she coined herself and kept meaning to trademark), which meant that the company that put together Lindoviento covered her travel and lodging costs (the company made money by selling $5,000 tickets to Lindoviento and "microlending" to locals who failed to understand the fine print and astronomical interest rates associated with late payments).

She had also gone to teach yoga. She was Bikram and Iyengar certified. Her master class in confidence (notably, not MasterClass) did not net as much as her ninety-minute flows (yet).

But the main reason she'd gone to Lindoviento—the main reason she went anywhere, really—was to build out her roster of potential pave-the-ways—men, women, and nonbinary individuals who could, say, pave the way for her to attend Paris Fashion Week, by money, connections, or some combination of both. Pave-the-ways were people who wanted to be associated with bohemian creative types but only knew bankers, lawyers, doctors, and sales reps. V had a way of sniffing them out, of discerning who would get off on spending money on her, not in a sexual way, necessarily, more in a "we have no cultural capital and we could use some interesting women of color at our Cannes Lions party so that we don't get canceled" kind of way.

Less conscious individuals might call such people sugar daddies or mommies, but V didn't see gender (or eat sugar, if she could help it). She liked to think of the people who subsidized her life as benefactors. Benefactors and creatives had a rich tradition. Would there be Michelangelo without the Medicis? Jackson Pollock without Peggy Guggenheim? What was she, if not a new kind of artist, someone whose existence and documentation of it qualified as a body of work?

This was what she told herself when she transferred her Venmo balance to her bank account. Though, lately, her benefactors preferred to grease her wheels in less obvious ways: first-class tickets to Tokyo, a Cartier Tank with an alligator strap, a Kate Spade purse that had clearly been rejected by another woman and by top-tier department stores before her. (She had blocked the benefactor who sent her that sad thing. It came from Marshalls with the tags still attached, an insult if there ever was one.)

The problem with this line of work was that you could not pay your rent in handbags and airline miles. So, in addition to teaching Conscious Confidence and yoga and catering to pave-the-ways, V worked as a hostess at Laffa, a zippy Middle Eastern restaurant in East Hollywood that charged $18 for a glass of natural wine and $27 for a kebab. That was also a venue for pave-the-ways. She was happy to accept a crisp hundred-dollar bill (or, who was she kidding, a few crumpled twenties) in exchange for an express pass to the top of the wait list. (People who thought that a Resy notification could get them a prime four-top on a Friday night were so very wrong.) It was a job where she could rack up $21 an hour—God bless California's mandatory minimum-wage laws—when her Venmo account dwindled into the single digits, something to bridge the gap between who she had been and who she was becoming. A homeowner. An occupant of a live-work space above Sunset Junction whose down payment required $50,000 more than she currently had in any of her accounts, Venmo or otherwise. (Though, if things went the way she hoped they would in Napa, by Sunday that would no longer be the case.)

Carl, on the other hand. Carl was a twenty-four-year-old actor who would be spending August in a four-bedroom villa in Mykonos that would be split by nine other actors, all of whom were vying to be extras in the reboot of *Lindsay Lohan's Beach Club*. Carl had no relation to the organizers of Lindoviento—she had programmed him into her phone in the manner of previous acquaintances, using identifying details that made sense solely to her, for example, Gary Vegas Drug Dealer. Carl would not be meeting V in Mykonos.

She swiped away his message, popped a level 3 grain on the sunrise photo, and wrote:

> New morning. New day. New moon. New you. Conscious Confidence [trademark emoji] V23 coming soon. Where do you want to rise?

(In lieu of a trademark, she figured, an emoji would do. She really ought to file those papers, though. After wine country.)

V had already set the wheels in motion to host her next workshop in Capri in August, but it never hurt to ask your followers—she had around sixty-five thousand, across all platforms—where they wanted to go. Market research, engagement, et cetera. A new hotel on the north side of the island had offered to host her and extend a 50 percent discount to the workshop's attendees on account of her social media presence . . . and on account of V having spent the better part of the most recent Art Basel Miami with the founder of the Italian real estate conglomerate that owned the hotel. She got him into a VIP preview hosted by Ruinart and it flowed from there.

As she posted the photo, she saw, below it, a new post: two round yellow *laddus* on a gold-rimmed plate, candlelight casting the whole composition in an amber glow. "Sweets for my sweet." What a caption, Shilpa89. Really reinventing the wheel.

V did not follow Shilpa89—that would be creepy, stalkerish, only slightly more stalkerish than looking up Shilpa89 on average twice a day, but at least the latter was known only to the stalkerish and the stalkerish alone. She did follow Shilpa89's new fiancé. He happened to be her ex-husband, Dev. She couldn't not follow *Dev*. That would be petty, small, avoidant. The opposite of conscious and confident.

She closed her eyes and allowed herself a moment of sorrow. How could he go from rainbow sherbet with holographic sprinkles (monk fruit–sweetened, all the way through) to vanilla, and probably low-fat vanilla, at that? She exhaled, opened her eyes, double-tapped the photo, and commented:

> [heart emoji] [shooting star emoji] Wishing you both eternal happiness [shooting star emoji] [heart emoji]

She believed that if she projected goodwill into the world, it would come back at her tenfold. It was also important, as a life coach, to be well adjusted and happy for your exes, or to at least appear that way.

A loud buzz pierced the arrivals area; a light on the baggage carousel began flashing red. V slid her phone into the pocket of her wide-legged Ulla Johnson pants and paced the length of the carousel, doing long, loping arm circles. In her previous life, she'd elbow her way to the black hole where the bags came out, the better to snatch hers up *first*, as if there was an award to be won for getting out of the airport the fastest. Now, she was pretty sure that sort of high-strung behavior was to blame for the single line that creased her forehead, that she filled in with periodic injections of Botox and Dysport, alternating so that the nerves never knew what was coming next. (Was there science behind this theory? She had not bothered to find out.) Besides, according to the itinerary sent around by the party planner, her flight from Manzanillo had landed before the New York flight that Anjali, David, and Hari were on, and they would all be heading up to the estate together.

Better to stretch, get the blood flowing, lean her smartphone against the telescoping handle of her carry-on, and film, for her followers, a tutorial about how they could reinvigorate themselves after a long flight. "Time is what you make of it," she said into the camera, before backing up and commencing another lap.

~

Anjali remembered why she had sworn off day-drinking. The dry mouth, the unquenchable thirst. The cocoon it spun around her brain and her motor skills, as evidenced by the number of times she tripped on a people mover at SFO (four). The pounding in her head that felt like it might burst through her temples, the bad attitude it bred within her until she slept it off or reengaged with alcohol to the point that she was at cruising altitude again and not mired in the muck, cursing her bad decisions, her lack of self-control.

Who *is* that weirdo doing arm circles? she wondered, descending the escalator into baggage claim. California was full of freaks, no question about it. Even the New Yorkers who moved here turned into something else, their edge worn away by perpetual sunshine and a lack of weather to fight against. Their quick wit withered; they stopped reading and paying attention to current events. They took up strange pursuits like transcendental meditation and crystals and breath-work workshops. One of *Highbrow*'s editors had moved to LA. Within a year, she'd quit and started weaving baskets. Her latest line had been featured in *T* magazine.

Maybe the freaks were onto something.

Anjali realized, by the time she stepped off the escalator, that the weirdo doing arm circles was Victoria Chou, Rachel's sorority sister, the only other woman of color in their Delta Gamma pledge class, the former wife of Raj's frat brother Dev. She was wearing the emerald-green Kismet Cellars hat that had come with their invitations. On Anjali, the hat looked silly, like she was trying too hard to be an age that had long since passed. On Victoria, it looked like the kind of must-have item for which hypebeasts stood in line while clutching iced matcha lattes.

"Here we go," she murmured, loud enough for David to hear but lacking the context for him to understand what, exactly, she was talking about.

"I just can't be bothered anymore," Anjali remembered Victoria telling her, the last time they'd had a real conversation. They were at Raj and Rachel's wedding reception at the Hotel Bel-Air, post-salads, pre-entrées, and Victoria was telling Anjali about how she'd quit her job at a preeminent public relations company that specialized in crisis management to pursue her true passion, confidence. "Well, teaching people to embrace their conscious, confident self."

"How . . . do you do that?" Anjali had replied.

"Workshops," Victoria had said, with a shrug, like it was obvious. "Social media tutorials. Festivals are the best." She grabbed a chunk of baguette from the basket between them and tore into it with gusto. "I had a waiting list of five hundred at Burning Man last year. You're not supposed to exchange money on the playa, but this one guy rolled up with a gold bar, like, an actual brick of gold—who would say no to *that*?" She held a piece of bread in either hand and arranged her face in an expression that said, Can you believe my life? I can't.

"But, you're so good at your job," Anjali had said. Victoria had been tasked with cleaning up the mess after an ill-advised commercial in which a reality TV star extended a can of Pepsi to a bunch of activists; the turnaround she orchestrated, in which the reality TV star led a march on Washington, had earned her a profile in the Up Next column of the *Times*' Style section. "You got that award!"

Anjali felt violated and couldn't figure out why. She wasn't especially close with Victoria; they only knew each other through Rachel. But she would never quit a job, let alone one for which she'd been publicly praised.

Victoria rolled her eyes. "You mean the one from ASS? Asians of Society and Service? The only reason they named me a rising star was because the president was accused of sexual harassment and wanted a discount on my retainer. Classic. God forbid one of our people ever pay full price for something that didn't come out of a Gucci store."

Anjali had quietly admired Victoria's ability to change her mind and own it, to march to the beat of her own drum. It was a feature of her personality that had, over the years, grown more angular and apparent, like a pair of wings emerging from a slab of marble. But for some reason, seeing her strut around now, doing arm circles, irritated Anjali to her core. Maybe it was Victoria's ability to be carefree. As a mom, as a rule, you were never truly carefree.

"Anj!" Victoria called out happily, sashaying over to her and David. Anjali noted Victoria's low-slung pants, the wide strip of midriff between where her pants started and her tank top—was that a tank top, even? Or a bra?—began. Victoria had topped off her outfit with a loose, unbuttoned shirt—in the same ribbed knit as her top and pants—and the Kismet Cellars hat. Anjali wondered what it would be like to move through the world this way, to be so comfortable in your own skin that you showed a good swath of it to strangers at the airport. Didn't she get cold? Or did her burning confidence give her all the warmth she needed?

"Victoria," Anjali said, letting herself get wrapped in one of those empath hugs—chest to chest, oozing with emotion, always a beat longer than you wanted it to last.

"It's V now," Victoria said, pulling back and smoothing a strand of Anjali's own hair off her face, a gesture Anjali found maternal in a way that made her uncomfortable. "V the Victor. You on Insta?"

Anjali quickly shook her head. "No . . . well, only for work. Which reminds me—sorry, I need to check on something."

V—the gall of a woman to go by one initial—and David made small talk while Anjali pulled up her message thread with Priya. Anjali had called Priya upon landing; when Priya didn't pick up, she'd texted, Just checking in, all good? No response. Did Priya understand what it was like to be a mother and leave your children in the care of someone other than yourself for four days, for the first time in . . . ever? Of course not. Of course she had no idea of the brand of anxiety coursing through Anjali's veins, an anxiety that would not abate until she held her son and daughter in her arms again, but Priya could throw her a bone, a photo of Ryan and Lucie frolicking on Sunset Beach, a *yep, all good!* Even a thumbs-up emoji. Priya couldn't spare half a second for a thumbs-up emoji?

She overheard V telling David about a cacao ceremony—whatever the hell that was—as she turned away and lifted her phone to her ear.

It rang five times, her heart kicking up with every repetition of the tone.

"I can't believe this thing rang. I never get service in here."

"Pri, what the fuck? You can't go dark."

"I'm not *going dark*, we're in Rufus's studio. You know how he is. They're painting. They're *fine*."

Rufus did not own a smartphone. Rufus spent only fifteen minutes online a day. Rufus did not—Anjali remembered this now—equip his studio with Wi-Fi and blocked the signal that came from the house with some kind of device. Rufus was an *artist*.

"Put Lucie on," Anjali said.

She heard Priya dramatically announce her presence on the other end of the line, and then her daughter's voice, which cut through her enmity toward Rufus and Priya like a kite through a clear blue sky.

"Darling," Anjali said, "how are you? Is Auntie Pri treating you well?"

"Did you know that the internet rots your brain? That's what Uncle Rufus said."

"Uncle Rufus rotted his brain a long time ago by putting things up his nose," Anjali said. "How is your brother?" She could hear Ryan babbling happily in the background. "How are *you*?" She couldn't help but ask again. "Are you taking your medicine like we talked about?"

"*Yes, Mom.* Can I go now? Uncle Rufus mixed up some paint that he said is cooler than acid."

Did her nine-year-old know what acid was? The horror. People who'd never had kids thought a weekend with them was a write-off, a chance to present themselves as the parents they might've been without any consequences or real responsibility. Free babysitting, the more charitable part of her brain reminded her. Free luxury babysitting. It was fine. They were fine. She'd deprogram them after they got home, and unless her sister and brother-in-law gave them actual acid, which would be a felony (at least), there was no way they'd be able to keep Ryan from watching that kid who unboxed toy trains on YouTube. The internet was a fucking godsend; Uncle Rufus had no idea what he was talking about.

"Of course, sweetheart. Be good."

"She's thriving." Lucie had already given the phone back to Priya. "Go, relax, get shit-faced on Mumm."

Anjali lowered her voice. "Please tell me if she starts using that thing more than once a day, okay?" She could hardly talk about Lucie's new treatment in private, let alone in this airport, where, not ten feet from her, two girls about Lucie's age bounded happily by a pile of luggage, smiling, laughing, clearly well adjusted. She felt like the worst mother on earth. "It's important."

"Is it? You only told me eighty-seven times," Priya said.

Anjali ended the call and pulled up her email. The chardonnays had temporarily succeeded in suppressing her impulse to archive, delete, or reply to every missive as soon as it hit her inbox; still, the sight of that red bubble above the envelope and the number it contained, 257, filled her with angst anew. What was she missing? What was going on without her? Who was getting ahead? Was she being left behind?

Did some of this anxiety stem from the fact that she currently had no control over her children and felt the need to control something else? Perhaps. Fine, yes. But knowing that didn't make it abate.

Before getting on the escalator, she'd scanned her inbox and seen nothing dire. Now, she saw a new message from her boss, Charles Morgenstern, *Highbrow*'s editor in chief, rumored to be retiring at the end of the year. He'd be naming his successor, who would have to be approved by the board of *Highbrow*'s parent company, but given that he'd elevated the magazine from a fusty bathroom-rack staple to a *must-have* bathroom-rack staple, whomever he picked would likely get the job. It was the next logical step in Anjali's career, which meant every time he reached out to Anjali, she tried to beat her own response time.

There was no subject, only a message:

How's Moran looking? SCOTUS piece dead. Need to fill a hole in A.

"A" referred to the issue of the magazine coming out the following week. The Moran story was nowhere near ready. Getting it ready would require Anjali phoning Moran, hand-holding him through the rewrite process, overseeing the fact-check—essentially remaining glued to her laptop and/or phone for the entirety of her "time off." Would it be a drag? Kind of. She'd complain about it, but inwardly she'd savor the challenge and the affirmation of her expertise. The brownie points she'd accrue. She could practically taste them.

She tapped out a reply: "I'll get it done."

People talked about the importance of switching off, of spending time with friends and family, uninterrupted by the buzzes and blue light of your devices. They talked about how no one, on their deathbed, ever wished they'd worked longer, harder, put in more hours at the office. But the thing none of those romantics got was that you didn't *get* to grow old and wistful if you didn't have money, that spending time with your loved ones was expensive, that if you blithely switched off your notifications and let the cogs in the wheel turn, you would be replaced. Especially if you were a mother. You would be replaced by something younger, faster, and cheaper. A shinier, newer cog. Probably made of flimsier stuff than you, but replaced nevertheless.

"Anj?" David called out. She looked up and saw that half a dozen silver Rimowa roller-boards had accumulated at V's feet. Anjali and David had stuffed everything they needed for the weekend into their carry-ons (nameless, brandless, the color of sludge, and fraying around the zippers), loath to pay extra to check a bag.

"Everything okay?" he asked as she rejoined them.

"Work," she said, sighing dramatically. "They need me to get that Italy robot story ready for next week."

"But you put in for the time off," David said. "This is supposed to be our weekend together." He lowered his voice. "Remember what Carlotta said?"

She gave him a pointed look. "What choice do I have?" The gall of him to invoke the couples counselor, especially after he had breezily informed her, shortly after boarding, that he planned to "take some meetings" while they were out here. When husbands had business to handle on vacation, it was fait accompli; put a wife in the same scenario and she was sabotaging her marriage, her family, being selfish instead of serving the greater good.

"I hear you, girl," V said. "That used to be me."

She said it with the tone of someone who's given up drinking when you tell them that you're hungover: I've seen the light; you can too.

Anjali scrutinized V and her suitcases, in all their bohemian bourgeois glory. What did she know, besides what hat to pair with what outfit? What concerns did she have, besides whether to go to the original Burning Man or the remix in Africa?

"And look at you now, the carbon footprint queen of the world," Anjali said. Snark was her preferred defense mechanism.

"Honestly, I almost never check a bag," V said, either unbothered by Anjali's dig or unaware of it entirely, "but I was hosting a workshop and needed my singing bowl and ocean drum, and those take up a trunk each . . ."

An ocean drum? What the fuck was an ocean drum?

"By the way, I didn't know that your hubs had started his own lit agency," V said. "That's really cool."

Anjali looked up at David, who had crossed his arms over his chest and was smiling tightly. She heard his message loud and clear: I am not into this woman. I am on my best behavior. I am only making small talk because it's the socially appropriate thing to do.

"It's something," Anjali said, resting her hand on her husband's arm. *It could be something* was more accurate. It could be something if he signed authors who could sell enough books to turn a profit, if he chose wisely, if he didn't fuck up the way he did at the bigger, extremely established agency where they'd thought he'd spend his career.

In spite of her annoyance at David bringing her up at all, something the couples counselor had said flitted into her mind: "You choose your attitude." She didn't like to think about those sessions, or the reason they'd begun, but she couldn't deny that there was truth to the advice, simplistic as it was. She could choose to be jaded and competitive and worried . . . or she could choose to be open and receive whatever this weekend had in store. Let V live out her nomad-gone-wild fantasies. What difference did it make to Anjali? What was the point of closing herself off, of judging every little thing, of worrying if (when?) David would slip? She was going to be open and live in the moment. Open, moment, open, moment.

"I'm sorry for that stupid thing I said about your carbon footprint," Anjali said. This seemed like a good way to cement her new attitude. "I'm a little stressed, between work and being away from the kids."

V batted away her apology. "But you know what you'd be perfect for," she mused, giving Anjali the once-over. "What are you doing in August? Have you heard of Conscious Confidence?"

Maybe there was such a thing as being too open. "Where's Hari?" Anjali asked, as if locating Hari was of utmost urgency. "He was in first class—he should've been out before us."

"I think that's him, coming down," David said, nodding at the escalator.

Anjali turned around and saw that Hari had changed from a sweatshirt and joggers—a *nice* sweatshirt and joggers, a matching set, probably from one of those direct-to-consumer companies that he advised—to a faded Steely Dan T-shirt, light-wash jeans, and espadrilles that had something written on their sides in a graffiti-ish scrawl. (Men wore espadrilles now? She could not keep up.) His hair was slicked back, like it was wet.

"Did you shower?" she asked when he joined the group, by way of a greeting. She wasn't being snarky. She was genuinely confused.

"Just a quick refresh at the Flagship Lounge," Hari said, with a disarming smile. "Standard practice." Was it? Anjali wondered, but Hari had changed the subject. "Everyone got everything?" he asked. "I think I saw our guy."

They followed Hari through a set of sliding glass doors and met Adolfo, who wore a vest and bow tie and held an iPad as a sign, who commandeered their bags and radioed to someone else to bring around the car: a fifteen-passenger Mercedes Sprinter van wrapped with "Kismet Cellars" on both sides. Adolfo handed out frosty bottles of Fiji from a cooler near the front as they climbed aboard and claimed their own rows.

"So," said Hari, twisting open the cap of his bottle as the Sprinter pulled away from the curb, "does anyone know why they bought a winery?"

4

Thursday afternoon
Atlas Peak Road, Napa

Fish out of water. The phrase had run on repeat in David's head during the two-hour drive up to Napa, over the Bay Bridge, past the larger-than-life cranes that looked like something out of *Star Wars*, past the big-box shops that gave way to verdant hills striped with picture-postcard vineyards that rose and fell with the swell of the road.

He hated that a saying so trite summed up his current mental state, but there was no other way to put it. He didn't want to admit that he'd never been to California. He knew, given his line of work, entertainment industry adjacent, that he ought to have been, should've made some trip to Los Angeles when he was at the agency, but for whatever reason, it hadn't happened. (Maybe the higher-ups intuited how awestruck he'd be, how he'd shed his "New York or nowhere" shell and turn gooey beneath the unobstructed sun.) He had not attended Raj and Rachel's wedding in LA. Lucie was so young then, and Anjali's parents didn't think they could handle her on their own (Priya was a non-option at the time, hopscotching between Berlin and Ibiza, never not raving). David had offered to stay back and let Anjali make a weekend out of it—after all, Raj and Rachel were her college friends; he didn't *need* to go.

Now, watching the vines whip past, their leaves Technicolor green, their rows extending on to infinity, he thought of how he'd written off overtures about Big Sur, Monterey, Malibu, all the supposedly scenic points on Route 1, as hyperbole, diversions in a state ridden with tent cities, traffic, and people who refused to read. Could those glorified rest stops really compare to London, Paris, all the great cities of Europe (not that he'd been since his daughter was born) that took the same amount of time to get to from New York? Well, in a word, yes. How wrong he'd been. How he'd love to commandeer the van and keep it for a week, a year, see it all. As their plane had descended over San Francisco Bay, he'd fought the urge to jump out of his seat and press his nose against the nearest window, entranced by the way the fog rolled over the Sierra Nevada, like the fingers of a hand closing in, taking, taking, taking.

Maddie had posted about Napa, hadn't she? Maddie in her short-shorts, romping around a vineyard. Had he saved that post? He must've. He slid his phone out of the pocket of his zip-up vest and lost himself in the scroll.

"You good, bro?" Hari's voice came from across the aisle. It took David a minute to return to reality. It always did. The world on his phone, a bubblegum-scented fantasy that never failed to enthrall him. He had installed a subsidiary app that was supposed to limit his time on this one, where you paid a monthly fee to keep up with content creators of your choosing, but he had disabled the subsidiary app, because technically, this was work: search and discovery.

"Just catching up on email," David said, giving Hari a tight smile. This *was* work, but he didn't feel like explaining that to Hari. You couldn't argue with email. He pressed his fingers into the base of his neck. It had been bothering him all day and he couldn't figure out why.

"I hear you, dude," Hari said. He wagged his phone in front of his face. "Never-ending. I'm usually on calls the minute I touch down, but I cleared my schedule today except for this one at four. Can't get out of it, unfortch." Hari squeezed his empty Fiji bottle hard enough to make it pop. "Super-needy CPG client, demanded the MP."

From this, David deduced that Hari was a managing partner and had an insecurity complex. It was nice to know that he wasn't alone.

"I get it," said David. "The beauty of running your own business"—he gestured at himself—"you're never truly off."

"Serious props to you, man, leaving Archetype to start your own shop. For books, yeah?"

David nodded. "We focus on authors that old-school agencies"—such as Archetype, the multinational behemoth where he had previously worked—"don't take seriously." He'd found that "we" was generally better received than the truth. "There's actually a potential client I'm hoping to sign while we're out here. Have you heard of the Guerrilla Somm?"

"That twenty-one-year-old who tie-dyed a sweatshirt with a bottle of Pétrus?"

"That's the one. Takes guts to eviscerate a $5,000 bottle that every other critic gushes about. I feel like he could write the new wine bible, call it the *Guerrilla Guide*, something gutsy, for the countercultural kids." It was the first time David had elucidated the proposition out loud to someone besides Anjali and the Guerrilla Somm's publicists (he had three). It sounded solid, if a little fusty. "Countercultural kids" surely did not refer to themselves as such. What did ascendant anarchists call themselves, these days? He made a mental note to Google it.

Hari bobbed his head, chewing over what David said. "Is there much money in that, though?"

How quickly the MP had discerned David's pain point. The problem with edgy, iconoclastic, and (often) quite young clients was that their fans didn't read books—who needed books when the never-ending wonders of the World Wide Web beckoned?—and the last thing their detractors wanted was to buy something that would make the enemy richer and more relevant. David had thought his agency, Unsung, could do for unlikely authors what other agencies had done for social media stars—he could give them credibility and a wider platform, and they could give him 15 percent.

But 15 percent of $45,000, the grand total of the book deals he'd brokered in his first year of business, was barely enough to pay for a month of childcare (the cost of which had recently spiked, thanks to Lucie's new medication). Which meant that Anjali had to support them. Which meant that Anjali had no time to do the things that Anjali wanted to do—go to yoga, work on her novel, "go on a girls' trip like every other mom at drop-off." (Who she would go on such a trip with, David did not know, since she didn't have many girlfriends and every time Rachel invited her someplace, Anjali declined, even though David offered to pick up the slack.) Which meant that Anjali was unhappy, and specifically, unhappy with him.

"How did I let this happen?" he'd heard her mutter to herself the week before. She was chopping an onion into ever smaller bits, bringing the knife down with a rhythm and force that he found alarming. He was telling her about a tattoo artist that he had previously pegged as the next Glennon Doyle (a former churchgoer and addict with a Tracy Anderson body, she seemed to have it all). She had contractually agreed to ink her book on the backs of a small army of female followers. It was a brilliant marketing tactic, a viral sensation lying in wait, a stunt that would stun the publishing industry and move physical books by the boatload . . . if it ever happened. She had absconded to Bali to "rebalance."

"She's not responding to email or WhatsApp. My calls are going straight to voice mail," he'd told Anjali. "What should we do? Alert the authorities?"

"*We* are doing nothing," she'd said then, driving the knife into the cutting board so hard that it stuck.

Their therapist would later implore Anjali to spell out her frustrations instead of going for a zinger, and Anjali would half-heartedly vow to avoid placing blame, preface statements with "I feel." David felt good about none of this. David *wanted* to be the provider, or at least hold up his end of the bargain. He had every intent of making Unsung a no-holds-barred success; he just needed one big hit. The Guerrilla Somm. The Guerrilla Somm could be his Mike Piazza.

(Despite growing up on the Upper West Side, in die-hard Yankee territory, David had always rooted for the Mets. He loved an underdog.) The Guerrilla Somm could net him a commission and a publicity coup that would get Unsung off the ground, which would prove that, despite his less-than-honorable discharge from Archetype, striking out on his own had been smart. Wise. The right move.

"That's the beauty of books," David said to Hari now, slapping a smile on his face. "You never know what'll sell." You really didn't, and he preferred not to fixate on that fact. He looked for a conversational out and found one up ahead. "Wait—is this . . . are we here?"

Adolfo had slowed to a stop in front of a stately birchwood gate. He pressed a button on the call box, and the gate parted in two, revealing a long, undulating gravel drive lined, on either side, with oak and manzanita trees. The sky: cornflower blue. The birds: chirping. The overall effect: like something out of a Tuscan fever dream.

"Damn," V said, from the row behind Hari. "They are not playing around."

~

Established soon after the Sprinter hurtled out of SFO: no one knew why—or how—Raj and Rachel had bought a winery. "I mean, they've always *liked* wine, I guess," Anjali had said, suppressing the memory of her and Raj sharing a bottle of Two Buck Chuck that she'd brought back to campus after fall break, freshman year. She'd snuck it out of the cardboard box in her parents' basement and felt briefly invincible, showing up at his dorm room and whipping it out of her Kipling backpack with a coy "Guess what I got . . ." until he ruffled her hair, lifted up the edge of his duvet, and revealed a full case of Yellow Tail shiraz, which, at the time, in their unformed minds, was to Trader Joe's wine what gold was to plastic. "Nice of you to think of me, though," Raj had said, piercing the foil of the Two Buck Chuck with a corkscrew. It had a leather handle and a logo embossed in gold: "Ranjani Realty." Below that, in smaller, italicized letters: "Est. 1979, Los Angeles, California."

"I knew their fund was doing well, but not *that* well," Hari had said. Anjali noted the "their" and felt a pang of possessiveness, unexpected and unwanted.

"I'm here for a good time, not a long time," V had said, which didn't really make sense, but then Anjali looked over and saw that V was talking into her phone, recording a video.

Now, the three of them joined David in gazing, stupefied, out the windows of the van, which was approaching a sprawling compound at the end of the path's final slope. Looming into view: a contemporary Craftsman of warm wood and wide walls of glass. To its left: an aquamarine infinity pool, a sunken Jacuzzi, a boccie ball court, and a firepit ringed with Adirondack chairs. Past that, a guesthouse, a miniature version of the main residence, and an undulating vineyard, rolling hills of green. Finally, there was Kismet Cellars, which comprised two buildings—a winery and tasting room—perched on a swath of sandstone.

"Ten mill, at least," Hari said, as if estimating the price of the property would enable him to make sense of how it belonged to his friends. Anjali had seen him play this game. To her, the sight of this place, even though she'd Googled it, even though she'd watched the YouTube teaser announcing the arrival of Kismet Cellars and a "new era in Napa" no less than two dozen times, was stupefying in that it made her feel stupid. She did not know a person could live like this, let alone any person—people—with whom she had grown up and come of age.

Adolfo came to a stop in a semicircular driveway and hopped down to unload the bags; the group filed out, Anjali trailing David. She noticed it first: the broken glass by the front door, the brick in the entryway, the sound of a woman's voice, distant but shrill, refusing to relent. "Wait," she said, grabbing David's arm. She turned to the driver, as if he had all the answers. "What's going on?"

~

"Can you *please* keep your voice down? They're going to be here any minute."

Raj knew that telling Rachel to, in essence, be quiet was on par with "calm down" as one of the top ten worst things to say to a woman, but he'd reached his wits' end. First the broken glass, then the note on the brick that had gone through the window at who knew what hour, because the godforsaken "state of the art" security system had yet to be installed; now this, his wife, apoplectic, mad at him for something that was not at all his fault, every trace of her earlier obsequiousness gone, just like that.

"I *knew* something was up, I fucking *knew* it." She tensed up like she wanted to punch something—a pillow, a wall, him. Most likely, him.

They were in the primary suite, one long flight of stairs and another long hallway away from the rest of the house, in a space that would normally be soundproof, but with the broken window he couldn't be sure. This was not how you welcomed guests. If his father had taught him anything, it was to host with aplomb, immense graciousness, to offer the best of the best. Now, their friends would be arriving to broken glass and a brick that he wanted to move but knew he shouldn't. If he wanted to put a stop to this—and he did want to put a stop to it—he'd have to have the thing dusted for prints.

That ex-NYPD guy, what was his name? Ralph. Yes, Ralph would know what to do. Ralph would offer, at least, the illusion of safety, and Ralph owed him one.

He called Ralph, explained the situation, and told him to keep a running tab. He'd pay Ralph later.

The first step of damage control: avoid future damage. The second: clean up the mess.

"Where's the broom?" he asked, striding purposefully out of the suite and down the hall, opening closets that he was pretty sure contained linens and not the broom, but you never knew, and maybe the action would distract Rachel, or redirect her rage to the fact that he could never remember where the cleaning supplies were in this house (or any of their houses, for that matter). At least he could deal with that kind of rage. "Where's Jany? Isn't she supposed to be here?"

"Do not try to change the subject," Rachel said, storming after him. "You cannot get away with this. You think I'm shallow, that all I care about is *Instagram*, that I'm so self-obsessed, but you're the one, *you're* the one who's obsessed, obsessed with—"

"Hello?" A voice he'd know anywhere, live from the ground floor. It made him feel . . . something. He couldn't put his finger on it.

"Raj, Rachel? Are you guys okay?"

No, wait, he could. It made him feel eighteen again.

Raj whipped around to face Rachel and caught a flash of her almond-shaped fingernails, painted an iridescent pink, such a lovely shade, such a stark contrast from the woman they were attached to. He wondered how sharp those tips actually were, if he ought to steel himself. But Rachel didn't have it in her, to act out like that. She talked a big game, but in the end, she never got her hands dirty. God forbid she break a nail.

"Sweetheart," he said evenly, pressing his palms together, "our guests are here. Why don't you take a minute, pull yourself together, do what you need to do, and come on down?"

She blinked at him, then at the framed photo hanging next to them, a moody black-and-white panorama of the vineyard just before harvest. She yanked it off the wall, dropped it on the floor, and stuck her Valentino heel through the glass, shattering it with a crisp *snap*.

"Done!" she said, flashing him a saccharine smile. "Jany doesn't get back until two. Ahmad will be here at three. You can take care of this"—she gestured at the mess at her feet—"when you're done with that." She gestured at the entryway, where the broken window and their guests awaited, and strode ahead of him, down the stairs. "Anjali!" he heard her call out, happily. He took one breath and then another. He clenched and unclenched his fists. He could do this. He knew what to say. It would all be fine.

"What's up, guys?" he bellowed as he came down the stairs. He could hear the smile in his voice, the genial, jovial air. He adopted a similar tone whenever he had to fire someone, a "you can't get mad at me because I'm so goddamn likable" kind of ease.

"Our friends were just wondering about the mess," Rachel said, batting her eyes at him like Bambi. Evil Bambi. Bambi with devil horns and pitchfork tongue.

"Oh, *that*," Raj said. He shook his head as he made eye contact with each of them, measuring their level of discomfort. Minimal. None of them looked spooked enough to leave. A Howard Backen–designed home had that effect. You'd be amazed by what you could get away with.

"Minor inconvenience," he continued. "I'll tell you all about it." As he spoke, he crossed the foyer and closed the space between him and Hari, the most obvious person to hug first, if not the one he wanted to.

"Bro! Been a minute," he said, slapping Hari's back. From the feel of Hari's Steely Dan shirt—soft, too soft to actually be from the seventies, when they made band T-shirts with stiff cotton and not whatever this jersey blend was—Raj could tell that Hari hadn't changed a bit. Still striving. Still vying for acceptance. Still not entirely convinced that he belonged. Still the type of guy who spends $200 on a "vintage" T-shirt from Dover Street Market that was actually made in Vietnam the previous year.

"Looking good, my man," Hari said. Raj saw Hari's gaze flit to his biceps as he made some kind of assessment. Probably wondering who could bench more. Raj could bench him under the table. He'd bet a grand on it. Easy money.

"So, when do we get to taste your juice?" Hari asked, rubbing his palms together. Raj wondered if the homoerotic allusion was intentional or if Hari was just that un-self-aware. This was the guy who thought "Harry V" was preferable to sounding out his actual name. Poor kid. You had to feel for the folks with eighteen syllables, who ran out of room on standardized forms. To think what it did to your sense of belonging. You couldn't blame him for wanting to fit in.

"It'll be seven years before the first vintage is even worth trying," Raj said, "but we've got plenty of stuff to tide us over."

From there, he moved on to Victoria (divorce looked good on her, he thought, mentally apologizing to her ex-husband, with whom he was actually closer, but Dev was in India and V had RSVP'd yes, so what could you do?) and David. He saved Anjali for last. "Hey, loser," she said when he brought her in for a hug, which made him laugh, which made her laugh, which intensified that feeling of . . . whatever he felt when he first heard her voice, in real life, after nearly a decade. Youth? Virility? Possibility?

He pulled back and held her at arm's length. Same old Anjali. Same old whatever clothes, because she couldn't be bothered to follow fashion trends, busy, as she was, being intellectual, wading in the world of the mind. He could see her assessing him, a smirk playing at her lips, probably coming up with some crack about his shirt or his shoes or his watch, a Patek, though she probably had no idea what a Patek was, poor thing.

"How those Skechers working out for you?" he asked. Would he allude to another woman's butt with her husband within earshot? Never. But this was Anjali. Anjali could take it. Anjali knew how to banter. Anjali *liked* to banter, he knew that. And David . . . well, David had the spine of a jellyfish. It didn't take a genius to figure that out.

"Not as well as doping seems to be working out for *you*," she shot back, brightly. "What are you on these days? HGH? Baby blood?"

Oh, how he'd missed a worthy adversary. He mentally patted himself on the back for doing supersets that morning. His transformation from skinny-fat beer-pong champion to ripped beer-pong champion (old habits die hard) had been the product of a rigorous weight-lifting regimen and the occasional burst of cardio, nothing more complex than that.

Well, there'd been one round of CoolSculpting. Okay, two. For his abs. He was Indian. There was no other way.

They all had their things. Rachel had her running, the periodic shot of filler in her lips, and while she did not look like the nineteen-year-old he had met in the North Campus cafeteria twenty years ago, she had kept it tight. He saw how Hari looked her up and down and felt pride and possessiveness mixed with something else. He toggled his gaze from Anjali to Rachel. Skechers to Valentino. Funny to crazy. Well, perhaps that was putting too fine a point on it. All women were crazy, in their own ways.

~

Something wasn't adding up, but Anjali told the part of her brain insistent on adding things up to give it a rest. She had spent the early hours of the afternoon ticking things off her never-ending list. She talked to Priya. Talked to Lucie. Talked Moran down from the ledge during the drive up to Napa, sent him her edits once she got on the Wi-Fi at the house (after the first glass of Champagne), sent a memo to graphics (after the second), sent a status update to her boss (the third). Now, she was off. The autoresponder was on. There was nothing to worry about. There was only more Mt Tam to eat, caviar to bump, Dom Pérignon to drink.

"Racism," Raj had said, shaking his head defeatedly, like he couldn't believe racism still existed. This was after they'd said their hellos when they were all still in the foyer. "What can I say? I'm sorry you guys had to see this."

According to him, while most of their new Napa neighbors had welcomed them with open arms, there were a few who weren't thrilled by people of color acquiring prime vines in the valley. "You know how few Black-owned wineries there are in Napa? They've dealt with this too," he said, leading the way to the open-plan chef's kitchen, which was anchored by a farmhouse sink and a stone island the size of a small country. As he slid a magnum of Dom out of the Sub-Zero, David slid the last of the broken window into a dustpan. ("Please, cleaning is my thing," he said when Raj protested, and it was true—David's saving grace was that he seized on opportunities to wipe down counters and floors, though Anjali suspected that was because those were the low hanging fruit of household tasks, the grapes that grazed the ground.)

"Never mind that the previous owners defaulted on their loan," Raj had said, easing the cork from the bottle with a satisfying *pop*, "and this land, this primo cabernet sauvignon soil—did I mention that some of the vines date back to the 1800s?"

"No shit," Hari had said, leaning against the fridge. Anjali could practically see him trying to crunch the numbers in his head. Loan default plus rarefied real estate—did that equal less than $10 million? More?

"So, if we hadn't come in," Raj went on, "this all would've gone back to the government, and God knows what *they* would've done with it."

"Low-income housing," said Hari.

"Exactly," said Raj, placing the Dom on the kitchen's marble island. "And wouldn't these racist white pricks have loved that? Sorry, David," he said immediately, holding up his hands, as if he'd forgotten David was there.

"No harm done," David said, leaning the broom against the wall. Another saving grace of David's: he was used to being the only white guy in the room, disappearing into the background. He allowed for the world to not revolve around him.

"Do you know who did it?" Anjali asked. "Or how they got through the gates?"

"Yes, dear, do you know?" Rachel echoed, returning from some other part of the house with a box of champagne flutes. "Sorry," she said to everyone else, "I meant to put these out earlier, but wouldn't you know it, I got sidetracked."

"And doesn't it count for something that your wife is basically Barbie?" Hari asked.

"Hari, you were always my favorite," Rachel said, giving him a campy bat of the eyes as Raj filled a succession of flutes.

"Oh, that makes it worse," Raj said. "It's like I took one of their own."

"Isn't that your specialty, darling," Rachel said, "raping and pillaging?" Silence. Uncomfortable silence. "Oh, come on," Rachel said, "I'm talking about markets, *obviously*." She dissolved into laughter.

To Anjali, the tension between Raj and Rachel was as obvious as Rachel's lip filler (heartening to know that filters had their limits), but Raj seemed unfazed. He explained that the CCTV security system was supposed to have been installed the previous week, but the dispatcher had called and said they were missing some crucial component and had to postpone two more weeks. Raj figured that given their remote location, on sixty acres of land, and keypad-coded gate, they could make do.

"But given recent events, clearly not," he said. "I know a guy. Ex-NYPD. I've already called him. Someone will be patrolling the grounds round the clock. I promise," he said, passing the last glass to Hari and lifting his own, "you all are safe with me. And Rachel, too, of course." He smiled and nodded in his wife's direction.

Rachel raised her eyebrows at him and downed her glass in one gulp.

But then she pulled out a charcuterie and cheese board, and Raj opened up a 500 g tin of Petrossian Royal Ossetra, and V taught them all how to do caviar bumps—"like coke but you won't die"—and a familiar buzz flooded Anjali's veins. Hadn't some of her happiest days been with this very group of people? The Slope Day of their junior year, the one with Kanye West, when she and Rachel mixed Everclear and Kool-Aid in a thirteen-gallon garbage bin; the Slope Day of their senior year, the one with Snoop Dogg, when she and Hari snuck into Sigma Phi and stole a bag of weed. She needed to let go. She needed another glass of Champagne. She needed to send one last email from the confines of her suite and then shut her laptop as she flopped on the duvet, as soft as a cloud; she needed to kick off her shoes and slide into the monogrammed slippers that had been left in every room, like some fabulous hotel.

She needed to talk to Rachel, properly *talk*—it was clear that she and Raj were fighting, that hers was the voice Anjali had heard upon arrival. It was easy to dismiss Rachel as a Beverly Hills Housewife when she appeared on Anjali's phone, but seeing her now, in the flesh, reminded Anjali of the depth of their friendship, the Mariana Trenchness of it all. (Also, weren't some of those housewives unequivocally successful, more so than Anjali herself?) Anjali wanted to help, to be a shoulder to lean on, should Rachel need one, to make up for having been a selfish, spiteful friend.

But now was not the time. Now was the time to listen to V's bizarre encounters from a music festival in Thailand and let Rachel educate her on the modern miracle of laser hair removal, which gave Anjali an excuse to unabashedly gawk at her old friend's new physique and wonder just how many procedures, and what exactly, she'd had done. Now was the time to gaze fondly at her husband as he played beer pong—well, Dom pong—on the dining table on the deck, holding his own against Raj and Hari because he'd gone to Colgate and participated in his share of Natty Light–fueled drinking games like all self-respecting graduates of upstate New York educational institutions ought to.

Lunch was decreed unnecessary, on account of the spread—Époisses, Calabrese, mortadella, Midnight Moon, and that was just the south end of the board—and the group's upcoming reservation at Upsilon, "Napa's most exciting new restaurant," according to *Eater*, where dinner comprised twenty-one courses.

"So, really, how *are* you?" Anjali asked Rachel as they hunched over the island and dragged Tostitos through a vat of hummus that Jany (the wonder of having a live-in housekeeper) had picked up at Oxbow Market.

"Oh, *fine*," Rachel said. Anjali couldn't read her eyes, hidden, as they were, behind a pair of oversized Celine sunglasses. "I mean, trying to figure out if I married a monster, but who's not, right?" And then V darted over and grabbed both their hands because this Rüfüs Du Sol song that she loved had just miraculously found its way onto the sound system and that was a sign, that meant they *had* to dance, and Anjali had to tell herself that now was not the time for a heart-to-heart with Rachel and keep herself from pointing out that V had synced her phone to the sound system, so why *wouldn't* a Rüfüs Du Sol song that she loved come on?

She was open and in the moment, just as she'd vowed to be. That was an achievement. That was something.

As the late-afternoon sun filtered through the manzanitas and painted splotchy puddles of light across the lawn, she found herself outside, alone, with a half-full glass, twirling, lightly, to the tropical house music that was coming from the estate. She heard Hari yell that he was going to put on Coldplay and laughed to herself. Some things never changed.

She leaned against a wide, wizened oak and let her back slide down so that she was sitting at its base.

"Is this where the Bollywood song comes in?"

She turned her head. "Raj?"

He sidled out from the other side of the tree, head wagging, Champagne sloshing, singing, in a lilting voice that could've been mistaken for that of a sari-clad starlet, *"Dil hai chhota sa, chhoti si asha."*

She doubled over laughing. He smiled down at her and shrugged. "It's pretty much a rule—if you're Indian and under a tree, a Bollywood dance number can't be far behind."

"Oh, you dance now, too?" she said, wiping a tear from her eye.

"With the right partner," he said.

She met his gaze. "I'm pretty sure what you just sang translates to 'my little heart desires.' What on earth could your little heart desire?" She gestured around the lawn. "You have more land than Elon Musk."

"You, of all people, should know that Elon Musk does not believe in owning land anymore. That bird"—a sparrow flitting between blades of grass—"owns more land than Elon Musk."

"Fair," she said. "I guess I just meant wealth. Riches." She wanted to take it back, seeing the look on his face. "Sorry, too much Champagne, my head is not on straight."

He held out a hand to help her up. "Hydrate. We have an IV nurse on call, if you want."

"Of course you do," she said, rolling her eyes and dusting herself off.

"Riches," he repeated, laughing. "Do you always talk like an eighteenth-century English lord?"

She playfully slapped his arm. "You know what I meant: money. God, now it sounds so classless, I shouldn't have said anything at all. Your little heart can desire whatever it wants. Have at it."

He glanced at her coyly. "Okay."

5

Thursday evening
Upsilon, downtown Napa

It was criminal, what you could get away with once you had a Michelin star, Anjali thought, glowering at the plate in front of her, course ten of twenty-one. "Course" was a generous way of putting it. Atop the disc of porcelain was a mound of something crumbly and brown.

"Dirt," a soft-voiced server had said as she set down the dish with the precision of a Juilliard-trained ballet dancer. "Chef encourages you to use your hands."

This fucking chef. Seamus Matheson had been a struggling actor picking up shifts at a La Colombe on the east side of Los Angeles when Gaggan Anand, he of two Michelin stars, asked to meet the man responsible for brewing the most delicate blonde roast he'd ever had the pleasure of tasting. Gaggan had taken Seamus under his wing, to Thailand, to the temple of theatrics and haute cuisine that he had named after himself, and put him in charge of the pour-over situation, then the entire bar program—Seamus had a flair for shaken cocktails and the muscles to match—and finally, given him the role that, on the twenty-two-hour journey from LAX to BKK, he had dreamed of one day inhabiting: sous chef. In Gaggan's universe, a sous chef did not need to know how to cook—the back-of-the-house folks did the mincing, the searing, the heavy lifting. A sous chef was a *star*. (Well, costar. Gaggan headlined.)

The two would preside over a chef's table shaped like a boxing ring, with twenty seats on the outside and them in the middle. While shaving truffle onto masala-marinated Wagyu and dusting garlic prawns with crystals of dehydrated *tom yum*, they would riff on current events, rib each other, and—the impetus for one Netflix special, several articles, and thousands of online reviews—make fun of every person at the table. Nabbing a seat at the Bangkok restaurant (prepaid, $700, plus a 30 percent service charge) required completing a questionnaire that asked, among other things, about the most embarrassing thing that you had ever done. Toward the end of the night, once the majority of the table was swaying from overconsumption in one form or another (a pairing of natural wines cost an additional $300, and almost all the diners sprang for it), this information would be skewered and served up as entertainment, to the (general) delight of everyone involved.

The truth about people who pay $700 for a dinner is that they don't often get made fun of, at least in public. Sometimes you want to be torn apart. Dominatrix logic.

Anjali had read the *New York Times Magazine* profile of Seamus Matheson, knew from whence he came, was aware of how he had adapted Gaggan's formula to suit his own strengths and the appetites of the gourmands who fell on Napa Valley more frequently than rain. She had familiarized herself with Upsilon's accolades, had known that this would be a slog but figured it would also be a story, an experience, something worth doing if, for nothing else, than to say she had done it. She was aware that she might be enjoying all this more if she had tucked away her skepticism someplace unreachable, beneath the folds of her Spanx, which were somehow still visible through her jersey maxi dress, one of those affairs that can be tied in twenty-four different ways, that she had bought off Instagram. (Was she "on" Instagram? No. Did she sometimes get suckered into the eerily prescient "explore" page of the app when she was looking up Rachel or something work adjacent or one of the moms at Lucie's school or—*yes*, yes, a thousand times yes.)

The thing was, Anjali needed her skepticism. It made her viable. Who would she be if she simply accepted this plate of "dirt" with a smile and a nod, if she murmured thoughtfully as she sampled what very well could've come from the potted marijuana plant that this chef surely kept in the back, if she . . . *licked up* the crumbs like Victoria was doing while batting her eyes at the chef?

"Smart," Seamus said, now watching Victoria, arms crossed. He was in the donut hole in the center of their table, which was on an elevated platform in the middle of Upsilon's bustling dining room—Seamus's version of a stage, inspired, unabashedly, by his mentor. "Easy to do that with this dish, though."

"Oh, I'm just getting warmed up," said Victoria, "in case there's anything . . . *girthy* later." She winked, a fan of eyelashes dusting a dewy cheek.

Disgusting. These people were disgusting, Anjali thought to herself. *She* was disgusting, taking part in this unabashed display of disposable income and depravity. If she was being honest, though, it wasn't Victoria or Seamus or the Michelin committee or even the "dirt" that was at the root of her irritation, although, whatever was on her plate, it wasn't helping—the few morsels she'd tasted, with a fork, brought to mind burnt potato skins and made her yearn for the baggies of Goldfish and Babybels that she kept for the kids in her vegan leather carry-all. She could *live* on Goldfish and Babybels. Happily.

What actually disgusted her was Raj, or more specifically, the sensation that Raj had aroused in her that afternoon, that she had not felt in many years, certainly, not at the hands of him. He was not supposed to want her. She was not supposed to want him. Rachel's arrival on campus, upon transferring to Cornell the spring semester of freshman year, had blocked that path as effectively as an overturned eighteen-wheeler in the middle of I-80. Anjali could not get around Rachel and, over time, had come to respect that. Raj and Rachel were made for each other. The Maharaja and his blonde-haired, blue-eyed Rani, a *Baywatch*-era Pamela Anderson crossed with Kelly Kapowski. An Indian American boy born in the late twentieth century could not have dreamed bigger.

And yet, something was very wrong. Wrong to the degree that Rachel had called Raj a monster. Wrong to the degree that glass had broken in some other area of the house—Anjali had heard it, as well as the strain in Rachel's voice, as the group had tentatively entered the foyer. (Did one of them drop a glass? Punch a mirror? The more she thought about it, the more unsettled she felt.)

Wrong to the degree that Raj had all but invited Anjali to . . . what? What *had* he invited her to do under that oak tree? They were close enough to kiss, but he had remained where he was, and she, freaked out by his frankness or attempt at flirtation or whatever it was, had awkwardly said she had to run to the restroom and booked it across the backyard. Maybe she was making too much of it. Maybe he was just drunk.

Maybe it was a power play, his way of demonstrating that he could still manipulate her emotions like a puppeteer, pull a string just for the thrill of knowing he could.

She hated that her heart responded. That her skepticism, in the moment, had vanished.

"Not digging the dirt?"

She turned to David, next to her, and shook her head at both his question and his dad joke. She reached over and squeezed his shoulder. David had his flaws but at least emotional manipulation wasn't one of them.

Inside the donut hole, Seamus clapped his hands together. "What you just had," he said, "was the pulverized remains of our heirloom root vegetables, a kind of"—he wiggled his fingers in the air, as if searching for the right word—"*cremation* of the cold winter months."

"It's July," said Anjali.

"And every restaurant in this uninspired town is serving tomatoes," said Seamus. "Tomatoes are expected, tomatoes are *safe*. We don't *do* safe." From a shelf beneath the edge of the circular table, Seamus unearthed a meat cleaver and began banging the blunt side of it against his palm. "'*Ooo*, tomatoes and *burrata*,'" he said, raising his voice an octave, imitating some stereotype of a Napa tourist, causing heads around the restaurant to turn. "'*Ooo*, tomatoes and capers,' '*Ooo*, tomato carpaccio,' as if, if you slice a tomato *whisper*-thin"—a theatric expiration—"it magically turns into a piece of meat." He locked eyes with Anjali. "You can go to Whole Foods and get that shit: $3.99 a pound."

She smiled at him sweetly. "How far is that from here?"

"Funny," Seamus said, cracking a smile and pointing the meat cleaver at her. "*Funny.* I like this one." He turned to Raj. "Where'd you find her?"

"College Ave., orientation week, vomiting into a bush," Raj replied. Rachel said his name in an admonishing tone and Hari whooped; Raj smirked but his eyes told a different story, finding Anjali's, asking for permission after the fact.

"Marko," Seamus called out to his beverage director, "shot of mezcal for this one." He pointed to Anjali. "My special bottle."

While Seamus prattled on about his logic for the "B side"—the second half of the menu; they had eleven courses to go—Anjali nursed her shot of mezcal (to her Goldfish-trained palate, it tasted like wood warped by rain and left to rot) and stirred the murky cauldron of her heart and mind. She and Raj hadn't spoken, one-on-one, in years. Since before he and Rachel got married. It was one thing to act like no time had passed with friends, but she and Raj were more complicated than that. "Former lovers" was a stretch—albeit a glamorous one—and it elided the point. For a brief period of time, they had known each other like the backs of their hands, and then he had gone and fallen for Rachel—everyone always fell for Rachel—and that was that. The banter, the inside jokes, the degree to which he was trying to be close to Anjali were inappropriate, especially since she was, in theory, better friends with Rachel, and more than that, married.

What mattered, though? In theory or in practice? Because in practice, despite the fact that Rachel basically told Anjali that Raj was a monster, Anjali could not stop herself from fixating on Raj and how he made her feel. What if this was what Rachel was talking about? she wondered now. Was this who he'd become? Did he prey on unsuspecting women who wanted to feel wanted? Was he a serial cheater? A sex addict? Did he want to have sex with *her*?

And if the answer was yes, what did she want to do with him?

"Sorry to interrupt." A voice from behind broke Anjali out of her inward spiral, and she watched as a man in a navy sport coat and striped shirt climbed up the steps separating their pavilion from the dining room floor and walked around to shake Raj's hand. "I saw you from my table and I just had to come up and thank you in person. You've single-handedly saved my practice."

Anjali watched as Raj performed a show of modesty. She tried to hear what they were talking about. Who was this guy? What kind of practice would owe a debt of gratitude to Raj? Real estate? Wouldn't that be called an agency or a brokerage? Unless this guy was talking about a yoga practice. The thought of Raj doing yoga. The only thing more absurd was the idea that he was into her.

~

"Seriously, though—I knew Ranjani Realty was printing cash, but I had no idea it was doing, like, racks on *racks*."

Raj grinned into his lap but shook his head, as if Hari had been haranguing him about money all day (which Hari kind of, sort of, had). "Bro, come on. We're at dinner! At Upsilon! Can we please talk about literally anything else?"

Typical, Hari thought. In all the time they'd known each other, Raj had hated to talk about money. At least, Raj had hated to talk about money with *him*. He knew that, back in the house they shared at Cornell sophomore through senior years, Raj and Dev had had long, winding conversations about the privilege and pain of coming from wealth (as if there were any real pains), waxing poetic about the burden of having to work for their fathers once they logged a few years in the corporate world. These conversations would inevitably arise after a case of Natty Light had been crushed and scattered about the parquet floor, after so many rounds of beer pong had been played that they'd lost count, after Raj had packed the hookah and commandeered the first dozen puffs.

"Do I want to do commercial real estate? Sure," Raj had said, feet kicked up on their ring-laden coffee table, like he owned the place (technically, he did—Raj's father had bought the house for "couch cushion money," deeming it as worthy an investment as any, and they were all paying Uncle Ranjani rent). "But I don't want to be my dad's little bitch boy, have him watching my every move."

He paused to blow out three perfect Os of smoke. "Like, let me start my own branch in New York, let me take the fucking, whatever the fuck"—he twirled the pipe in the air, searching for the word—"*jitney* to the Hamptons, let me bang some chicks at Bungalow, let me *live*."

"Bro, you ain't taking no jitney," Dev had said, laughing as he reached for the pipe.

"Yeah," Raj said, smirking in a self-deprecating way, "I'm not a bus bitch, but if the bus is where the bitches be at . . ." He turned up his palms as if he were actually thinking about taking the jitney at some point in the conceivable future. It was January with a windchill of negative four; more importantly, Uncle Ranjani owned a helicopter.

"I get it, man," Dev had said, after blowing out his own set of Os. "You think I want to go back to ATL and run a bunch of Holiday Inns? Money's good and the chicken's bomb—seriously, we're going to Magic City next time you come; your beef with strip clubs is wack—but like, to have your future written when you're a baby?"

Hari had sat glumly in the navy-blue beanbag chair, waiting his turn. (He always wound up last in the smoking rotation; Raj, who owned the hookah and supplied it with premium tobacco that one of his "boys" in Los Angeles shipped to him every other Friday, was always first.)

It was not true that Hari came from nothing: his father had a fine job as a mechanical engineer in Cleveland, Ohio, a gold-watch-after-thirty-years type of gig; his mother had stayed at home. Hari and his younger sister had grown up with zero complaints or trauma beyond the usual first-generation stuff (seemingly barbed questions about multiarmed deities and redolent Tupperware contents that, in retrospect, were mostly justified expressions of curiosity from sheltered kids who didn't know a lot of Indian people).

Then he got to Cornell. Then he met Raj, his freshman-year roommate, who arrived in High Rise Five suite 2410 wearing a two-tone 1983 Datejust.

"You for real with that Rolly?" Hari had asked, awed. He had never seen a Rolex in real life.

Raj had narrowed his eyes, as if making an assessment about Hari right then and there. "Nothing fake about me, dawg," he'd said.

Hari felt like Raj had placed him in a box that day, the Middle-Class Friend box. The Will Never Be a Master of the Universe box. The Will Always Be Second to Me in Matters of Taste, Money, and Women box. (Maybe that last part was in his head. Maybe.) How he yearned to break out of that box, or better yet, not give a fuck about being in the box at all. He'd been trying for years to just get over it. He had plenty of other friends: coworkers at MCG, classmates from business school, the guys in his squash league at the New York Athletic Club. Yet Raj had always exerted some gravitational pull over him. Hari chalked it up to the length of time they'd known each other, how, from day one, Raj had set a bar that Hari yearned to reach, and every time Hari got close, felt like he was *right there*, Raj moved it up again.

What can you do? Hari asked himself now, easing a steak knife across a breast of Szechuan-peppercorn-crusted Sonoma duck. ("Chef wants you to feel the thrill of the kill," a wisp of a server had said, setting the plate down along with a jade-handled weapon of minute destruction from Japan, "so he asks that you slice it yourself." Way to delegate, Hari thought.)

He paused as the breast released a pool of blood the color of Barolo. Raj was Raj, set in his ways. If he refused to let Hari out of the box he'd put him in two decades ago, so be it. Hari couldn't deny that Raj had forced him to level up. To live bigger. To dream bigger. To want more. Had he even known what Barolo was, before he met Raj? Not in the slightest. So, fine, his friend would never tell him how much was in the bank or where exactly it came from because Ranjani Realty was not, *could not* be liquid enough to justify the purchase of a winery and estate as lavish as Kismet. He didn't need to know Raj's net worth. He just needed a tiny portion of it, the most incremental of investments, a smattering of chum to get the institutional sharks interested, and judging from the looks of this weekend, what he was asking for would be "couch cushion" money, in Raj's book. Like father, like son.

"Okay," Hari said. "Top five restaurants you've been to this year. Off the top of your head. Not including this one. I'll start—Bo Innovation."

Raj made a face like the duck had turned. "That glorified Panda Express in Hong Kong? Not even glorified—I'd rather eat at Panda Express than that scam castle."

"You've been?" asked Hari.

"Couple months ago," said Raj, "regrettably."

"You should've given me a heads-up. I spent, like, half of Q1 there. Would've sent you my spreadsheet." Hari prided himself on his spreadsheets of recommendations in various cities and airline lounges around the world. An ex-girlfriend had once likened him to the Points Guy, favorably, he thought.

"Last-minute," Raj said, wiping a dollop of yuzu-Parmesan glaze from the corner of his mouth. "Had business in Shenzhen."

Hari mentally tallied things made in Shenzhen: smartphones, semiconductor chips, tablets, headphones, vapes—what business would the head of LA's largest commercial real estate firm have in Shenzhen?

"Where'd you stay?"

"Upper House."

"Sexy."

Raj laughed. "It's what was available on Fine Hotels & Resorts."

"Didn't want to cash in some Bonvoy points?"

"Bro, you know I don't fuck with Marriott."

Hari knew, from his own frequent trips to Hong Kong, that Upper House—with its plethora of velvet and track lighting so dim, you needed the flashlight on your phone to find your room—was a favorite of high-end escorts and the men who could afford them. It was not a business hotel, unless you were in that sort of business. (He went for the golf, both at the Royal Hong Kong club and to advise a golf club manufacturer that was based in the central business district.)

He glanced at Rachel, next to Raj and easily within earshot. He could save this line of questioning for later. Surely, Raj still smoked. Surely, there would be a hookah session at some point this weekend. He asked Raj to get on with his list.

"Well, Osteria Francescana, obviously." Raj and Rachel had gone to Italy for their most recent wedding anniversary. Modena, Florence, Milan, and finally, Lake Como, where they had fought so vociferously that a security guard at Villa d'Este knocked on their door to make sure that everything was okay. (Hari knew the first part, not the second.)

"Massimo is the man," Raj said, swallowing his last bite of duck and placing his knife over his fork on his plate. "Invited us to stay at his place next time we're in town."

"No way, René told me the same!" Hari said. He was not on a first-name basis with René Redzepi, and his exact words to Hari had been more along the lines of "Come back sometime," but Raj didn't need to know that. "There's a house on the new compound, kind of like your place up here. You been?"

"Noma? More times than I can count," said Raj. "You been to Narisawa?"

"Best three-star in the world, in my book," said Hari.

"I mean . . . ," said Raj, swirling the remains of a 2012 Marcassin pinot noir (wine pairing No. 13). "It's good, but it's hard to top a Trust Me."

"You're tripping," said Hari. He could never figure out Raj. Three Michelin stars one night, Sugarfish, the McDonald's of sushi, the next. "You been to La Cime in Osaka? Legendary. Their *uni* will make you weep."

"You want to weep?" Raj pushed back from the table, as if about to throw down a trump card. "Mole at Pujol."

"Ten years ago called and wants its favorite restaurant back."

"Oh? Where you eat in Mexico City?"

"Quintonil, obvi."

"I'll take your Quintonil and raise you Septime."

"Mugaritz."

"Piazza Duomo."

"Hof van Cleve."

"Eleven Madison Park."

"Vegan EMP? No way, man," Hari said. "You could not pay me to go there. Not even because of the vegan thing, but the way he treats his staff—a regular despot."

"A despot that dates Demi Moore," said Raj.

"Is that still happening? I thought she'd moved on," said Hari.

"I bet V would know." Raj set down his fourteenth glass of wine—a Harlan cabernet to pair with course fourteen, "brain," a croquette of lamb and cassava shaped like its namesake and served atop pages printed with algebra formulas (also made of cassava).

"Yo, V," Raj called across the table. "Have you been to Eleven Madison Park?"

V nodded. A date with a New York–based daddy, a professor of French literature who, afterward, asked her to put on over-the-knee leather boots and elbow-length leather gloves (both Balenciaga, both purchased by him for her) and give him a sponge bath. No sex, just a sponge bath.

~

Thanks to the acoustics of the dining room and the ridiculous donut-shaped table, Anjali could not help but overhear as Hari, Raj, and V name-dropped high-end restaurants and the famous people who worked at and/or frequented them. Revulsion churned in her stomach. Who cares, she thought. She knew they were superficial but didn't realize how out of place she would feel in their company. She thought she was in the know, working at *Highbrow*, having an office at Rockefeller Center, but the truth was that even if she liked this sort of food, even if she had the time, she didn't get paid enough to treat Eleven Madison Park like the local Applebee's and cultivate a first-name-basis relationship with Daniel Humm. The things they got to do, Anjali thought, turning down her mouth. The fantasy worlds they inhabited.

David checked his phone for the eleventh time. For someone in the business of books, he spent an awful lot of time on his phone of late, forever tugging and releasing. He had applied a "screen protector" that purportedly blocked blue light but also made it impossible to see what was on his screen unless you were looking squarely at it. It irritated Anjali, this screen protector, but the thought of bringing it up and asking him to remove it, of displaying for him the depth of her insecurities, of mothering the man she had married, irritated her even more.

She looked at Rachel, who looked like a *Vogue* model. V too. Raj and Hari, yukking it up, ragging on each other as usual. Seamus, at the center of it all, fucking Victoria with his eyes.

She needed to get out of here. She needed a slice of pizza. She needed to leave before the infuriatingly poised servers dropped another course—what would it be? Toad? Tree branch? Toenail?—and before Seamus began the dreaded sharing of the questionnaire responses. The chef had taken a cue from his mentor and former boss but whittled the list of asks down to one:

"What's the worst thing you've ever done?"

Anjali had laughed when she saw the email from Upsilon. What kind of person would answer honestly? She had nearly forgotten to respond, then dashed off an answer during the ride up to Napa that morning, after receiving an URGENT: RESPONSE NEEDED IMMEDIATELY follow-up from the restaurant. "Forgotten our wedding anniversary," which was a lie on two counts: she hadn't forgotten; she had chosen not to remember or acknowledge it because it had fallen two weeks after David had revealed to her why he had gotten fired, and it wasn't the worst thing she'd ever done. Not by a mile.

Seamus, Hari, Raj, and V were in a heated discussion about the relevance of Michelin stars when Anjali stood up, pushed in her chair, and strode away from the table. She considered posting up at the bar and ordering a gin martini, extra dirty, the drink she thought she should like but had never had the gall to order, but kept walking, past the hostess stand. She pushed through the heavy oak door to the sidewalk outside. Air. Fresh air. Air untainted by Seamus Matheson and her idiotic friends.

She found a patch of brick wall next to the restaurant and leaned against it, taking pressure off the balls of her feet, which felt like fire in the Aldo heels she'd stupidly changed into before dinner. They were her nicest shoes. Rachel probably wouldn't deign to clean the house in them. (Rachel had probably never cleaned a house.)

It was Thursday. If she was going to last through the weekend, she was going to have to change something: her attitude, her behavior, her reaction to everyone else. Her location? Could she change her location? Could she piss off and check in at some luxury hotel and just get massages all weekend? Work on her novel, maybe, work wine country into her tale about a time-traveling henna artist—could the henna artist work a wedding in wine country? Why not?—or find a story worth telling, something like what she had assigned Moran but bigger, better, something uniquely hers?

She had never been more fulfilled than when she was chasing a story, when she was accumulating the pieces and on the cusp of figuring out how they fit together.

She thumbed at her phone. The Montage in Healdsburg (where was Healdsburg, even?) had one room left. It was $1,274. She could not afford the Montage. She probably could not afford a massage at the Montage. She could afford . . . pizza.

She was mapping out the distance to the nearest pizza place as well as the distance from the pizza place to the Montage—what if they had an unpublished rate? What if the woman at the front desk was also an overworked, underappreciated mom and took mercy on her? What if she commandeered a couch in the lobby and refused to leave? What would they do, throw her out?—when she sensed someone approach.

"You're missing ass," Raj said.

"You can't be serious," Anjali said, a grin blooming on her face in spite of herself.

"Pork butt. Pretty standard Korean preparation. Actually—the place I go to in K-town does it better and for about eight times less."

"Wasn't it your idea to go to this horrible restaurant?" Rachel was not a foodie. It was one of the things she and Anjali saw eye to eye on: Goldfish over everything.

"Gotta sample the local holes-in-the-wall, you know?" Raj said, turning to face her. "If I'm going to be mayor of this town one day, I ought to know my neighbors."

"You? Public office? You can't afford your lifestyle on taxpayer dollars, sixteenth-century Barolo and mansions up and down the coasts."

Raj shrugged, genially. "Trump figured it out."

"Modeling yourself after the greats, I see," Anjali said. She enjoyed this. There was something transgressive about it, but she could not deny that she enjoyed it.

"'Make Napa Great Again.' Has a nice ring to it." Raj moved a step closer. The tip of his John Lobb loafer touched the pointed toe of her Aldo heel. "You could run my campaign."

"Now I can't tell if you're kidding or not." She could smell his cologne. Montblanc, a woodsy musk that brought her back to freshman year, High Rise Five, all those feelings that felt palpable enough to burst through her skin.

"Dead serious," he said. He placed his palm on the wall next to her.

"Well, you can't afford me," Anjali said. He had to be kidding. He had a history of doing this, of taking a joke too far.

"I can try," he said, and then pressed his mouth into hers.

6

Friday morning
Kismet Estate, Napa

Rachel awoke to an empty bed, Raj's overstuffed pillows propped up against the headboard, which was a live-edge slice of oak as wide as a boat. Below them, a note, on his creamy Smythson stationery, apologizing for his abrupt departure the night before, citing a fire at the winery that had to be put out, a promise to return soon. Hastily scribbled. When wasn't there a fire? she thought. When wasn't there something more important to attend to than her?

She ran her hand over the fitted sheet, as if to conjure him from the mussed, fog-hued Belgian Linen, and felt the weight on her wrist, a cuff of cool metal against her hot, drowsy skin. Oh, right. Oh, *that.* She almost laughed in disbelief, but when you knew Raj as well as she did, there was no reason to not believe—it totally tracked. She couldn't be mad at him now, and wasn't that the point?

The previous evening, not long before they were due to leave for Upsilon, he had ambled into their bathroom and leaned against the lip of the long Calacatta marble sink, interrupting her application of emerald-green eye shadow and their hours-long streak of not speaking. He had apologized for what she had seen upon arriving at the estate: the brick, the note, the broken window, and the fight that had ensued. He said he was "looking into it," that the group that had filed a complaint against his—*their*—lab had no idea what they were talking about, that there were no causal links, that the science was on his—*their*—side. The Oxnard lab, the latest addition to his—*their*—portfolio, pioneered "game-changing medicine," and these hiccups, these haters, were to be expected.

"The ups and downs are unavoidable," he said.

"Aren't they always, with you?" She was leaning into the amber-lit mirror above the sink, trying and failing to line her right eye. What she'd drawn looked less like a wing and more like a tail, and not even the tail of a bird. Of a terrier, maybe.

"Isn't that why you love me?" he said. "The constant thrills?"

"I could use a little more rom-com and a little less suspense," she said, daubing her eye with makeup remover. "Look—I don't ask a lot of questions because you don't seem to want to talk about it."

"Not your circus," he said. Not her monkeys. She knew the rest. It was a favorite saying of Raj's late father.

She thought about Monday evening, when Raj had come home from Oxnard—such a murder of a commute, there to Beverly Hills, she didn't know why he couldn't delegate someone to check in on the lab, but you couldn't keep Raj from his control, the blanket that kept him warm. She thought about her marabou-trimmed "floor decor," as the Money Honeys called it, the Dodgers, his dismissal of her like she was a notification to be swiped away.

"But I *want* to be involved," she said, turning around so the small of her back pressed into the sink's marble lip. "I want to help. I'm not some delicate flower that's going to shrivel up and die if something goes wrong."

"I'm just trying to protect you," he said, sliding open a drawer on his side of the vanity.

She sighed, then turned back to the mirror and pulled the skin at the corner of her right eye taut once more. There was a time when his old-fashioned values read as chivalry; those times had passed. "I'm not some damsel in distress. Even this ex-NYPD guy—what's his name again, Ralph? Should we, like, feed him?"

Raj snorted. "He's not a fish."

"Well, it feels a little *much*, you know, with our friends, having this guy patrolling the grounds like we're in some kind of prison," she said. "Just please make sure that whatever's happening at the lab is aboveboard. You saw what happened to the Sacklers, God forbid that becomes *us*—"

Another snort. Were the Sacklers too lofty of a comparison, or too low? "If you'd let me finish," he said, revealing what he'd extracted from his drawer—a black leather box—and opening its gold-embossed lid. "I found something that might help. Protect you. According to the Romans, anyway."

She saw, squealed, and brought her hands to her face.

The latest addition to Raj's stack of Get Out of Jail Free cards: a Bulgari Serpenti watch in eighteen-karat rose gold, inlaid with diamonds and a malachite face the color of the eye shadow that Rachel had accidentally knocked into the sink in her frenzy of excitement. The watch's name derived from the ancient Roman belief that serpents provided protection from evil spirits . . . and also, Rachel remembered, as she gazed at the watch's glimmering bezel, rebirth. And fertility. She'd read this in an article on *Town & Country*'s website while dreamily clicking through various Serpentis in a Google-shopping tab next door.

He slid it onto her left wrist. She eased herself onto the marble slab between the his-and-hers faucets, their fixtures gleaming gold. She pulled him toward her with her smooth, toned calves, all evidence of hair long ago removed by the Beverly Boulevard location of a laser hair removal franchise endorsed by the Kardashians. She cocked her head to the side and let the tie of her silk dressing gown come undone.

"How can I ever repay you?" she asked.

He had kissed her on the mouth. "Venmo," he'd said. She kicked him. "Later," he said, pulling her off the sink. "Don't want to keep our friends waiting."

"Later" had failed to materialize. Raj had texted the group saying that Anjali felt sick and he was escorting her back to the estate in the Sprinter: Dinner's all taken care of, I'll meet you at Cadet.

The plan had been to go to the beer-and-wine bar in the alleyway with the gender-inclusive signage, the moody lighting, and enough drapey ferns to make you wonder if the place also sold plants (it did not). But as Rachel stepped out of Upsilon's revolving door and onto Main Street, she heard, two blocks away, the unmistakable opening riff of "American Girl," by Tom Petty, and felt a sudden yearning for an America she never knew: cowboy boots and Daisy Dukes and NASCAR, an Americana far-flung from the central New Jersey suburb where she'd grown up, with its soccer fields and split-level Cape Cods. Cadet, after the au courant overload of Upsilon, felt like more of the same. Too bougie. Too self-satisfied. The night needed a vibe shift. Bounty Hunter would do it. She texted Raj to let him know.

She was delighted to discover, upon swinging open the bar's mahogany door, that there was a deejay. There was a crowd. There was a lone, unclaimed high-top. All excellent signs. Raj would be so pleased. He loved this place. Cadet had been her idea, it was newer and felt more fresh, more appropriate for their cosmopolitan friends, but Rachel was beginning to understand that what seemed like a good fit in the abstract did not always make sense in real life. After hours of "dirt" and "brain" and "tongue"—a mousse made out of locally grown marionberries and oyster mushrooms, truly the most revolting of all—Bounty Hunter's proposition of blue-cheese-slathered chips and house-smoked wings sounded practically revelatory. With a margarita? Even better.

For a while, she toggled between looking at the door and looking at her new watch and looking at her phone, which was in her hand, half listening as Victoria flirted with the couple at the high-top next to theirs and Hari and David talked about sports or some true crime show or whatever it was that men talked about among themselves.

She excused herself to call him, twice. No answer. She texted him and Anjali: All good? Need anything? Again, no response. She asked

David if he'd heard from Anjali. He shifted his eyes as if it had only just occurred to him that he should be concerned about his wife's wellness and whereabouts and looked at his phone. "Oh yeah, she texted—she's lying down. Probably just needs to sleep it off. We're out of practice," he said with a half-hearted laugh, setting his phone down on the sticky high-top table. "We don't get out much anymore."

It was around that time that the effects of that first margarita, compounded by however much wine she had drunk before, began to make themselves known.

Maybe Anjali wasn't sick. Maybe Anjali had a thing for Raj. Maybe Anjali was still jealous of her, as Rachel always suspected she had been. Anjali had feigned support for their relationship when Rachel and Raj began dating freshman year, had cooed and clapped when Raj presented Rachel with a bouquet of roses after a particularly trying microeconomics exam (who was she kidding, they were all trying), but anyone could see that Anjali felt slighted. Rachel had felt for her. Anjali had never had a boyfriend. But Rachel didn't ask Raj to fall in love with her. She had simply matriculated at the best college afforded to her by her grades and means. Anjali couldn't expect Rachel to stay away simply because she'd arrived at Cornell first. This was America. If you wormed your way in and the check cleared, you were welcome.

But Anjali never stopped trying to impress Raj with her supposed wit, always cooking up some comeback to demonstrate how clever she was. It was sad, really, how Anjali still craved Raj's validation after all these years.

Now, as Rachel lay in bed, the clouds shifted in the skylight above the California king. A beam of sun struck the face of the Serpenti. Brilliant. Anjali could try to *be* brilliant, but this watch was the very definition. Anjali didn't get a watch. Anjali didn't get a ring—well, she got a ring from David, if you could call that speck of a diamond a ring (Rachel felt awful, assessing it as such, but facts were facts). If Anjali needed twenty minutes alone with Raj so badly that she was willing to fake being sick, so be it. Wouldn't be the craziest thing she'd ever done. Rachel trusted Raj. Besides, if Raj was going to cheat on her, the last person he'd choose was Anjali. He had once told her he didn't find Indian girls attractive. They reminded him of his sister.

She'd decided, the night before, that she could either spend her remaining waking hours worrying, wondering, and waiting in vain, or she could order another margarita, or a round of tequila shots—or both, why not, tequila was her friend—and sidle up to the flannel-shirt-wearing deejay beneath the taxidermied moose head. She could slip him a twenty. Or a hundred. A hundred was better than twenty. She could kindly ask him to play "Where the Party At," take Victoria's hand, and reenact the dance that they used to do on the tables at Johnny O's. She could engage in behavior that she usually would not, if her husband was around, and by all indications, her husband was not around.

"Where the Party At" led to "Low," which led to "Pony," by Ginuwine, which led to Victoria and Rachel grinding against each other while all four of them, and the vast majority of the bar, sang the chorus off-key. She had no agenda, aside from reclaiming the night as her own, recasting herself as the main character rather than Raj, at least in her own mind. She could feel and see the eyes on her as she sashayed and whooped and flipped her hair, and thought, Let me enjoy this. Let me *live*. Let me indulge in the fantasy of being single and desirable and young and vibrant. What was the harm?

But midway through an Outkast song, she found herself draped over the edge of the mahogany bar, asking for water, turned to the right, and saw that Hari had materialized next to her with two waters, giant Pizza Hut–size plastic tumblers filled with crushed ice, one of which was outstretched to her, and she wondered if she had subconsciously put on this whole show to confirm that Hari still remembered what she could not forget, even if she wanted to: that night at the Chateau Marmont, over a decade ago.

She and Raj had been on a break, and she had found herself, for the first time, alone in Los Angeles, in a one-bedroom in that apartment complex by the Grove. Hari had been in town from New York. He had organized separate catch-ups with each of them, and while hers had started chastely enough—hours before dark, on the leafy Moroccan-tiled patio of Eveleigh—it had progressed up Sunset Boulevard to Skybar at the Mondrian, and then to the bar at the Chateau Marmont, and then Hari's bungalow for some more wine, and then things happened with him that had stopped happening with Raj, and they had talked until four and slept until seven and swore to God that they would never tell anyone about what had happened, and then it happened again, and they ordered breakfast to the room, and Rachel had almost hurled her plate of scrambled eggs at the wall, after Hari tore himself from under the duvet and jumped in the shower, apologizing a million times, citing a client meeting at ten, so profound was her frustration. She wanted the morning to go on forever but knew it could not. Hari lived in New York. Hari was Raj's *boy.* She could not be that woman, the one who drove a wedge between two friends.

At least, she could not be that woman any more than she already was.

She'd done right. She'd been smart. Look at me now, she thought as she stretched her arms, the left newly heavier than the right, toward the wood beams overhead. She let the Serpenti snake down her forearm, the diamonds glinting in the morning sun that streamed in from the skylight. If her subconscious had made her peacock around Bounty Hunter to get Hari's attention, then her subconscious was pretty pathetic. All the guy had done was offer her a glass of water. Not like he had said anything. Not like he put a hand on her. They hadn't touched, besides compulsory hugs of greeting and retreat, all shoulders, clavicle to clavicle, since that night at the Chateau, all those years ago. It was like Hari made an active effort *not* to touch her, not to be left alone with her, not to conjure any hint of intimacy that would remind him of their time in that bungalow.

And she had this watch. This $77,000 needs-its-own-insurance-policy watch. And the man she was married to, who gave it to her.

She had to post a photo. The Money Honeys would absolutely die. She reached for her phone on the nightstand, angled her wrist in the crystalline light.

it's time . . . to find u a man who treats u like mine

They didn't need to know what preceded and followed the Serpenti. They needed something to aspire to. These poor things, bogged down by the cruft of life.

They were in heated debates that morning—about guns: one of the Honeys had asked which designer handbags were "CCW friendly" because "the regulation concealed carry purses are so ugly"; about whether to tip an aesthetician who owned her own practice: "if I'm paying $200 per injection it's all going to her, right?"; and about which was better: the Four Seasons Punta Mita, in Mexico, or the Four Seasons Ocean Club, in the Bahamas. A member had asked for recommendations on where to redeem a Four Seasons gift certificate for "some much needed me time. Going through a terrible divorce, husband has been cheating on me with one of our friends for like, six years [tears streaming down face emoji]."

A pang of paranoia: What if Raj was with Anjali right now? He had been in bed when Rachel had stumbled into their suite, after two, still chewing a slice of the Domino's thin crust that Hari had ordered from the Uber. She had felt both annoyed and relieved to see him there. He couldn't have called? Texted? Let her know that he was alive? But as she discarded her slip dress in a pile on the floor and got under the covers, the need to sleep overrode the need for immediate answers, plus there was the watch, and this house and the other houses and what trouble could he have gotten into, really, if he was here, softly snoring, draping his arm over her as she curled her body into his?

When had he woken up? Where was he? What kind of "fire" required his attention? Weren't there a dozen people under him who could deal with it? Ahmad? That ex-NYPD guy?

She called Raj. It went to voice mail.

She scrambled out of bed, telling herself that it was because she needed to get ready for Megan's live run, which would start in an hour, and not because she wanted to run downstairs and locate her husband and Anjali and confirm that nothing untoward was going on between them. Getting ready now would give her time to French braid her hair like Megan, take a pre-workout selfie and tag Megan as Megan instructed her #Machines to do. "Be seen," Megan had said last week, during a forty-five-minute hip-hop run that Rachel had woken up at 4:00 a.m. to take. (Megan taught from Peloton's New York studio; if Rachel wanted a shout-out, and Rachel always wanted a shout-out, she had to adjust her schedule to Megan's.) "Show me, show our tribe, show your friends, your family, your haters, how far you've come. Show *off.*"

Rachel devoured Megan's morsels of #MachineLearning like the Domino's thin crust she only allowed herself to eat when she knew she could run it off the following morning. "This prime real estate, right here?" Megan had said the other day during an Instagram Live, pointing at her head, from which a veritable fountain of a ponytail cascaded. "*High* demand. *Many* hopeful occupants. But no one, *nothing*, gets to live here rent-free. Not in my head, and not in yours. What are you dwelling on? Is it worth your time? Is it worth your energy?"

Megan's soliloquies always looped back to how she quit her job as a criminal defense attorney to "take a chance" on becoming an instructor for a "small, stealth fitness start-up," and how finding her purpose, as well as her husband (Peloton's CFO), and becoming a mother (they had a son, Swoosh), made her allergic to anything, and anyone, that did not lift her up. As she raked a comb through her hair, Rachel recalled another line of Megan's: "I audit my circle like the IRS did Wesley Snipes."

With her free hand, she jabbed at the screen of her phone and scrolled through her recent calls until she found the event planner. It rang eight times. Seven more times than it ought to, for what they were paying this woman. They should've hired Mindy Weiss.

"Did Megan RSVP?"

"Who, sweetie?"

"Megan, the Peloton instructor."

The event planner apologized, she was having a hard time hearing Rachel, she was at the ice sculptor's studio. Apparently, there were conflicting opinions on whether the ice sculpture of Bacchus, one of several installations Raj had insisted upon for the opening, should have a beard.

"Dealer's choice," Rachel said, rolling her eyes. Ice sculptures in the heat of summer, in a region plagued by drought. Practically a war crime. She asked again about Megan.

"Oh, no, sweetie. I think we have to count her out."

The comb hit a snag at the nape of her neck. Rachel pulled harder. She felt her eyes well as the follicles gave way.

~

Hari awoke fuzzy, in need of more than caffeine. A shower. A fire hose, of sorts, to wash the bad energy away.

He didn't go into the shower with the intention of doing what he did, but as the steam rose, he forgot where he was, whose house he was in, and he saw her, twirling in that slinky dress that she probably knew would drive him crazy, that would drive anyone attracted to the female form crazy—she was the goddamn epitome of it; statues ought to be erected in her name.

The things he would do, if he could. (Could he? Would he? That look that she had given him during that Ginuwine song—a lark? An invitation? The cumulative effect of excessive amounts of wine and Ginuwine?)

He was back in that suite at the Chateau, with two of her, three of her, in positions that the human body could not conceivably achieve, doing things that would probably get him arrested, when the sound of someone calling his name brought him back to reality, and he replied,

"One sec," because he was so close and, honestly, what on earth could possibly be so urgent that it required his attention now, and then there was a knock and the bathroom door cracked open and the vision in Hari's head evaporated, like so much steam.

"Dude," Raj said, "why—*whoa*, okay, my bad!" The door slammed as he left.

Presumably, enough steam had evaporated that it was now clear what Hari had been doing.

He said "fuck" a million times and turned off the shower. Only then did he remember that, at dinner the night before, he and Raj had said they'd go for a run before heading out for their first wine tasting.

Fucking Raj, barging into wherever he pleased, like they were back in college.

Though, this was his house, and Hari had neglected to lock the doors to the bathroom as well as his suite. Still—privacy? Didn't Raj pride himself on being polite?

Or was it some twisted attempt at a power move? Hari wondered, seething. Yet another way for Raj to assert his dominance, to demonstrate that the whole world was his domain. Well, fine. Let him barge into rooms like a bull in Brunello. Raj didn't get to barge into his *brain*.

Raj couldn't have known what he was thinking about. Raj didn't *deserve* what he was thinking about.

He turned the shower back on. No way could he run, pent up like this.

Hari rewound the proverbial tape to a point before the Chateau. Before they were thrust into the real world, when they were still in Ithaca, senior year, halcyon days, the week between exams and graduation, the time that a bunch of them were supposed to have a picnic down by the gorges and everyone bailed, everyone except for Rachel, who had shown up at the house on Blair Street with a paper bag of Pita Pit and a pout that failed to rouse Raj from his hungover stupor—sake bombs at Plum Tree the night before—but worked wonders on Hari.

Who could say no to a face like that? He couldn't understand how Raj could let her down. He would never want to let this woman down.

They had gotten into Hari's Toyota Camry and driven down to Buttermilk Falls, blasting "Wonderwall" as loud as the stereo would go. They stopped at Wegmans. They picked up a six-pack. She took off her shoes. She crossed her long, bare legs over the dash. He did what he could to keep his eyes on the road.

"So what's your deal, Hari?" she asked, after they'd downed two beers each. They sat at the base of the falls, dangling their feet in the water. "Why do none of your girls seem to last?"

"I'm too nice," he said. "They want guys who put drugs in their drinks and hook up with their best friends."

"You *are* too nice," she said. "You should be more of a jerk."

"Got any pointers?"

"Well, you live with exhibit A."

Hari thought of an African proverb: When elephants fight, it's the grass that suffers.

"Blame it on the sake bombs," he said. "I'm sure he'll make it up to you."

"Oh, sure," Rachel said. "Syracuse Mall with Daddy's Amex, Thai Cuisine on the way back. We've got it down to a science."

Hari had to laugh.

"But sometimes I want to make him *really* mad, you know?"

She had turned to him then, chin pressed against a newly bare shoulder, her too-thin, too-big T-shirt having slipped past the point of no return, and given him a look that said she wouldn't tell if he wouldn't. There was no one else around. Just the rush of the falls and the rustling of maple leaves and the sound of his own blood going south.

"We should probably go," he said.

Now, he played out what he would've done if he'd had the courage. What he could still do, if he had the courage. He was older. He was wiser. He was no one's fool anymore.

7

Friday morning
Kismet Estate, Napa

Victoria was supposed to be meditating, was supposed to be listening to the prompts of the mindfulness coach, gently exhorting in his sonorous, slightly accented, could-be-English-or-Scottish-or-Welsh-but-can't-quite-put-your-finger-on-it voice, was supposed to be delving deeper into the black hole of her mind, or finding a point of light within the black hole, or lifting herself out of the black hole on a string of light—she wasn't quite sure. She hadn't been paying attention. She opened her eyes, ripped out her AirPods, and exhaled hard enough that the wisps of hair beside her cheekbones momentarily took flight.

She had woken up with a question running on repeat, in her mind, and despite several sun salutations, a few detoxifying twists, and now, a guided meditation (which she generally tried to avoid; she prided herself on her ability to drop into her subconscious on a dime—she'd once astral projected while sitting on the runway of SFO, two hours delayed), she could not get it out.

Had it been enough?

"It" was her marriage to Dev, seven years extinct according to the Superior Court of California. She rarely looked back at it in anything but anger: anger at how long it took him to sign the papers, anger at his hubris, thinking that moving to the Bay Area would be good for their marriage, their careers. Anger at herself for trusting him, anger at herself for denying his offer of stock options, something to set her up, save her from the Laffa hostess stand.

But last night, watching Anjali and David and Rachel and Raj in all their glorious imperfection, like watching the hot but daft new bartender at Laffa fuck up a Negroni Sbagliato yet again, V let herself wonder, for the first time in a long time, if she had given up too soon. If it would've been wiser to have made do with what she had. A Negroni Sbagliato with Pellegrino instead of Prosecco wasn't standard, for sure, but it wasn't *bad*. It was drinkable, maybe even preferable, depending on what you wanted.

The divorce had been her idea. Burning Man. Burning Man was what did them in. They'd been invited by Dev's boss, the head of a rent-to-own real estate start-up based out of Oakland, the "Brooklyn" of San Francisco (if you removed everything worth going to in Brooklyn from Brooklyn), that Dev had joined after graduating from business school at Wharton. Dev's destiny of taking over the family business had never come to pass. Three years after he graduated from Cornell, while he was "working" for Sotheby's corporate and spending a not-insignificant amount of his salary on Sunday brunches at Bagatelle and bags of cocaine, his father sold his collection of Atlanta-area hotels to Holiday Inn's parent company, cashed out, and moved back to India with Dev's mom. "You kids have it too easy," he'd told Dev. "You see what it's like to start something from scratch."

The kick in the ass had its intended effect. Dev took stock of where he was and what he wanted. He stopped doing coke (for a time). He stopped going to Bagatelle (it was getting old, anyway). He brought up the idea of business school to his dad, who offered to cut a check if Dev "got in somewhere worth going." Three years later, Dev was moving fast and breaking things. He returned to New York. He got hired by a Bay Area start-up that needed a man on the ground back East. He was declared "the Man Who Might Make Manhattan Livable Again" by *New York Magazine*. Then his boss decided that the company would move faster and break more things if they were all in the same room. (Supposedly this had nothing to do with *New York Magazine* heaping praise upon Dev instead of him. Supposedly.)

"So you want to move to . . . *Oakland*?" Victoria had said, treating the name of the city like the soiled paper bags she would soon get used to avoiding on her way to BART, to go to the Battery, to go to the De Young, to go anywhere that reminded her, albeit for the most fleeting of moments, of downtown Manhattan. The timing could not have been worse. She had been on the verge of leaving Edwin McCormick and starting her own crisis PR firm, in New York, where she knew not only the editors and columnists of the sections that mattered at the *Post* and *Daily News* (Page Six, the *Daily News*'s equivalent of Page Six) but also the names of their pets, their significant others, their drink orders.

She had recently resurrected the career of an artisanal pizza maker accused of using moldy dough. She had taken the dough to a food scientist, who had determined that the mold converted the dough's gluten into protein without altering the taste. The pizza maker had to hire the door guy from 1 Oak to manage the resultant line of customers. He was thinking about franchising. It was among her greatest professional achievements. She had earned her stripes. Her time had come.

"You can start your own shop there," Dev said, when she brought up all of this. "Tons of potential. Tech firms are always in crisis, in need of damage control. Give it a year and *you'll* be the one in magazines, you'll see."

Except, she'd only had a few clients in tech. Except, Google, Facebook, and Apple all had their own in-house crisis PR teams. Except, no one understood what she did—what do you call a lauded crisis communications professional without a crisis to handle? A woman unemployed. A woman adrift. A woman trying to figure out why she was in a part of the country that was billed as "better" than New York but seemed worse in nearly every way: more expensive, more dangerous, less art, less culture, largely because the people who produced art and culture could no longer afford to live there.

She, like Rachel and Anjali, had grown up in New Jersey. In her heart, as in so many hearts of the tristate born and bred, "the city" could not be replaced. It wasn't Oakland's or San Francisco's fault, really. The Bay Area never stood a chance.

Their new environment had rubbed off on Dev. He had taken up mountain biking, swapped his Brooks Brothers for Patagonia, become a fixture at the local Socialists' society, which met at a "pay what you want" bar (really, the garage of a member who brewed their own beer). She had gone once, at Dev's urging. The amount of ungroomed facial hair and ear gauges disturbed her to the degree that she excused herself and walked around the Bay Place Whole Foods for an hour, soothed by the presence of the olive bar, as resplendent and overpriced in Oakland as it was in TriBeCa.

More disturbing: Oakland Dev displayed none of the edge of New York Dev or college Dev before that. None of the bravado that had attracted her to him. He grew soft and sensitive, started calling himself a "change maker" and wearing blue-light blockers. There was something undeniably unattractive about men when their youthful swagger burned off and adult-onset anxiety set in. This hand-wringing about society, other people, "doing good." She couldn't help but think that it was Dev's attempt to overcorrect for his privilege. But she *liked* his privilege. She thought she had married an alpha male. He turned out to be a beta, and bumbling.

The invitation from Dev's boss, to hole up with him and a camp of other start-up founders and C-suite executives at Burning Man—"air-conditioned RVs, showers, a private jet to Black Rock, the whole nine"—felt like the first glimpse of blue sky after a storm. Finally, an occasion for her to dress up, go out, wil' out, meet people. Planning their outfits (sequins, wings, a headdress of questionable political correctness) and their contribution to the camp (several butane grills and a trunk of pre-marinated meats from H Mart), Victoria let her hopes rise. Maybe four days in Black Rock City was just what they needed. Maybe it would bring them back together.

It brought them to the Orgy Dome. If you ever want to end your marriage, go to the Orgy Dome.

"Look," she said now, pushing up from the rug of her ground-floor suite, which overlooked the estate's expansive patio, infinity pool, and vineyards beyond. "If you had stayed with him, you'd be a mother of two living in a glorified shack by Lake Merritt, getting your kicks by flirting with the spinach guy at the Sunday farmers' market—a *great* farmers' market, the only thing you miss about living in Oakland, but still." (Talking to herself, out loud, in times of trouble was a technique that Scarlett, the "desert nymph" they met at the Orgy Dome, had taught her. "Technique" might've been a generous way of putting it.) "You wanted this life. You asked for this life." Flitting from festival to festival, glomming on to whoever had cash to burn and an ego to stroke (another tried-and-true Scarlett "technique," although you didn't need to spend long at any of these gatherings to figure out that they were over-indexed on rich people who were basically begging to be financially exploited), all in the service of turning Conscious Confidence into a profitable entity, one that would grow beyond her, because personality-driven companies could only grow so much before the personality that sparked them burned out.

It was Scarlett who'd said, "Babe, the age of crisis is over. People want brightness and light. People want to feel *good*," and then she'd given Victoria her first hit of a drug that, per word on the playa, was basically Viagra for horses. (This happened the night after the Orgy Dome, in a Bedouin-style "fantasy suite" to which only Victoria was invited, not Dev.)

After Burning Man, Victoria had moved to Los Angeles to share a room with Scarlett in a collaborative house near Venice Beach. "I thought you hated Socialists," Dev had said, darkly, when V told him her news. "It's temporary," V said. "While I figure things out." The truth was that she could no longer live in a city to which she had only moved because she was someone's wife.

She'd revealed none of this to Anjali when they'd seen each other at Rachel's wedding the following year. She'd lied through her newly whitened teeth, slipping into Los Angeles's standards of beauty's full-fledged fakery like a well-worn pair of jeans. She could not own up to her current situation, an award-winning crisis communications specialist in a crisis of her own making. The irony.

"Stop," she said now, and clapped her palms together. She had to stop spiraling. She had to stop dwelling on the past. She was $50,000 shy of making that down payment on the live-work space in Silver Lake, and she had come to Napa to make up the difference. She could ask Rachel and Raj. She knew she could ask Rachel and Raj. But things between them seemed strained, and everyone else in the house also seemed to want something from them. She didn't want to pile on.

There was also the humiliation factor, confessing to your friends that you weren't doing as well as your social media presence might suggest. She didn't want to admit defeat. (This was also why she could not return to New York, at least not yet.) Certainly not with Dev riding high, Dev and his new bride, "sweets for my sweet." Barf.

Better to look in the margins, she thought, like the chef at Upsilon, who'd recently signed a deal with Miele that she knew included a fat cash payout in addition to the shiny new appliances, or the couple she had met at Bounty Hunter, who would be at the grand opening of the winery the following night, weathered swingers from Santa Rosa who'd made their money in run-of-the-mill chardonnay and looked at her like she was an over-oaked bomb of butter that they'd just love to taste. She had to stop thinking about what might have been and keep her eye on the prize.

She sometimes thought of herself as a truffle-hunting pig, trained to root out the richness of the earth. There were whole fortunes to be had, if you knew where to look.

There were also alternative tactics.

She could consider a more aggressive approach with Raj and Rachel than she would with other marks, given how well she knew them. Rachel especially. Who wore a Serpenti to a dive bar? The woman moved through the world as if ensconced in a glossy, protective bubble. Like nothing untoward could touch her. Like any potential disaster would stand down in the face of her lithe frame and sculpted cheekbones. Like bad luck would pass her by.

Victoria wondered where the Serpenti was, how quickly Rachel would notice if it went missing. Rachel probably had drawers full of "country house" stuff—"Oh, this old thing?"—throwaways that would no longer cut it in the rarefied circles of LA but would fetch bank on StockX, the RealReal, the whole pantheon of secondhand sites and stores. Victoria had taken note of the way that Rachel flung down her quilted YSL purse after reaching home, letting its gold chain slide off the back of a linen-wrapped dining chair and onto the floor, paying it no mind as she shoveled slice after slice of Domino's thin crust into her Juvéderm-enhanced mouth. (You'd think you'd be judicious about what you put in that thing, after pumping a thousand dollars' worth of filler into it. You'd be wrong.)

Victoria had gotten into the habit of ringing up a great variety of merchandise as bananas at the Whole Foods self-checkout. Avocados? Bananas. Gluten-free English muffins? Bananas. Shiitake mushrooms? At $11.99 a pound versus 20 cents a pound, *definitely* bananas. Would filching a YSL and listing it online be so different from the subterfuge in which she already engaged? Didn't some people believe that there was a finite amount of money on earth and all anyone was doing was bartering? That "new" wealth was a fallacy?

Her phone pulsed. New activity in the group's text message thread. Rachel was going for a run on the treadmill in the home gym. Raj and Hari were going for a run outside. The primary suite, and its walk-in closet, would be unoccupied, for a time. The thought of getting caught, though. Too risky. Too early in the game for that bold a move.

If she wanted to prove that she still had it, there were other ways.

She glanced in the mirror, readjusted her sports bra, and fluffed her hair. She pulled taut the skin beneath her eyes and wondered what she could trade for enough units of Botox and how many good years she had left. The problem with banking on your looks: the well inevitably runs dry. Not today, though. Not yet.

She looked around the suite for a "morning" type of prop and found a birchwood cup that was meant to hold a toothbrush but could easily read as a mug. It felt cheap and disposable, like those bamboo plates that were theoretically better for the environment than plastic. Rich people were so weird. The things they spent money on, the ways they tried to scrimp and save. She picked up her phone, sank into a bouclé armchair that swiveled, and tucked her legs beneath her. She tapped until she was broadcasting live.

"Hi, lovers," she began. "Peaceful morning here in wine country. Seeing the vines makes me feel really grounded, you know? Really at one with the universe and the natural flow of things. Come here, I'll show you."

She got up and opened the sliding glass door that led to the backyard. She padded down the grass with bare feet, past the pool, to the firepit, which offered a view of the vines that splayed out across the land. She panned over it, silently thanking the sparrows for amping up the ambiance. Their warbles were key. She'd pay them if she could. (Well, given her financial situation, probably not.)

As she turned the camera back around, she pressed it to her cleavage.

"Something about nature, you guys," she said, looking into the lens again. "It truly makes my heart swell." She settled into an Adirondack chair and went on for a while about how falling asleep to the sound of the waves at Costa Cara medicated her brain stem—she wasn't entirely sure where her brain stem was or if it could be medicated, but no matter, no one fact-checked Instagram Lives—and how the quality of light in Napa was having a similar effect on her "sur-consciousness," which, again, she wasn't sure was a thing but *subconscious* was, so why wouldn't it be? "But anyway, I thought I'd throw it out there: What do *you* want to see today? What should I do? What can I show you? You can respond in the comments, and, oh yeah"—she giggled, as if she had almost forgotten—"for those of you that have asked"—no one had asked—"my gratitude cup has not yet run over."

A Venmo notification popped up.

"Okay, MackDaddy89, I see you." She giggled again and bit the tip of her pointer finger. MackDaddy89 wanted to see the founder of Conscious Confidence "get ratchet with blondie." For a hundred bucks now and the potential of more later, she would happily make that happen.

~

"Drink up, sweetheart, it'll help."

David handed her a tall glass, still fizzing. Alka-Seltzer. David thought Alka-Seltzer could cure anything. The first time he'd handed her a glass had been at *Highbrow*, where they'd met, when he was in ad sales and she was the assistant to the then editor in chief. She had not fathomed that a white guy could be interested in her, let alone someone as all-American as David, what with his ZogSports and Sperry Top-Siders and dog-eared Penguin Classic paperbacks. She had not dated anyone seriously before him, but if she had asked any of those Akshays or Rahuls or so-and-so's auntie's family friend's nephews if they had read James Joyce or Raymond Chandler or Virginia Woolf, they would have given her a blank look. These were men who owned one book: *Blink*. It was doubtful they'd even read that.

She knew, upon seeing David's Upper West Side studio for the first time, she had struck gold. Franzen. Murakami. Austen. The old masters; the hot, new talents; a wall of spines that showed signs of wear. She drank too much, that night. David had put on a jazz record and made Manhattans. Between the books and the presence of a music-playing device that was not made by Apple, she hadn't known what to do with herself. The Alka-Seltzer the next morning—after he had chivalrously called a black car to ferry her back to her place in Hell's Kitchen—sealed the deal, along with the kiss that he wrapped her into after he opened the passenger-side door, before she collapsed into the back seat. She would marry this man. She would do whatever it took.

For a while, it hadn't taken a lot. They read. They watched independent movies. They went to book parties. They moved in the same circle, a circle that made up for what it lacked in monetary wealth with intellectual capital. But two people could only live in a room built for one for so long. They needed cash. David went the agency route. Anjali jumped to another publication that promised a pay raise and more high-profile assignments. The circle that had once felt like a Paris salon in a city of finance bros began to feel insular. Immature. Disconnected from the real world. There was nothing like getting pregnant to reacquaint you with the needs of the body, the value of practicality, the urgency to grow up and get your life together.

"Thank you," she said to David now, propping herself up against the headboard and taking the glass. She never stayed in bed this late. Even before Lucie and Ryan, she liked to rise before dawn, read in peace, get a head start on work. (She still got up at five thirty in the morning, but now the hours that formerly felt dewy and full of potential were spent rushing around, packing lunches, getting the kids up and dressed and fed. Those hours no longer belonged to her.)

She felt like a sloth. Did sloths get drunk? Did sloths get hungover? Did sloths stray from their sloth husbands-slash-wives? Did sloths eschew the convention of mating for life like any animal with any common sense probably should?

David perched on the edge of the bed and patted her thigh. "Think you're up for wine tasting? Hair of the dog, could help."

"Ugh," she said. The thought of wine made her insides roil. "Where are we going again?"

David reached for the agenda on the nightstand (annotated printouts had been placed in every suite). "First stop, Peninsula, 'A winery unlike any you've ever experienced, nestled within the hills of western Oakville. An architectural landmark and Napa's premier producer of cabernet sauvignon.'" The remainder of the day's itinerary frothed to the front of Anjali's mind: another blah-blah, "once in a lifetime" wine tasting after Peninsula, then a winding drive back to the estate, where Sammi Ali, the "Allah of shawarma," according to a much-hearted Yelp review, would cook for the group. She didn't know if she could stomach any of it, but she also didn't want to miss out. What was that Rihanna song? Wasn't this what she came for?

"You think they'll give me a premier bucket if I need to throw up?"

David smiled. "Probably something made of marble, designed by Frank Lloyd Wright." He reached over and smoothed her hair, a gesture that stirred in her a cocktail of equal parts comfort and guilt. "I'm gonna see about breakfast—want to come? A bagel or banana for what ails you?"

If only simple carbs could solve this problem.

"You go. Let me get myself together."

He stood up. "Holler if you need me."

She put the glass down once he closed the door and knocked the back of her head against the upholstered headboard, twice, in tune with the song that had not stopped playing in her head since the previous night, the one by the Killers, the one about a kiss.

Not the whole song, actually. Just that part.

Only a kiss, her ass.

The fact that her mind had chosen to fixate on this particular refrain, of all refrains, annoyed Anjali; it was too on-the-nose, too obvious, brought too easily to mind all those nights at dank, dark New York dive bars, belting out the chorus of "Mr. Brightside" while throwing back a fifth vodka soda.

Well, she hadn't had *that* many nights like that. She had stood by and watched and judged as *other* people had nights like that, cavalier young professionals with last names and family friendships to anchor their positions, no matter how many times they called in sick or showed up late or simply not at all, without an excuse. She had always kept it together. She had always stayed in control. She had commandeered their drunken nights for her own files; it was funny, how you could do that, subsume someone else's past into your own, rewrite history, be the bad bitch you never were, if only in your own mind.

Until last night.

She would love to say that Raj forced himself on her, and if anyone had seen them, that's what she would've done, thrown him under the bus. But the truth was that she had kissed him back, she had leaned in, she had liked, *savored* even, the plush feel of his lips against her own, the familiarity, the briefest sense that no time had passed since they had last done this. When *he* pulled away and said, "Let's get out of here," she had given him the same girlish look of acquiescence that she had in High Rise Five, twenty years before.

They had sat next to each other in the Sprinter on the way back to the estate, the back of her hand curled loosely into his open palm—that his hand stayed there, that it did not draw back, was its own quiet thrill—in a silence alternately fraught and soothing. At first, she worried that Adolfo would see them and say something. But then she reasoned that Raj was effectively his boss and he probably didn't want to risk his job, and if she was *that* concerned, she ought to take away her hand and place it in her lap, or sit on it, or ball it up into a fist—do anything besides interlace it with the hand of this man who was *not her husband.*

It's okay, she thought, eyes fixed on the tinted window and the darkness beyond, holding hands isn't illegal. A kiss isn't illegal. Look at what David did; you're allowed an indiscretion, you're allowed to have fun.

But she wasn't having fun. She would tell Raj, as soon as they got out of the Sprinter, that it had been a mistake. That she was drunk, that she got wrapped up in the moment. That it could not happen again. Rachel was her friend, after all, and his wife; it was beyond inappropriate, their behavior. They weren't in college anymore.

And yet, as this line of reasoning entered her brain, she felt a perverse thrill at having usurped Rachel, if only for a moment, at having reclaimed what was once hers. God, she was a terrible person. A horrible feminist. A very, very bad friend.

Raj jerked his hand from hers as the Sprinter came to a stop in the gravel driveway. She pretended to feel nothing and followed him out. In their absence, the broken window had been fixed, the glass replaced with a new pane, the brick that had greeted them in the foyer removed. A single strip of police tape was wrapped around the entryway, and the guy that Raj had hired to patrol the compound was leaning against the side of the house near the front door, vaping. Anjali shuddered as she watched him blow out a cloud the size of a small tree. Upsetting, how pervasive vaping had become. Was he even allowed to do that on the clock?

"Boss," Raj called out as he approached the house, "is that necessary?"

"If you want to know who did this," Ralph said, shrugging.

"It's a bad look," said Raj.

"Rules are rules," said Ralph. Anjali realized they were talking about the police tape, not the vape. So everyone vaped. Whenever they wanted. Cool.

Raj nodded in a sign of seeming solidarity and left it at that.

"Look," she began as soon as he closed the front door behind them, but he interrupted.

"Wanna smoke?"

She hadn't expected that.

"What? Where?" She knew he meant hookah. With Raj, it was always hookah.

He cocked his head in the direction of a wing of the house she had yet to explore. The floor's gleaming oak planks formed an arrow that led down the hallway, as if encouraging her to follow him. As if she needed encouragement. Just for a second, just to see where this leads, she told herself, just to fully submerge in this momentary escape from mom world, just to try to wrap your head around how the other half lives, how Rachel lives, how these people who you grew up with grew to inhabit completely different worlds from you. It was like going on safari, really (not that she ever had). She was just . . . seeing the animals. Seeing all the animals she possibly could.

She wasn't going to smoke. Not after getting on her mental high horse about the ex-NYPD guy and the vape. She would take a peek, say her piece, and leave.

He slid open a barn door, and her train of thought came to a halt. A library. They had a *library*, and not just a spare bedroom with an Ikea shelf of GMAT prep books and unopened mail but a vision of walnut wood, shades of burgundy, and gold that glinted in the glow of a stone fireplace that was somehow already roaring. A chandelier of amber bulbs and cascading crystals hung from the ceiling; below it sat an art-deco-style coffee table of smoked glass topped with, as promised, a three-foot-tall hookah. Four cushy, clubby chairs were centered around it, the types of seats you could curl into and stay forever.

Almost against her will, Anjali drifted to the floor-to-ceiling bookshelves lining the walls. They were packed, to the brim, with books in every shape and size. Not color coordinated. The shelves of a true book fiend. Her eyes darted to spines bearing names she knew and loved. Raj read? Since when?

"I thought you'd appreciate it," he said, watching her.

"Tell me you've opened even one of these."

His lack of response said it all.

"So your decorator ordered them by the foot."

"From the Strand," he said. "Someone's gotta keep them in business."

She had dragged him to the Strand during college. Not just him—Rachel and Hari, too, the time that she drove the four of them down to New Jersey for Thanksgiving break. Raj had said they could all crash at his father's place the night before the holiday: "Do it up, biggest going-out night of the year." "Crashing," to Anjali, connoted a patch of floor and a sleeping bag, maybe a couch. Instead, Raj directed her to the residents' entrance of Trump Tower. His dad's "place" had park views and four bedrooms.

They had taken the N to a noodle shop in Union Square with a laissez-faire stance on carding and a five-dollar lychee martini special. Afterward, before the next bar, she had insisted on showing them "the best bookstore in the world." Raj and Rachel diverted from her tour; she eventually found them making out in the Erotic Literature section.

They had gone to the Strand one other time. When he visited Anjali in New York, when he and Rachel were on a break, when he wanted to read his way out of a pit of grief. "Through," Anjali had said, handing him a paperback of Joan Didion's *The Year of Magical Thinking*. "The only way out is through."

Now, she braced herself against one of the clubby chairs and turned to him. "Look, Raj, what happened—"

He held up a hand. "Say no more. It was my fault. I lost my head. I don't—I would never disrespect you and David like that."

Except that you did, she thought. And she did too.

"But—and please, stop me if I'm out of line—I have to ask, as your friend, as someone who's known you for twenty years—are you happy?"

There was a knock at the door. Her heart spiked. She'd thought they were alone. Was it Rachel? David? Whoever-slash-whatever had thrown a brick through the foyer that morning? (Why did her thoughts go there? The sight of that ex-NYPD guy and the police tape?)

"Come in," Raj had said, unfazed. He took a seat in one of the clubby chairs as a young man in joggers and a T-shirt entered, carrying a tray that held a bottle of Pellegrino, a bottle of pinot noir, a bowl of popcorn, and what Anjali recognized as a steel carrier for hookah charcoals. They glowed a menacing orange.

"This is Ahmad," Raj said. "My right hand. I'd be lost without him." He smiled at Ahmad in the ingratiating manner of someone who holds all the cards. Ahmad kept his head down and nodded curtly at Anjali. She got the sense that Ahmad was trained to see certain things and not others. He placed the tray on the smoked-glass table and saw himself out. "Thanks, bro," Raj said as the door shut.

Raj gestured for Anjali to take a seat, picked up the sinuous, velvet-wrapped pipe, and looked at her, awaiting an answer.

The happiness question. No one had asked her that in years. Her mother was afraid to; the last time she had tried—before Anjali and David got married, when they were in the throes of wedding planning, trying to decide between a run-of-the-mill Sheraton and an even more run-of-the-mill Marriott, Anjali had snapped, "Happy? *Happy?* Who is happy, honestly? No one is happy; everyone is compromising. We should all just admit it and get rid of this ridiculous expectation." Her wish came true. Even the couples counselor had not used language that straightforward—it was all "Do you feel heard?" "Are your needs being met?" and other fanciful ways of avoiding the big question that felt too complicated to answer.

The response she had started with in the library, "Things haven't been easy," led to an unintentional outpouring about the "incident" she'd divulged to no one else, not even Priya.

"Wow," Raj had said, trying to hide a smirk with the heel of his hand and doing a bad job of it. "I don't know what's worse, the fact that he claims he hasn't actually cheated or the fact that you believe him."

She'd untucked her foot from beneath her and kicked his thigh. "So I pour out my heart and you make fun of the mess," she said. "Is this your hobby? Psychological warfare?"

"Oh, come on, Ji. Don't you think you deserve better?" He passed her the pipe.

She knew smoking was bad. She knew smoking was wrong. She was a mother, for the love of God; she had her children to think about.

And yet.

She inhaled. She had forgotten that heady sensation that hookah brought on, an internal free fall, like the first dip of a roller coaster. She blew out a cloud that almost obscured Raj's face and the look of satisfaction that had taken it over. He had always liked it when she smoked, when she behaved in a way that she would generally characterize as bad.

Her mental high horse rode off into the sunset.

"Your turn," she said, passing the pipe back to him. "Are you happy?"

He snorted. "Does it look like I am?"

"Um, a winery, a driver, a Mercedes Sprinter, Ahmad . . . what else: Did that cardigan of yours come from your own personal cashmere farm?"

What started as a genuine laugh withered into resignation. "Looks can be deceiving," he said. "All this really is is gambling."

"You're the house," she said, "and the house always wins."

"From your mouth to God's ears," he said. "Times have been tough."

His vulnerability disarmed her. She had built him up, in her mind, as the antithesis of her husband, all certainty and brawn, but in the library, in the glow of the bucket-sized Diptyque candles positioned in the four corners of the room, she saw the human side of Raj. Riches aside, he was hustling just like the rest of them.

He talked about how he wanted to grow the real estate company and his venture fund in "unconventional" ways but kept getting push-back. "There's so much that I didn't bargain for, miles of red tape and regulatory oversight." He shook his head. "It's a free market. Why I shouldn't be allowed to flex . . . it's un-American, really."

"What does that mean, 'flex'? What are you trying to do?"

"Believe it or not, I'm trying to help children," Raj said. The look on his face signaled that he expected an award for this.

"As in, people not yet old enough to sign a lease?"

He laughed. "This isn't about real estate. Well, not in the typical sense. Real estate of the mind. The final frontier."

This type of conversation was generally too life-hackery for Anjali's tastes, but she was pleasantly surprised that Raj had expanded his horizons beyond profit and loss. She wondered if he had ever had these conversations with Rachel. She guessed not.

That fucking kiss.

Nothing else had happened. Nothing else *would* happen.

The ringing of her phone brought her back to her present state—in bed, hangover peaking, reeling in more ways than one.

Priya's face lit up the screen. *Priya.* What would her sister say about her lack of judgment? She'd probably sympathize. Surely, she'd engaged in plenty of ethically questionable behavior during her Ibiza years. Surely, she'd kissed a man who wasn't Rufus. Probably while Rufus watched. Anjali picked up.

"Tell me you packed another one of Lucie's vapes," Priya said.

"What happened to the one she had? Did she drop it in the toilet?" That had happened, once, at a bowling alley off Route 22, and the mere thought of retrieving it made Anjali want to retch.

"I'm looking at it right now. Doses remaining: zero."

"Are you sure?"

"Listen, dear sister." Priya jiggled the vape back and forth, and Anjali heard the telltale sign of an empty cartridge rattling around the chamber. "There's nothing in it. And she is on one today. She tried to bite me when I asked her to please pass the syrup at breakfast."

Anjali put Priya on speaker and dropped her head into her hands.

The psychiatrist had warned her about this. While Puff, the first FDA-approved vape for children, had been proven to treat the particular type of social anxiety from which Lucie suffered, in clinical trials, some subjects went from getting by on one hit per day to needing two, four, even eight hits to maintain their serotonin levels. "It's not that the vape is addictive," the doctor had said, "it's that the anxiety changes shape and form, which can require an increased dosage."

Anjali had had many questions. (David was supposed to come to the appointment, too, but David had double-booked himself because David could not multitask. Anjali had yet to find a man who could multitask half as well as any of the women in her life.) Why a vape? A vape for a child? How could that possibly be safe?

"Think of it as an inhaler," the psychiatrist had said. "It's not all that different—both devices deliver medication to the bloodstream faster than a pill can, but there's a crucial difference." Anjali had understood then, but she'd allowed the psychiatrist to lean back in his Aeron chair, tent his fingers, and go on. "Look at Juul. Not that it is Juul, but if the cure is packaged in a form that's palatable to the patient, they're more likely to take it and get better, and isn't that what we all want?"

"What's in it?" Anjali had asked, turning over the glossy pamphlet that the doctor had handed her. Key words jumped out: "groundbreaking," "plant-based," "above all, safe."

"A distillation of plants from the Amazon that are most effective when consumed in this form," the psychiatrist said. He took off his glasses. "Look, I know how it sounds. It's out there. It's a new technology. There are other options. We could try SSRIs . . ."

"Absolutely not," said Anjali. The potential for Prozac or Lexapro to stunt Lucie's growth had been enough for her to postpone even going to a psychiatrist until it was absolutely necessary.

"It could just be a phase," the psychiatrist said. "It's possible that in a few months she won't need medication at all. But as it stands . . . if it's gotten to the point where she won't go to school, I'd advise that we at least give Puff a try."

It all sounded so ridiculous at the time. Beyond outlandish. Anjali could not imagine Lucie vaping like those teenagers who hung out in the parking lot of the Dunkin' Donuts, clutching their toilet-paper-roll-sized devices as if, if they sucked on them hard enough, they'd divine themselves into TikTok gods. But Anjali also could not have imagined the anxiety attacks that had left her formerly gregarious daughter unwilling to go to school, to Girl Scouts, to her friends' houses, to pretty much any venue that required interacting with other people. Until they happened. Her fear, elucidated to Anjali and David after much cajoling: that she'd say or do the wrong thing, make someone mad. It seemed so easy to upset someone these days.

The effects of Puff—advertised, online and on TV, with a commercial in which preteens frolicked to a Kygo remix of "Puff the Magic Dragon"—were immediate. Within a week, Lucie showed signs of her old self. Within a month, she was attending Girl Scouts again. Within two months, she wanted tickets to see Taylor Swift, and what were girls who wanted to see Taylor Swift, if not socially well adjusted? She had even adopted a can-do attitude for tackling chores that she had avoided before: folding her clothes, cleaning her room, offering to help Anjali and David prepare dinner.

Puff had side effects, like anything else. You built up a tolerance. You came to depend on it. And when you didn't get it, your demeanor could change—Lucie had never been a biter, a sniper, the sort of child prone to dark and broody spells. Of course, every kid had their moments. Especially preteen girls. Anjali had noticed that Lucie's mood swings had gotten more dramatic; whether it was because of her dependence on the drug or impending adolescence, she couldn't tell.

Two Puffs a day, one after breakfast and one before bed, had sufficed. How had she needed so much more, so soon?

Anjali mourned the loss of Lucie's innocence. She was always mourning it, even as she took pride in the fact that her daughter was coming into her own. Parenting was a never-ending process of wanting to hold on and knowing that you couldn't. Of wading into unknown waters and praying to every force in which you had faith that you'd both come out on the other side.

"There's another vape in the side pocket of the duffel," Anjali told her sister now, tearing back the covers. If she couldn't fix her daughter, in this moment, she could at least fix herself. "But seriously—can you please monitor how much she uses that thing? It's not a toy. It's not a fun-times-let's-do-drugs type of vape, okay? Three hits a day, max."

8

Friday morning
Peninsula, Oakville

Raj loved to watch Peninsula wash over the uninitiated. The quiet delight as they stepped out of the Sprinter and onto the pea-gravel drive fringed by firs, oaks, and olive trees, where sparrows bounced from branch to branch. The realization that this was not one of those . . . pile-out-of-the-stretch, pile-into-the-bar, and take-five-splashes-of-wine-straight-to-the-face-type places, where you were elbow to elbow with bachelors and bachelorettes and all manner of sloppy human specimens hell-bent on getting sloshed.

The bewilderment, as they entered the arcade with its impossibly long reception table, a live-edge slab of a once-majestic tree, beckoning them to the part of the pavilion where the sun streamed through the thatched arches. The hushed exclamations of gratitude as they accepted a complimentary pour of vintage Krug, served in a gossamer-thin glass, as they moved, as if guided by some unseen force, to the place where the stone walkway ended and the lily-pad-laden pond—one of several at Peninsula, although they didn't know that yet—began. Finally, the sheer astonishment, taking in the narrow column of water that jutted out over a canyon and the thickly forested Mayacamas Mountains beyond, creating a river suspended in the sky.

Then the cameras came out and ruined the mood, but that was to be expected. You didn't see places like this every day. Though, maybe, when he ran this town, that would change.

He had first come to Peninsula with his father, when he was fourteen. They'd taken the jet—back when there was a dedicated jet, onyx with "Ranjani Realty" splayed across the side in gold, not one of the rent-a-ride affairs to which he was now accustomed. He had been as bowled over as anyone else, both by the surroundings and the unctuousness that ran down his throat and warmed him from the inside out, the notion that the contents of a bottle had the power to change your worldview entirely.

He had sheathed that visit in a snow globe, and every time he saw something that rubbed against his memory of wine country as a refuge for all that was rich and right, he felt a jolt of rage. Public Storages and 7-Elevens had no place in this world, this haven of the haves. The single-story homes with their postage-stamp yards, the AutoZones and Walmarts and tent encampments along the trail that cut through downtown Napa—those were the worst of all. Yountville, the town north of Napa, had done it right. Bouchon and Jean-Charles Boisset and nary a Dollar Tree in sight.

On this particular visit to Peninsula, he watched one member of their group more closely than the rest. How did she handle opulence? Did she fall all over herself, OMG-ing, taking it all in with a phone in front of her face, or did she take it in stride, as if she inhabited modern marvels of architecture and design all the time?

She had shat the bed the night before, dashing out of Upsilon like that. Good thing he and Seamus played poker together. He knew Seamus couldn't care less what the average diner thought about his food, as long as the critics continued raving and as long as he got paid. (For this reason, Seamus also paid the critics.)

But as Rachel and Victoria posed before Peninsula's perpendicular waterfall for two, five, now more than a dozen selfies, instructing Joy, their eminently obliging host, to turn their phones this way, that way—"Try portrait mode," "Do one from below, looking up at us," "Can you make it so that we're not backlit?"—Anjali had stood to the side, hands behind her back, phone nowhere to be seen. Raj had thought about approaching her, then thought better of it.

"May we start in the barrel room, Mr. Ranjani?" Joy appeared at his side, apparently dismissed from documentarian duties, though, surely, not for long. "Or would you prefer to start with the vertical tasting in the salon?"

"The barrel room sounds great," he said. "And please, call me Raj." He clasped her hands in his and slipped a fifty-dollar bill from his right palm to hers. A hundred would've been better, a hundred was what he had planned, but times being what they were, he had to adapt. He tried not to wince with apology as he did it.

She smiled with pursed lips and slid the bill into the pocket of her pants with the slightest of moves. A total pro, this Joy.

"Dude, are you kidding me with this place?" Hari said, nudging Raj in the elbow as they followed Joy through the courtyard, around another pond laden with lily pads, dappled by sunlight filtered through a hedge of firs. Another photo shoot commenced. "What's it cost to become a member?"

"There's no membership," Raj said. He took a sip of his Krug and watched Rachel mimic Victoria's pose—hand on hip, three-quarter turn toward the camera, one leg jutting out, foot arched. An emerald-green Birkin dangled from her forearm, its alligator handles brushing the tail of the Serpenti. He'd paid a hundred grand for that bag. Paris, one wedding anniversary or another. Fourth? Fifth? Boom times, either way. He wondered how much it would go for on the secondhand market. Less? More? He recalled reading something about how women were newly into beat-up Birkins. He could beat that thing up, easily.

"So how do you get in?" Hari asked.

"I get an allocation. Three bottles a year." Why not give the poor sap what he wants? Raj thought; all he cares about is how much things cost. "Twenty-one hundred dollars." Couch cushion money, compared with a Birkin, compared with what an expertly flipped pre-owned Birkin would bring in . . .

He could not stomach the thought of divesting and rationing. Not yet. Not necessary. There was still hope, oodles of it. Norman Vincent Peale's positive thinking—*come on,* Raj, don't fall down this hole.

Hari nodded, as if $2,100 was a totally normal amount to pay for three bottles of wine. "Gets you into the right circles, I'm guessing."

"Exactly," Raj said. "If I want to be taken seriously, this is a good place to be seen."

"Mr. Mayor," Hari said, snickering.

Raj elbowed him in the ribs. "I told you that in confidence," he said. "There's still a lot to figure out." He knew he shouldn't have divulged his plan to Hari, as he had done, that morning, jogging back through the Kismet gate, their cooldown mile. The shit you said after a run, when the endorphins were coursing. He was liable to give away all his secrets; he had to be more careful, shut the fuck up until the right time. Several parts had to align, like atoms in an element. One of the really complicated elements. Tungsten or titanium, or something.

"You take yourself so seriously, bro," Hari said, turning his glass upside down, letting the last drop of Champagne fall to the pea gravel. Joy and the influenzas had started walking again; Anjali and David trailed behind. Raj turned around and took heart in seeing that they were on opposite sides of the pond. "You're about to launch Kismet. Why not kick back, chill, enjoy life up north for a while?"

He didn't expect Hari to get it. Hari hadn't received the phone call that Raj had prior to the trip, about the complaint that had been filed—the veritable brick that came through his phone before the actual brick that came through his window—about the investigators, about the need to divest—in a major way, not a "list your closet" way—about how it would be prudent to take the money that had been funding the venture on the brink of imploding and put it into something solid, something that would be less susceptible to regulatory scrutiny. Something that, ideally, would not be on him. Something that he could recoup later.

About how, perhaps, it would be advantageous to rehabilitate his image. Take up a cause that did not increase his bottom line. Join the board of a B Corp. Start a nonprofit. Both options seemed so . . . pussy-ish, to him. Public office, something with power, that was more his speed.

Hari also had the benefit of zero beneficiaries. No one to provide for but himself. Though, he'd probably *love* to provide for Rachel, that commandment-breaking son of a bitch.

Raj knew it would be easier if he only had himself to look out for, given that he now had one iron in the fire and a bank account bleeding out like a victim on some terribly predictable procedural show. Easier but lonely. He liked companionship. A worthy adversary.

"I'll chill when I'm dead," he said.

More oohs and aahs and "Can you take our photo?" as they reached the entrance to the barrel room, where the stone walls of the winery framed a panoramic view of the Mayacamas, creating a dramatic play of light against dark. He watched Anjali take a photo of the view, unmarred by three-quarter turns and hips and hands.

"We keep this building temperature controlled to fifty-five degrees, year-round," Joy said, pushing in the door to the barrel room. "You'll notice the dip."

"And y'all might notice my nips," Victoria stage-whispered, into her phone. Going live, he should have known. Was nothing sacred? She had linked her arm through Rachel's and they were giggling like schoolgirls, or more accurately, like sorority sisters. Trash. It was a bad look for him, for them. He had forgotten how bad of an influence Victoria was on Rachel. Or maybe it was Rachel who was too impressionable, so unsure of who she was that she just took the shape of whoever happened to be nearby.

The door closed with a heavy thud; darkness swallowed them up. A loamy, earthy smell emanated from the barrels along with the ever-present aroma of red wine, the kind that rises up from the drain when you dump that bottle that you opened two weeks ago and let languish in the back of the fridge.

At the center of the room was a flat-topped boulder arrayed with six sparkling Zaltos, the Aston Martin of glassware, the only vehicle Raj used for wine, if he could help it, and above it, a spotlight. As they got closer, Joy explained that the boulder had been excavated from the mountain beneath the winery. "We are big believers in sustainable architecture—"

"Can't not be, not in these times," Raj interjected, nodding gravely. He felt the need to compensate for his wife and friend's frivolity. Joy had no way of knowing that he'd imported the teak for Kismet's doors from Bali. Must've been a Sasquatch of a carbon footprint on that one.

Joy acknowledged him with a wan smile. "So we found ways to integrate what we took out of the earth in the architecture and design of the winery. But to really get a sense of our terroir—is everyone familiar with that term?"

"Of course," said Raj.

"Actually," said David.

"I mean, a li'l explanash wouldn't hurt," said Victoria, turning her camera toward Joy. Was she drunk? Raj wondered. Or high? Or drunk and high on the inflated sense of self-worth brought on by the sycophants and spam accounts that followed her on social media?

"'Terroir' refers to the holistic natural environment in which a certain wine is produced—the climate, the topography, the soil," Joy said, "which you can actually feel for yourself." She reached down and placed a smaller hunk of rock on the table. "Pass it around—you can see bands of iron, slate, quartz."

The rock. The shape of the rock. It was uncanny. It couldn't have been intentional. But it was so obvious. It couldn't have *not* been intentional.

They all exchanged a look. Hari started snickering. Victoria grabbed the rock, held it in front of her phone like an Oscar, and said, "Damn, which one of y'all out there is hung like this?"

The rock was shaped like a penis. Undeniable. It even had balls.

"Wait, V," Rachel said, grabbing the rock out of Victoria's hands and positioning it like she was going to put it in her mouth. Then she stuck out her tongue so it all but brushed the rock's side.

"OMG, yes, Rach, go *down* on that terroir," V said, zooming in.

"You know we Money Honeys roll deep," Rachel said, eye-fucking the camera.

"Ooh, she on *fire*," V trilled.

Mortified. He was mortified. There was no other way to put it. How was this an acceptable way for any woman to act in public, let alone his *wife*? But he was not in a position—no man was, anymore—to stop two women from being women, from goofing off, from eschewing formality, from living their #bestlife even if it meant debasing themselves (and, by association, him) in front of however many people were watching, besides the assembled company. Hari clapped and said, "Get it, girl." Anjali and David laughed with their eyes and covered their mouths. Even Joy tittered. He wondered who Joy knew, how many people Joy would tell. He doubted that anyone who mattered in Napa followed V, and even if they did, the odds of them watching her live stream at that moment were slim to none, but gossip could be vicious. Gossip could be even worse than the act itself. You never knew how stories got twisted as they telephoned their way through town.

He folded his mouth into a line and tried to keep heat from rising to his temples. He yearned for the bygone times when wineries went without Wi-Fi. Another thing he'd do as mayor: ban live streams from such hallowed halls as these. Let the bachelorettes at V. Sattui have at it, show all to whomever. Let some places remain sacred.

"How funny," Joy said. "I never noticed that about its . . . shape. We'll have to make sure we have a yonic sample, too, you know, girl power!" Her comment escaped the other women, who were making zero effort to compose themselves. "Now, if you'll grab a glass and follow me," she said, gesturing at the Zaltos, "we're going to pull a sample from our 2021 estate cabernet sauvignon, which hails from the west side of Howell Mountain, which you saw as you entered the winery. It's quite young—"

"That's how I like 'em," Victoria said, into her phone.

"But it'll provide a great point of comparison to the 2018 and 2013 estate cabs, which you'll taste—"

The sound of glass shattering on stone interrupted Joy's speech and reverberated across the expanse of the barrel room. Raj whipped around to see Rachel, wide-eyed, standing next to the boulder table, shards of Zalto surrounding her feet, terroir phallus in hand.

She said "sorry" several times. Too many. To the point where the apology felt cloying, interspersed with some lame explanation about how she was about to put down her glass and must've knocked into the table, and then she attempted to pick up the pieces, and the ignominy of Rachel squatting in four-inch heels and a miniskirt finally pushed him over the edge.

"What is going on with you?" he said, storming over. Under his breath: "You're embarrassing us."

Joy excused herself to get a dustpan.

"It was an accident," Rachel said, righting herself. Her eyes brimmed.

"Pull yourself together," he said. His eyes darted to the malachite on her wrist. "Act like you deserve that watch." Uncalled for? No more so, in his mind, than blowing a rock while the internet watched.

"Hey, guys," Hari said, striding over, butting in where he most definitely did not belong.

"I can't," Rachel said, wiping away the tears before they fell. She made a motion with her hands, like this was all too much, then turned on her heels—Gucci Mary Janes, glinty and gauche, he ought to throw them out, or put them on StockX, or give them to Ahmad to put them on StockX—and walked toward the door.

"Rachel!" Anjali called after her. She whipped around and glared at Raj. "It's just a glass. It could've happened to anyone."

~

Anjali found Rachel slumped against the wall that offered the panoramic view of the Mayacamas Mountains. How bucolic it seemed, when she had photographed it earlier. Well, actually, she thought, as she sat down next to Rachel and offered, in both senses, a shoulder for her friend to cry on, there was something sinister about the composition. The extreme dark of the shadows beneath the construction and the extreme bright of the sun on the far side of the canyon. Like hell and heaven, rolled into one.

"It's like I'm always doing the wrong thing," Rachel said, when she lifted her head. Anjali's formerly clean white T-shirt now bore smears of snot and mascara. "No matter what—either I'm being too stuffy when I'm supposed to be 'fun,' or I'm too ratchet when I'm supposed to be reserved, or . . . I don't know, whatever I am, in any given moment, it's just not good enough." She reached into her handbag and pulled out a tissue. Anjali wondered if Rachel had planned for this—or was she always on the brink of a breakdown and perpetually prepared? What a depressing thought.

"Have you ever felt like that?" Rachel asked. "Like no matter what you do, it's not right?"

Not long ago, Anjali would have professed to know not of what Rachel spoke. She had been so self-righteous, so sure of herself as she was building her career and doing everything the baby books and mommy blogs told her to, but the older she got, the more life came at her, the more she realized she was essentially bubbling in all the Bs on a Scantron and praying to the gods of probability that she'd pass.

"I know exactly what you mean," Anjali said.

"Do you ever wonder if it's too late to start over?" Rachel ventured. "To become a completely different person?"

"I mean . . . what kind of person do you want to be?"

Rachel sighed, her form collapsing into a crescent moon. She stretched her legs out on the slate pathway and arced her feet back and forth, the gilt horse bits of her square-toed heels clicking softly when they hit the ground. "I don't know, I mean, look, I know I'm privileged and I have it good—"

"A life a million girls would kill for," Anjali deadpanned.

"Right! Yes! Total cliché! But you know Raj, his temper, how hard he is to deal with." She paused and gazed out at the Mayacamas. "I mean, there's a good person underneath it all, right?"

Was there? Anjali wondered.

"He hasn't had it easy, you know?"

It was true. Anjali knew. He had suffered an unimaginable tragedy a decade ago, losing his parents and sister. But was Rachel really going to defend him now? After the way he'd humiliated her?

Maybe the person Rachel was really trying to defend was herself. Maybe she was trying, in her roundabout way, to justify why she was married to a man who treated her the way Raj did. You could practically see the tug-of-war going on in her brain: he's rich, but he's a dick. I love the trappings of my life, but the life itself . . .

There was also the tug-of-war between being vulnerable and protecting what dignity you had left. You never wanted your friends to pity you.

"He did take you home last night when you felt sick."

Anjali took note of the edge in Rachel's voice as she said this, the sense that she wanted Anjali to confirm that she had, indeed, felt sick.

"I'm really sorry about that," Anjali said. "That dinner"—she shook her head—"I don't know what it was, but one of those dishes did me in."

Rachel arched an eyebrow. "Only one?"

They laughed. The tension snapped. Some of it. A little twig of tension.

"I figured that place was your idea," Anjali said.

"Are you kidding? I'd rather have Domino's. Well—I *did* have Domino's."

"I'm jealous," Anjali said.

"I don't know why he feels like he has so much to prove," Rachel said. "I'm not pretending that I know what it's like to run a multimillion-dollar company or be that guy that all your friends reach out to when they want a dime—you know who he's working with now? Sid—"

"*That* guy?" Every group of college friends had one—the borderline creep whom no one trusts, the type of guy who decants Popov into Belvedere and puts the bottle back on the top shelf. "The one who went to med school in the Caribbean? What are they doing?"

"Some kind of lab," Rachel said. "A medical start-up, a departure for him." She lowered her voice as she mimicked Raj. "'Gotta diversify, market saturation.' Blah-de-blah, who gives a fuck? All he does is work." Another sigh. She knocked her head softly against the wall of the winery, once, twice, three times. Dejection, personified. "He's game to gamble on just about anything, except starting a family with me."

Anjali made a sound of sympathy, even though she had a hard time picturing Rachel as a mother. Or Raj as a father. They clearly had issues to work out between themselves before bringing another person into the world. Although, who was she to judge? She was practically a doorstop, driving a wedge between them. And it wasn't as if she and David had been perfect when she got pregnant with Lucie. People liked to think there was a perfect time to become a parent but that time did not exist; you could always be more stable, more settled, more ready, in theory. But nothing prepared you like the event itself.

"Is that . . . something that you've talked about?" Anjali asked.

"He says I'm too selfish," Rachel replied. "He says I don't know how to put myself second. Funny how I always manage to do it for him."

9

Friday afternoon
Peninsula, Oakville

It was always the ones with money, David thought, watching Anjali rush out of the barrel room, trailing after Rachel. Rich people could not be content. With their basic needs taken care of, they found other things to get upset about: foreheads, waistlines, jawlines, fault lines beneath their property that prohibited them from building a three-thousand-square-foot wine cellar, in the case of one of his former clients, an MMA fighter turned motivational speaker and author who claimed to be sober but was not in the slightest. Rich people got upset about housekeepers who talked too much and personal chefs who tripped over a Flamingo Estate farm box (spraining an ankle, crushing the tomatoes, Sungolds, the last of the season) and a wife who broke a glass that didn't even belong to them. That they weren't even on the hook for. That was a mistake, a mild faux pas, if anything at all.

Rich people could afford to get upset about saving face. The rest of the world just had to trudge on, chastened, embarrassed, humiliated.

He longed for rich-people problems. He longed for the commissions of clients who had money to burn, the types of people he used to represent at Archetype, before they kicked him to the curb. He longed for a daughter who could get out of bed without the help of a vape.

Maybe most of all, he longed for Anjali. Old Anjali. The version of Anjali that existed when they used to go to Shakespeare in the Park and book parties at McNally Jackson, when they lived on the Upper West Side and shared the Sunday *New York Times* and cheese-laden egg scrambles at that little place on Fifty-First, a hike from the UWS but a warm nook full of memories, before marriages and mortgages and moving to the suburbs, before he fucked it all up.

What's a man to do when his wife has not laid a hand on him for a year? When he comes home from work and she looks at him like a notice from the IRS? When it seems abundantly clear that the highlights of her day, the stuff for which she gets up in the morning, do not involve him? When meanwhile, back at the office, human resources needs an agent to pitch into the internship program, to mentor wannabe agents, to engage with them on social media? Was it so wrong of him, to have volunteered himself for that opportunity, to seek to fill his spare time with the mentoring and molding of minds that were young but not *that* young, all of legal age, all past the point of consent, he made sure. He always made sure.

Was it his fault that so many of them were female? Was it his fault that aspiring authors—also female, women like Maddie, Maddie with the short-shorts bounding among the vines, yes, he had saved that video, he'd made sure of that, too—began contacting him as well?

Well, perhaps that last part. He had told an internship applicant from Columbia to pass on his information to any MFA graduates seeking representation and had failed to understand how many aspiring, twentysomething novelists there were in New York City, and how many of them were female.

He had also reached out to Maddie first. But she'd shown up in his feed. Why would she have done that, if she didn't want to engage?

How was he supposed to know what was kosher to say to these women and what was not? He tried to use the language they did. He tried to conversate. If they sent him pictures, he hearted them. He said they looked nice because they did. What, was he supposed to lie?

It felt like women were constantly redrawing the borders of what was okay and what was not. He had nearly fainted when HR summoned him, produced screenshots—how did you even take a screenshot on a phone? Did you take a picture of it with another phone? All he had done was offer encouragement and advice. How could that be so wrong?

You couldn't call a woman a sweetheart or a slut, you couldn't say she was beautiful or big or small or smart—because what did that mean? That *other* women weren't smart? That you were astonished a woman could even *be* smart? You couldn't not respond because then the women would say that you ignored them, you didn't give them a chance, you didn't hold space, you were a fucking misogynist and probably racist, too.

So he developed a strategy: exclamation points and emoji. To *Would you maybe be interested in representing me?* he might reply, *Yes!!!!* [smiley face with hearts for eyes emoji].

How could you argue with the smiley face with hearts for eyes? How could that be construed as bad?

Anjali had laughed, in disbelief, when he told her. "Questionable communication," she repeated. "You got fired for *questionable communication*, David? You risked your career, your salary, our family's health insurance, to engage in some dirty DMs with girls that are barely older than your own daughter?" He had pulled up conversation after conversation, emphasized that he hadn't asked for anything untoward, that he had never even met any of these women, let alone done anything physical with them. "It's not like I cheated," he said. "Help me understand—how is this reprehensible?"

She had given him a withering look. "Do you not get how creepy and wrong this is? The abuse of power?"

She eventually admitted, at the coaxing of the therapist that he insisted they see, that *he* had found on the internet, that *he* paid for out of pocket, that part of her wished he had never told her. He could've lied about why he'd gotten fired, fabricated layoffs, faked a burning desire to break off on his own.

Yet another example of women redrawing the borders. He thought honesty was the best policy.

One of the most depressing parts about getting old was screwing up in all the ways that you said you never would. His parents, working-class Manhattanites who came up when one could afford to live in Manhattan and be working-class, had divorced because his father had cheated on his mother. Wantonly. He was a dentist. The hygienists—it was a revolving door. But his father and mother had never had anything in common besides their bridge group and gin martinis and the veritable religious belief that New York City was the only place one could live. He and Anjali had so much in common. Their love of the written word and the people who put pen to paper, the compulsion to carve out a life of the mind in a world hell-bent on building material wealth.

The problem, he supposed, was that you couldn't have a life of the mind and still live in the material world. Did he see a touch of younger Anjali in the girls—*women*, young *women*—that he had messaged with? Perhaps. Was it as simple as him feeling undervalued at home and superhuman in the eyes of a twenty-two-year-old MFA student? For sure. It was sad, truly, how much it came down to that—a stranger seeing you as you wanted to be seen because you'd failed in the eyes of your beloved.

He thought insisting on counseling was the right thing to do, the next step in the flowchart. He thought it would win him brownie points. He thought therapy would fix him, fix them—was he supposed to simply be okay with a sexless marriage for the foreseeable future? What did other couples do?

It had only served to further annoy his wife. "Truly, David, I don't have time for this," she'd said, after their last session, gesturing at the screen of his laptop—he'd thought she'd be happy about the virtual option, cheaper, more convenient—like she wanted to hurl the computer against the wall. "The fact of the matter is that we can't afford to get divorced. If you really want to make it up to me, stop sending these disgusting messages and get your agency off the ground."

He checked his phone again. This goddamn Guerrilla Somm. He had been active on social media that morning, David knew because he had checked; the Somm had his phone on him. *Everyone* had their phone on them. He'd read an article that said the vast majority of people read a text message within three minutes of receiving it. The Guerrilla Somm had said he was interested in the prospect of writing a book. "Into it." Those had been his exact words. He had given David his number and told him to text, which David had done with all the desperation of a teenager with a crush:

Fantastic!! Shall we meet Saturday?! Have a place in mind?!!

And then, several hours later:

Happy to come to wherever is convenient for you!!!

And then, this morning:

Hey!!!!!!! Still good for Saturday???!!! [smiley face with stars for eyes emoji]

(You couldn't fault the smiley face with stars for eyes. It was David's way of saying he wanted to make someone a star, and who didn't want to be a star?)

In David's mind, signing the Guerrilla Somm was the first thing he needed to do to set things right with his wife. Of course Anjali didn't want to sit through couples therapy. Of course she didn't want to talk about feelings, wring her hands, or more accurately, watch him wring his hands. She wanted him to perform, to provide. She wanted a winner.

He also thought that Maddie had what it took to write a sellable book. Self-help. She liked to advise her followers on their dating, friend, and career dilemmas while roving around the world on sponsors' dimes.

She had built her following in college, attending the University of Miami, president of her sorority, a big sister who expanded her flock. But he thought, given Anjali's concerns, that it would be wise to widen his oeuvre, to consider potential clients not of the female persuasion. There was also the flub with the tattoo artist. These girls, you couldn't trust them! You never knew what they would do.

The barrel room door opened, and Rachel and Anjali strode through, arms linked. She could be harsh, David thought, looking at his wife in appreciation, but it was only because her expectations were so high. Why shouldn't they be? She'd been on the honor roll since she had learned the alphabet. She'd made herself indispensable at the country's most prestigious magazine. She packed lunches and took care of the ones she loved. She had never done anything wrong.

He would be better for her, for Lucie, for their family. Forget sex. Forget interns. Forget MFA grads and lubricious content creators and Maddie. He would delete her messages. Delete them all. Block her number. He had been stupid enough; he couldn't afford another fuckup.

Anjali and Rachel joined Victoria, who had ceased her live stream. Victoria patted Rachel's back and gave her a sympathetic look; Rachel offered a wan smile that communicated all was okay, if only for the moment. "Shall we proceed?" Joy ventured. In one hand she held a wine thief, a long tube of glass designed for extracting wine from a barrel, and in the other, her own Zalto. Raj nodded in assent, barely flitted his eyes over the women on the opposite side of the table.

Joy hovered the wine thief over their empty glasses and unleashed a torrent of cabernet. They swirled, they inhaled, they searched for words for what they smelled and tasted: cherries, freshly cut grass, wood chips after the rain. "Maybe . . . Gobstoppers?" David offered. "The purple ones, before you get to the center."

"That's a good one, man," Raj said, tipping his glass in David's direction. David murmured a thank-you before he could parse whether Raj was being genuine. But why wouldn't Raj be genuine? What could Raj have against him?

He felt his phone buzz.

Guerrilla Somm: can you do tonight?

Oh dear. The Sammi Ali dinner would commence at eight, and he knew that was the part of the program to which Anjali was most looking forward. He didn't want to miss it, or skip out early. He could try for after? But he would not be on his game after, what with the wine here and the next place and the bottles that would surely be uncorked at dinner.

He turned to Raj. "Would it be all right if someone joined us for drinks at the house before dinner?"

"Who?" asked Anjali, voice serrated with suspicion.

"That sommelier," he said, locking eyes with his wife: Look what I can do, look how I can fetch. "Tonight's the only time he can meet."

"The Guerrilla Somm? Absolutely," said Raj. "I've been trying to get him to preview Kismet. Tell him to come for drinks, stay for the meal." David inwardly did a fist pump and thanked whatever God or universal force was at work. Finally, it felt like things were aligning. Finally, he had done something right.

~

From the barrel room, they had migrated to the salon, an expansive, high-ceilinged room with a long, repurposed-boulder table laid with six place mats, spindly breadsticks in squat ceramic jars, and four more wispy wineglasses per person. The women sauntered ahead of the men, heads huddled together. They settled into low leather chairs along one side of the table, the side that offered the view. Hari was dismayed to see that Rachel had flattened like champagne popped and summarily abandoned on a countertop. So she had broken a glass. So she had been a little goofy. She didn't deserve to be harangued by her husband. He would never do that to his wife.

Joy excused herself to get a carafe of water. The six of them sat in silence. The air felt like it had edges. Hari took out his phone. Maybe the Wine Spy app would loosen them up. Give them something to talk about. He'd been meaning to show it to Raj, to see how Raj could work it into his portfolio. Now felt as good a time as any.

"Yo, check this out," he said, nudging Raj and David, training the camera of his phone on a bottle of 2013 estate cabernet at the center of the table. The bottle itself was empty; its contents had been poured into a bulbous decanter, and its cork, purple at the edges that had lapped against the wine, stood next to it. As the app "read" the wine, cross-referencing details from the label of the bottle with the thousands of similar bottles in its database, the screen of Hari's phone showed an illustration of a vine growing leaves and grapes before shedding both: his version of the hourglass, the rainbow spinning wheel.

"Did you code that?" David asked.

"I hired the Bangalore coders that did," Hari said.

David made a sound of admiration.

Raj watched, fingers to his lips, in silence. The app made a *thunk* sound and played an animation of a cellar door slamming shut.

"Yikes," Hari said. "'Not ready yet. Needs two to four more years to mature.' Sounds like my ex-girlfriend!" He laughed and took in the looks of mild contempt. "Oh—I'm not knocking her, that's what she said to *me*." He continued laughing to show that he didn't take it personally, even though he very much did. She was a twenty-seven-year-old flight attendant on the JFK-to-BOM route who had inducted him into the mile-high club.

"Well, given that it's an estate cab from an undeniably good year and it's been triple decanted, I guess we're just going to have to suffer through it," Raj said. He turned to Joy, who had returned and was making her way around the table, filling up their water glasses. "Don't mind my friends; they don't get out much."

Hari had to ask himself: Would Raj ever see him as an equal? All signs pointed to no. This, despite the fact that Hari had built something out of nothing. This app. His abs. His ConciergeKey status. Hari didn't grow up with a multimillion-dollar company bearing his last name.

Raj ought to *respect* Hari. Not dismiss him like a prompt to rate your Postmate, at the very least.

"Not compared to this guy," Hari said, with an ingratiating smile. "We still fly commercial and wipe our own asses."

Raj shot him a look. Rachel choked on a laugh. Mission accomplished, Hari thought.

Now they were outside, on Peninsula's garden patio, surrounded by thickets of lavender through which honeybees buzzed. There was a picnic table laden with crudités and hummus that was made, for some reason, from fermented soybeans instead of chickpeas. (Why this compulsion to reinvent hummus? Hummus was fine.) There was a pizza oven, a magnum of cabernet franc that Hari had purchased from Peninsula despite, or perhaps because of, Raj's comment that he despised cabernet franc. A pepperoni pie would be out soon, a mushroom and asiago after that. Tensions had loosened as they'd worked their way through the vertical tasting; Raj was now chopping it up with Joy and David, gossiping about the Guerrilla Somm, while Anjali and Victoria were wending their way through a row of flowering bushes, with blooms in seemingly every shade of pink.

Rachel had taken a glass of cab franc and wandered out to the row of vines it hailed from, which began a few paces past where the garden ended. Hari topped up his glass and walked over to her.

She was looking off into the horizon, hugging her elbow to her side. A breeze kicked up the pleats of her pleated miniskirt just enough to reveal what she was wearing underneath, just for a moment. Hari took a mental picture, saved it to his favorites.

"Having fun?" he asked, when he got within earshot.

She whipped around and smiled at him. "Could be worse."

"Could always be worse," he said, closing the space between them as he came to stand next to her. "But"—he chewed the inside of his cheek, knew that if he said what he wanted to say, he would not be able to walk it back—"it could be better."

She said nothing at first, seemingly watching as a bluebird landed on a fir in the distance and then flitted off. "What do you mean?" she asked. He thought he detected a note of hope in her voice.

Hari shifted so that he was facing her. "I mean that you don't have to let him treat you the way that he does." It was an echo of what he had said to her a decade ago, that night in LA, when she had revealed to Hari why she and Raj had broken up and her hunch that maybe Raj was beyond reform, maybe they were not meant to be together after all.

Now, Rachel widened her eyes at Hari. It looked, for a moment, like she might burst into tears.

She inhaled sharply. She took a sip and rearranged her face into an expression of steely reserve.

"Oh? What would you suggest?"

Hari had no words. He stuttered something to that effect.

"Exactly," Rachel said. "When you find out the formula for a happy marriage, I'd love to hear it. Until then, enjoy the weekend that my husband is paying for and keep your opinions to yourself."

10

Friday afternoon
Seven Senses Spa, St. Helena

The plan had been to go from Peninsula to Raging Sparrow, a cult winery in Napa whose cabs retailed for $4,000 a bottle. Normally, Raging Sparrow was off-limits to visitors, even those lucky enough to get an allocation—getting on the winery's waiting list required knowing someone who knew someone and putting down a $2,000 deposit to "reserve" your wine, the root product of which had yet to germinate and was but a glimmer in the eye of the label's century-old vines. You generally had to wait twelve to fifteen years to receive the wine, and another ten before critics deemed it "drinkable." (What it was in the interim remained a mystery worthy of discovery for someone with a lot of time and money to burn.) There were reams of Reddit threads devoted to dissecting Raging Sparrow's draconian policies and whether the wine was "worth it." "It's worth it if you're stupid-rich and need to open once-in-a-lifetime bottles to keep up with / piss off your stupid-rich friends," one user said. "For my money? Drop $500 on a '92 Stag's Leap and call it a day. If that doesn't impress your friends, find new ones."

But as the group gathered before the Sprinter, sated by blistered slices of Neapolitan and enough varieties of cabernet to fill a Costco shelf, Rachel made an announcement.

"Anj and I are going to go get massages. Anyone want to come?"

It wasn't a genuine invitation; Rachel had genuinely invited Victoria earlier, as they walked from the barrel room to the salon. Victoria had thanked her for the offer but said that she needed to see what Raging Sparrow was all about, which Rachel understood. It was a prime content opportunity, one in which she would've been happy to partake—she had thought up a post for the Money Honeys ahead of time, a midrange shot of her hand wrapped around a bottle, Serpenti glinting below, a caption about how you couldn't put a price on the good life—had it not been for Raj and Hari and the feeling that her every move and mood was being watched and judged.

Don't have too much fun but don't have *no* fun, look hot but not too hot, be easy, be accommodating, be authentic but not if you're feeling bad—no one wants to hear you bitch and moan. Swallow your ego, swallow your pride, accept criticism, take the blame, and smile. Don't forget to smile.

She needed a break, from men, from keeping up appearances, from trying so hard, from wine. Maybe not from wine. She'd gladly accept a glass of Seven Senses sparkling, complimentary with every treatment.

"What?" said Raj. It was the first time he'd addressed her since the barrel room. His mood had improved, over the course of their time at Peninsula, but no way was she going to talk to him first. He owed her an apology, a groveling, really. If he thought that giving her the watch meant that he could buy his way out of bad behavior, he was wrong . . . except, that was what he had done throughout their relationship, and every time prior, it had worked.

From a Tiffany's charm bracelet during their freshman year of Cornell—when she found out that he'd hooked up with one of her Delta Gamma sorority sisters before they knew each other, so it wasn't cheating, but she'd insisted on knowing about all his college hookups prior to her, insecure and new on campus as she was, and he had lied—to the Birkin dangling from her forearm, to the Serpenti wrapped around her wrist. This was his pattern. Fuck up, pay up, rinse, repeat.

Midway through their fifth-anniversary trip to France, they had met a fellow Dodgers fan at the bar of the Hotel du Cap-Eden-Roc, and after a magnum of rosé (Bandol, top-notch; that part, she hadn't minded), Raj and his new friend ended up choppering over to Monte Carlo to watch the final game of some hotly contested series and play blackjack for thirty-seven hours straight. While Raj had extended an invitation to Rachel—"Babe, come on, it'll be epic; we'll see the seagulls another time"—like her invitation in the pea-gravel drive of Peninsula, it was not genuine.

She had wanted to see the Chagalls. At the Chagall Museum. Where they had prebooked and paid for a private tour. She ended up going by herself. Afterward, she took the train to Paris by herself and ignored his Burgundy-fueled pleas to please call him back, followed by slurred voice mails instructing her to definitely *not* call him back—she was a bitch, she was ungrateful, she didn't know how good she had it—followed by the original pleas but remixed, subdued, slightly more self-aware but also strung out.

She'd arrived in the lobby of the Four Seasons George V and found him, hat in hand in the form of an orange Hermès shopping bag big enough to carry a goat across the border. (His Dodgers hat was, wisely, not in his hand. He had lost it somewhere between the Hotel Metropole and the private terminal of Charles de Gaulle.)

Here, now, in Napa, she was putting her foot down. Applying Megan's #MachineLearning. Making changes.

In front of the Sprinter, she reiterated her change in plans, despite knowing that he'd heard her perfectly well.

Raj laughed bitterly at the ground and looked to Hari and David for support, who averted their eyes. "Whatever," he said, with a dramatic shrug. "We're going straight to Raging Sparrow, though. I'm not making Jason wait again."

Once again, her husband was putting Jason's well-being above her own. She knew enough that she shouldn't have been surprised—Jason, the owner of the high-end wine bars, had grown up with Raging Sparrow's winemaker, and had also let the winemaker crash on his couch during the days when he was coming down from meth, before he went to rehab and discovered his talent at manipulating a different drug that didn't threaten to derail his life. (The winemaker didn't drink. Those hoping to get on Raging Sparrow's waiting list often sent the winemaker prized bottles from equally exalted wineries; those bottles got sent on to Jason and marked up to a level that would make the Cline's customers who counted themselves among the .01 percenters gasp but still pull out their Amex.)

"No problem," Rachel said. "I ordered an Uber." A Lux, but it seemed gauche to mention it. She glanced down at her phone, then up at an orange Aston Martin SUV winding up the pea-gravel drive.

Raj looked at Anjali, in the process of assuring David that she was fine, that he should go on ahead. He turned back to Rachel and sneered. "Your loss." He got into the Sprinter. The other three followed, David shrugging with resignation, Victoria blowing kisses, Hari standing a beat too long on the steps of the Sprinter, looking at Rachel, trying to say something with his eyes.

It wasn't that she didn't have feelings for Hari. It was that she didn't feel like destroying her life to examine them. If she followed that thread—what if she had chosen one instead of the other?—she would end up unraveling the sweater that constituted her life, and it was a nice sweater, a fine sweater, cashmere, alpaca, really quite soft, and sure, there were a few loose yarns here and there, but did she want to pull and nip at every single one? No. Not wise.

What Hari said had also felt like a test. She couldn't be sure that what she told him wouldn't get back to Raj. Better to play it safe, at least around those two.

Rachel tried to push the situation out of her mind as she arranged herself, face down, on a Saran Wrap–covered table at Seven Senses. She murmured her assent as a massage therapist explained what he'd be scrubbing over her limbs: a pulp of Sonoma sauvignon blanc (fruit, seeds, and skins), Central Valley olive oil, and salt from the Salton Sea.

"So, is this your secret?" Anjali asked, from the table next to hers, her voice muffled by a towel-wrapped face cradle, as another massage therapist was working the pulp into her back. "Is this the reason you probably still get carded while I get called 'ma'am'?"

"Oh, no," said Rachel. "That's all injectables. Come to LA and I'll make it look like you were never born."

They both laughed.

Her breakdown at Peninsula had lowered her guard, with regard to Anjali. She had been reminded of the girls they once were. Practically sisters, really. They had grown up across the street from each other, in mirror versions of the same suburban split-level. Born three days apart. Destined to be besties. Until the sixth grade, when Rachel moved to Paris for a year (her father, a linguistics professor at Rutgers, scored a fellowship at the Sorbonne) and came back changed: taller, thinner, with a worldview that extended beyond the Menlo Park Mall and the allure of one who has ventured far and returned to tell the tale. She got invited to sit at the popular table. She felt guilty about leaving Anjali to languish with the goths and geeks, but not guilty enough to say no.

Advanced Placement US History, junior year, brought them back together. Partner projects made easier by physical proximity and enough familiarity with each other's families that Rachel knew how and when to namaskar. It was with Rachel's family that Anjali had her first sip of wine. It was Rachel who lent Anjali her first pair of high heels, when Anjali's mom refused to buy her a pair for prom because they were "too raunchy" for a girl of sixteen, "like something fit for some exotic dancer." (They were black pumps with two-inch heels.) It was Rachel who Anjali ran to, when she got the acceptance letter from Cornell. It was Anjali who consoled Rachel when the thin envelope from Brown arrived, when Rutgers emerged as the best and most fiscally wise choice.

Until Rachel's father got a job at New York University, which meant that she could now apply to one of Cornell's public colleges as a transfer student and pay in-state tuition. She didn't tell Anjali until the thick envelope dropped. She didn't want to jinx it.

Rachel had thought that, in Ithaca, they'd pick right back up where they left off. She hadn't anticipated Anjali's standoffishness, her seemingly impenetrable circle of Indian friends, the South Asian Students Society that suddenly took up all her free time. Rachel had never known Anjali to be so Indian. Growing up, Anjali eschewed Indian food, would beg her mom to make spaghetti and Ragù. But Rachel could roll with them. After finding her footing with the French, Rachel could roll with anyone. She wanted to make up for lost time, forge the bonds that were supposed to last the rest of her life. When she finally met Anjali's friends, they welcomed her with open arms. Raj especially.

Once they started dating, and once they pledged their respective houses, Raj and Rachel became an entity, one never mentioned without the other, the way that Anjali and Rachel had been, way back when. Rachel and Raj went to frat formals and sorority fundraisers; Rachel found, in Victoria, the girlfriend that Anjali didn't seem to want to be, or maybe didn't have the bandwidth to be, busy, as she was, writing for the *Cornell Daily Sun* and editing a poetry journal and endlessly applying for internships, desperate to break into the magazine industry.

Rachel also suspected that, beneath the busyness, Anjali was jealous. Anjali had never been good with guys. She tried too hard to be one of them. Guys didn't want to fuck their best friend (unless, of course, they did). Guys wanted a chase, a conquest, a dainty princess to win. At least, Raj did. At one point.

It occurred to Rachel, now, that this was the closest she'd felt to Anjali since they were in high school. She'd missed it.

"If you'll slide down and turn over"—her massage therapist's voice came from above—"we can begin phase two. You're not claustrophobic, are you?"

Rachel rolled her eyes as she rolled over. "I wasn't before."

The massage therapist laughed gently. "We're just going to fold you into the treatment, to generate some warmth. If you'll keep your legs together and your arms by your side," he said, as he pressed the edges of the Saran Wrap over her body, "that will allow the scrub to penetrate into the deepest layer of the skin."

"How long do we have to stay like this?" Anjali asked.

"Twenty minutes at least," her therapist said. "Thirty if you want to get it to the hypodermis, the deepest layer of the skin. Thirty-three is the magic number, if you ask me."

"What if I have to pee?" Anjali asked.

"Do you?" Her therapist looked stricken. "Oh no, I should've asked before. We can undo the wrap now, but we'll have to reset, and the bee pollen is already in the infrared oven and there's only so much bee pollen, what with the shortage of honeybees—"

"Oh, Kevin, I'm just kidding," Anjali said. "We'll be fine. Or not. If anything happens, you can bill her." She wiggled her body in Rachel's direction. Though she knew it might crack the mask of pinot noir grapes, ginseng, and vitamin C that had been slathered on her face, Rachel could not stop a smile from blooming. Classic Anjali.

Rachel owed her. Rachel owed her a lot.

Kevin and his colleague excused themselves from the room.

"So this must be what it's like to be a burrito," Anjali said.

"Anj, I'm sorry," Rachel said. "I'm sorry that I was a jerk to you after I came back from France. I was just thinking about how long we've been friends, and I know that I haven't always been a good one to you."

Anjali said nothing, which Rachel took as an invitation to go on.

"This weekend has made me realize that I need to prioritize my friendships, my *real* friendships, not just the Money Honeys—"

"The who?" Anjali asked.

Rachel explained the concept of the Money Honeys.

"So they've got Pelotons and money," said Anjali.

"Presumably," said Rachel.

"Do you have to have a Peloton to join?"

"I mean, they're not running background checks."

~

Anjali kept asking questions about the Money Honeys. It *was* interesting—a forum of self-decreed rich people who felt they could ask each other anything, free of judgment—but the real reason she had latched on to the subject was that she did not want to respond to Rachel's apology, because if she acknowledged the apology, she would also have to acknowledge what an awful, terrible, no-good, very bad friend she was being.

The apology did make her feel warm inside. Weirdly justified for holding on to a dagger of animosity for upward of thirty years, clenching and unclenching it depending on where she and Rachel were at in their relationship. Or maybe the warmth was the result of the wrap and she was just a horrible person.

Of course she felt guilty about what happened with Raj. But she wasn't deluded enough to think that he actually wanted her, that he was in love with her, that he even liked her as more than a pawn. He wanted something out of her. *That* was why he kissed her. He was a master manipulator, had been since day one. A PhD in getting people to do what he wanted without them realizing it.

"What are they posting about today?" Anjali asked. Money Honeys was safer territory than anything going on in her brain right now.

"Oh God, what aren't they posting about? Bags, shoes, what to buy with the $5,000 their husband gave them for their birthday, whether Cartier Love bracelets are in or out. Family stuff—*tons* of complaining about in-laws and husbands and kids. They're always posting about their kids. 'This one's overweight, but I feel guilty for taking away his snacks.'

'This one's anxious, but I don't want to put her on meds.' I mean, can you *imagine*, anti-anxiety drugs for a nine-year-old?"

"Oh, sorry, before I forget—can I borrow a pair of shoes for tomorrow night? The ones I brought are murder."

"Totally," said Rachel. "I've got tons of options."

Had Anjali been facing Rachel, Rachel would've been able to see the emotion taking over Anjali's face, the way her features twisted, the way she folded her top lip over her bottom to stifle a latent sob. Anjali had needed to pivot. She did, also, have to borrow another pair of shoes if she planned to last for more than an hour at the grand opening party the following night, and the topic of shoes put them in safer territory—Rachel had Valentinos, Rachel had Guccis, Rachel had Manolo Blahniks that really were as comfortable as *Sex and the City* made them out to be (according to Rachel). Rachel had follow-up questions: What was Anjali wearing? What should *she* wear? She had one option from Armani and a second from Bottega, but if neither of those worked, there was something from Jeremy Scott's last collection with Moschino, "but it's pretty out there; I know Raj hates it," and . . .

Anjali was glad when Kevin and his coworker returned.

She could not confide in Rachel about Lucie's condition. She felt embarrassed. *Good* mothers didn't let their children get crippling anxiety, *good* mothers didn't give their children vapes; a drumbeat, self-taught, self-inflicted, had resounded in her mind since the diagnosis.

The massage therapists freed them from their plastic prisons and removed the remnants of the scrub with hot towels. Then there were soft, dry towels, to sop up any moisture left behind by the hot towels, then a change of towels for the table, which required them to stand up, in yet another set of towels, while the massage therapists made the switch, and finally, blissfully, the massage portion of the treatment, which involved bee pollen and locally sourced eucalyptus oil, during which Anjali attempted to make her mind go blank.

One thought knocked around like the lone Tic Tac in an otherwise-empty box: the mom in the Facebook group Rachel mentioned had to have been talking about Puff. Or had to know about Puff, at least. None of Lucie's classmates were taking it yet, at least none that Anjali was aware of. She wasn't particularly close with any of the moms in Lucie's class. She felt inadequate around them, their made-from-scratch snickerdoodles and gluten-free raspberry tarts consistently outshining the precut fruit trays she bought from the grocery store when it was her turn to provide snack. It couldn't hurt for Anjali to connect with this mom, to see if there were other parents dealing with the same problems as her. Maybe they could share coping strategies. Maybe she, and in turn, Lucie, would feel a little less alone.

She wondered if they worked, these Money Honey moms. Probably not. Probably poured all their energy into maintaining their looks and providing a happy home for their children and spouses who not only brought home the bacon but fried it up and served it on cage-free-egg sandwiches on Saturdays when Mommy had her mandatory spinning date with Cody Rigsby. You'd think that a three-hour-long spa treatment would have sapped her of bitterness. You'd be wrong, for while Rachel had followed the recommendation of the massage therapists to seal her therapy with a steam and sauna, Anjali had sat, wrapped in a towel, on the edge of the cushioned bench in the women's locker room, curving her spine into a tight, taut C, clutching her phone and firing off missive after missive to Moran, to Morgenstern, to the graphics team. If she couldn't fix her daughter, at least she could fix this piece, at least she could prove her worth in other ways.

They met again at the spa reception. "Well, that was *necessary*," Rachel said, plucking her Platinum Card out of her wallet, and Anjali had protested, half-heartedly, until she caught sight of the bill. Four figures, before tip.

"This weekend's on us," Rachel reiterated, giving Anjali's shoulder a gentle squeeze, "and you've been an angel. I don't think I'd be able to survive this opening gala, without you."

Anjali mumbled something to the effect of "thank you."

"By the way," she ventured, "can you send me an invite to Money Honeys?" It could make for a great story: the last place on the internet where women got to be themselves. Mostly, though, she wanted to connect with that mom Rachel had mentioned and find out if there were others like her.

"Of course," Rachel said, delighted. "Do you want a free month of Peloton, too? I can send you a code for the app. I have, like, a million; they're practically giving them away."

She didn't, but she said yes. It was easier.

Anjali took in Rachel's watch, her bag, her outfit that cost more than what Anjali made in a week. She thought about the time she'd spent on her phone instead of in the steam room or the sauna. She thought about how a down year, for the Ranjanis, would bring in more money than she and David would see in their entire lifetimes. Even if she was promoted to editor in chief. Even if David's agency took off. Unless she did something drastic, nothing essential about their situation would ever change. They would strive until they died.

In a Suburban, heading back to the estate—Rachel had ordered the Uber and said the Suburban was "just what showed up"—Anjali gazed out the window, watching the undulation of vineyards and hills. Every row between the vines looked like another potential avenue, when you whipped past this fast. Another path less traveled. Another opportunity.

Her phone lit up with a message from Priya.

> She took three. Still won't get out of bed. Not for ice cream, pizza, Taylor on the projection screen, nothing. What should we do? Another hit?

11

Friday evening
Kismet Estate, Napa

If it's not a hell yes, it's a hell no," a pithy adage that assumed gray areas didn't exist. What if it started as a "hell no" and then *Eater* came out with an article about how you allegedly bullied a line cook? And then a busboy chimed in, and then the somm you had lifted up from literal nowhere, from a trailer park in Redondo Beach, followed suit? And then a hostess told the *Chronicle* that you propositioned her, which, *yeah*, she gave you her number and told you to call her if you ever wanted to "play" on a Monday night—what else were you supposed to do?

And then you got fired. From the restaurant with your goddamn name on it. And then you had to reconsider your previous policy of never cooking for private clients, never attempting to turn tricks in someone's home, because that's really what this amounted to, a chef of his caliber cooking in this glitchy kitchen. Prostitution. Slinging shawarma instead of sex.

Shawarma. Sammi Ali hadn't made shawarma since he was eighteen. He used to have a guy for that. And now he was attempting to spit-roast 187 layers of thinly sliced lamb in an electric oven that had set off the fire alarm, twice, despite the fact that it didn't produce a flame.

He was inspecting the contents of the spit for even a hint of char when he heard the slap of slippers against hardwood, and then a voice.

"Question—can you cook with these?"

He turned around to see a woman in a silk pajama set and fans for eyelashes holding a plastic bag of what looked, unmistakably, like dehydrated mushrooms.

"Seriously?" he asked.

"It's only lion's mane, super-low dose," the woman said. She dropped the bag onto the kitchen island and leaned her forearms against it, shortening the space between them. "Everyone's so tightly wound, I want to, like, massage their insides." She moved her fingers in a way that reminded him of rubbing compound butter under the skin of a chicken.

"What's in it for me?" he asked, crossing his arms. He had a suspicion, but he was not about to make the first move. He would not make that mistake, again. At least, not yet.

"Mmm . . ." She cast her gaze over the three round orbs illuminating the island. "Well, I could let you come with me to this party later on at the Madrona"—she started walking around the island to his territory, next to the range—"or I could give you a complimentary one-on-one Kundalini session, which usually goes for a grand"—now she was standing in front of him, close enough to touch—"or . . ."

She looked like the type of woman who thought that the opportunity to go down on her was a gift. Maybe it was. He'd be happy to find out.

"I could introduce you to Morgan Stanley's head of nourishment."

In his head, a record scratched. "For real?"

"I worked with her directly when their global headquarters had that salmonella outbreak. She owes me one."

Sammi shook his head, remembering. The bank had had to launch a salmonella research fund. "You can never trust bagged spinach." He did need a next act. This was only his third private gig, and already, he was over it. His last client had asked him to make feta out of cashews and bacon out of cauliflower. Cauliflower could do a lot of things, but it could not become bacon.

"So, yeah?" She cocked her head at the mushrooms.

He laughed to himself as he doused an empty pan with olive oil and tore open the bag. He hadn't cooked with drugs since making a batch of weed brownies a decade ago. The high had lasted for two days and made him want to jump out of his skin. Never again, he'd said. Look at me now, he thought. Another hell no turned into a hell yes.

She said her name was Victoria, and she gave him her phone number before gliding away to "get ready." He couldn't imagine what more she needed to do, but perhaps he ought to give up on trying to understand the machinations of anyone he encountered. Everyone was more than met the eye.

~

"We have to go," Anjali said. She was back at the estate, in the suite that she and David shared, pacing the length of the window that looked over Howell Mountain, retracing steps that she had taken so many times in the past half an hour, the logo on the undersides of her sneakers had imprinted itself into the fibers of the rug. She held her phone and manically moved her thumb about the screen. "There's a red-eye that leaves at midnight out of SFO, but fuck, it's sold out. Oh, wait, there's a 9:00 p.m. that goes through Chicago—"

"We'd have to leave now," David said. He sat on the edge of the bed, head in his hands, staring at the floor.

"Great, fine," Anjali said. She kept shrugging as if everything was normal, doable, a foregone conclusion. She kept thinking of that meme, the one of a dog in a house, flames going up all around him, and the speech bubble above the dog's head: "This is fine."

"I'll order a car. Or borrow the Sprinter—since we're all at the house tonight, no one needs it. I'll run it by Rachel, but I can't imagine why she'd say no." She saw no reason to engage with Raj. The previous night's kiss felt like a force majeure, a glitch in the system, something that she might've done when she was twenty-one but could in no way justify now. She was a middle-aged mother. She had to get real.

"The Sprinter is picking up the Guerrilla Somm, who I'm supposed to meet."

"Seriously, David?" She stopped pacing and stared at the crown of his head, which was capped by a curtain of hair. Used to be thicker, that curtain. God, they were all getting so old. "Our daughter is sick. She needs us."

"She's not sick, Anjali," he said, throwing his hands into his lap. "So she needed a few more hits, didn't the doctor say that could happen? That she might build up a tolerance?"

"Yes, but—"

"Could it be possible that you're just not having as good of a time as you thought you would and you're looking for an excuse to go?"

Well, yes. Yes, that could be possible. But who was David to decide how much of this was genuinely about Lucie and how much was her own paranoia and compulsion to solve a problem that was out of her hands?

Did she hold her daughter to a higher standard than her son? Of course. Lucie was older. Lucie was her first. Lucie was a reflection of her, but better, because, unlike Anjali, she had been born to parents who knew how to navigate the terrain of growing up in America. And yet Lucie had ended up with this problem, which Anjali could not help but see as a result of her apparently subpar performance as a mother. Her deficiencies. Had she not spent enough time with Lucie? Had she been wrong to go back to work? How could she have prevented her daughter's anxiety?

She resented that the burden of Lucie's diagnosis rested on her shoulders, not David's. Of course he didn't think it was a big deal. Of course business came first, even when "business" constituted a deal that was not yet done, with a content creator who would probably flake out like the last one.

"You don't want to leave because you have this meeting that *might* get you a client that *might* write a book that *might* make more than what some desperate publisher pays for it. You're choosing yourself over our family. Again."

David exhaled roughly and raked his hands through his hair. "You know who's interested. You know how much money they're offering, if he signs. You know what 15 percent of a million is—that's *real money* for our family. You asked me to get my agency off the ground. That's what this is."

Right. Random House. A million-dollar advance. She had filed away that part as pie-in-the-sky stuff, something she'd let herself fantasize about if the meeting actually materialized.

Anjali thought about how David had reacted at baggage claim, when she said she'd have to work on the Moran story. Why was it that when men had to work, they were providing, and when women had to work, they were backing out on some unwritten promise to always put their family first?

"Fine," she said. "You stay. Take the meeting. Take all the meetings you want. You can't stop me from going."

She was one click away from purchasing a ticket, but even as she said it, she knew she wouldn't pull the trigger. The fare: eight times what it ought to be, one way. To arrive at her sister's place on Shelter Island, after the layover and the three-hour Uber down the Long Island Expressway and the ferry, barely a day earlier than originally planned. Part of her, a large part, yearned to hug her daughter to her chest, to simply see her with her own eyes, without the filter of a screen, to make her okay by force of her presence. Part of her wanted to believe David.

Priya had sent a video of Lucie dancing to Bad Badger, a Puerto Rican pop star born with a streak of white through his otherwise-black pompadour, an Elvis for the age of Instagram. Lucie had her hands in the air, all mirth and giggles. She looked like a normal nine-year-old. She looked happy. Did it matter that she'd had to take a little more medication to get there? If she had a fever, Anjali would give her Tylenol until the fever broke. No question. These things happened. She was growing up. You had to adapt and trust the process. Eventually, she would be totally out of Anjali's hands. Motherhood was a never-ending challenge of giving up control, of letting go, inch by inch, even when the animal within you wanted to reel back all the line you'd released and go back to when your child needed you to breathe.

David got up and clasped his hands around her arms, forcing her to stop pacing.

"I know you're worried," he said. "I am too. We're going to see the psychiatrist on Monday. They confirmed the appointment, right?" Anjali nodded; she'd called the practice that morning after getting off the phone with Priya. "Why don't we just try to enjoy the rest of the weekend? Just a dinner tonight and a party tomorrow. Remember when we said we'd kill for a party?"

She bit her lip and nodded.

"And I could really use my gorgeous, blazingly intelligent wife by my side for this wooing of the Guerrilla Somm."

"Gorgeous?" She rolled her eyes. "David, I'm wearing Skechers."

"I wouldn't have you any other way."

~

Raj thought the holy trinity of a shower, smoke, and espresso martini would set him right, but they were no match for the pile-on of Peninsula, Raging Sparrow, and the nerves triggered by the impending arrival of the Guerrilla Somm. He felt unsteady, unsure. He wanted to excise this anxiety, this parasite, from his body. He pictured it eating away his insides, infecting everything in its wake.

Do what you do best, he told himself. Pick the right glassware. Pour the right wine. One foot in front of the other. Too late to turn around now.

He stood back from the bar built into the dining area of the estate's great room and assessed the contents of its shelves. People failed to realize the importance of glassware. Average people, plebes, the types who drank Barefoot chard out of squat, stemless glasses that had indentations for squat, fat thumbs, not realizing that they were warming the wine with their hands (if you could even call Barefoot chard "wine"). Rachel had taken to doing that with her chardonnay, back at the Trousdale home, despite his protestations. Maybe because of them. She seemed to relish getting a rise out of him. (Where had she even bought those glasses? Bed Bath & Beyond?)

The Guerrilla Somm would not stand for stemless, not that Raj had any in the estate, besides the plastic ones meant to be used in the pool and Jacuzzi, and even then, he disobeyed his own policy and took a dip with a Zalto. He was careful. It was fine. Only losers played by the rules.

Zalto's entire catalog of glassware—the slim Universal; the hexagonal Bordeaux; the apple-bottomed Pinot, round and diaphanous as a balloon—gleamed beneath the bar lights, freshly washed, dried, and polished by Jany. (Presumably, with extra care. She knew, from having worked her washcloth too vigorously around the bowl of a past Pinot glass, that if she broke one, it would come out of her paycheck.) He was set on glassware. What perplexed him was the matter of decanters: Would the Guerrilla Somm find the U-shaped Amadeo fanciful or fusty? Would he appreciate the simplicity of the beaker-inspired Josephine, or was it too basic? What about the Boa, the Eve, the Simone Crestani that had a glass octopus growing out of its side?

If there was one skill Raj had picked up in his ascendance to the upper echelons of the elite, it was knowing what went with what, and what you went certain places for: London for Gymkhana, Paris for George V, Bangkok for the Banyan Tree, New York for Carbone. Rules of the lower classes, he broke with abandon, but there was a certain way to move through the world when you had money to burn, or wanted, at least, to look like you did. You had to present yourself properly. You had to present your status to *other* people properly.

He knew what decanter he would use if he were the person primarily charged with enjoying its contents, but you could never tell with these influencers. In his last video, the Guerrilla Somm had decanted a bottle of Kistler into a Nalgene and proceeded to swig from it while hiking the three-mile loop at Shiloh Ranch and disseminating his latest "in/out" list. (In: "palate parching," which apparently intensified the flavors of the wine once you finally took a sip. Out: tasting menus. "Give me a burger and fries and let me get the fuck on with it.")

God, how he hated currying favor from people beneath him, coaxing goodwill out of them like pulp from tamarind (it used to disgust him, the way his mother squeezed that turd-like thing). What a world it would be if he was king. If his mere name commanded respect.

He pushed up the sleeves of his Loro Piana cardigan—summer weight, a silk-cashmere blend that matched his Gift of Kings trousers, the only kind of elastic-waist pant he deigned to wear outside the gym—and reached for the Josephine decanter. He felt soothed by its symmetry. He silently prayed that the Mega Purple had done its work.

When he purchased Kismet Cellars, he had inherited sixteen barrels of cabernet sauvignon, enough for four hundred cases, as well as several unlabeled magnums and jeroboams, the big daddy of wine, three liters in one bottle. "You'll need at least seven years before any of this is drinkable," the winemaker who worked for the previous owners had said, and at first, that had been fine with Raj. He had other streams of revenue. He had all the time in the world. He could renovate the tasting room, winery, and the estate; win people over with the vibe of Kismet Cellars—with its partnerships, its cuisine, its events—and with the wine that would be poured in place of Kismet while the house vintage took on age—Raging Sparrow, Peninsula, Realm, Favia—the culty-ist of wines, hard to get anywhere but available here. Kismet would make the bulk of its money on a Soho House–type membership, and sure, some members would buy an allocation of the 2019 cab before tasting anything Kismet produced, lured by the lore of the vines and the promise of getting in on the ground floor of Napa's next ultra-high-end winery. People bought future shares of wine all the time. Raj wasn't reinventing the wheel.

Construction costs exceeded his budget. Story of his life. He'd sold off commercial properties in New York and Los Angeles that he maybe should've held on to. The medical start-up was supposed to be his saving grace—"Easy money," Sid had said—but the message he received after the afternoon tasting at Raging Sparrow confirmed what the lawyers had foretold earlier in the week, when they called him during his drive back from Oxnard. There was a problem. It was, apparently, major. The lab would have to shut down and recalibrate before he'd see any money from that venture.

He had to move wine now. All of it, to keep the lights on not just at Kismet but also in his life, in general. There was no other way. He had to work with what he had. Throw in some oak extract, some powdered tannins, some Mega Purple to take the cab's notes of stewed stone fruit from six to nine, to cover up the hint of green bell pepper that he abhorred (if he could cast one food off the face of this earth, it would be green bell peppers). Mega Purple wasn't illegal. It was developed by a subsidiary of Constellation Brands, whose portfolio included Meiomi, Kim Crawford, and Woodbridge. (Would he drink those wines? No. Would he like Kismet's returns to look like theirs? Most definitely.)

Was it unethical? Was it unethical for Gatorade to sell a flavor called blue raspberry when blue raspberries didn't exist? Raj didn't think so. It was marketing. Marketing was fine, and ethics were for people in ivory towers, who cared not about the material world and wore their moral superiority like a coat of arms.

After depositing his friends at the estate, he'd gone to the winery, uncorked an unlabeled jeroboam, added the Mega Purple, and run the bottle through the corking and labeling machine he'd inherited along with the preexisting wine. He had no way of knowing how the wine tasted now, but it had to be better than before. It tasted like feet, before.

If the Guerrilla Somm gave it a thumbs-up, he'd have Ahmad spike the rest of the batch. Simple. A seal of approval from the winefluencer of the moment would move product far faster than a splashy grand opening party (stupid, stupid of him to let the bill for the party run up as high as it had, but it was too late to do anything about that). Best-case scenario, he wouldn't even have product to move by the following night. Kismet would be sold out.

He looked at the jeroboam now, staring back at him from the lowest tier of the bar. If the best-case scenario came to pass, bottling and labeling would take all night and well into the following day. It would be advisable to start as early as possible, to not miss his moment. Kismet's moment. Fuck it, right? The Mega Purple had to work. Constellation Brands did not fuck around. They owned Corona, for chrissakes. They had Snoop Dogg money. He would kill for Snoop Dogg money. He dashed off a text to Ahmad. Best to get the ball rolling, best to fire up the jets. There would be no better indicator of Kismet's exclusivity than having nothing to offer at all.

~

Rachel had returned from the spa and gone for a run. Five runs, to be exact: five warm-up runs that were five minutes each: three from Megan and two from Sabrina, her second-favorite instructor, oldies but goodies, the ones that she did whenever she wanted to increase the total amount of Peloton runs that she'd done so as to hit a milestone sooner. Milestones got shout-outs. Milestones got love. Her desire for love superseded her desire to lean into the effects of her spa treatment. She had relaxed. She was fine. Going for a run (or five) after going to the spa was normal, totally normal.

Afterward, she showered and laid out two outfit options for that night's dinner with Sammi Ali. One: a faded Cornell T-shirt, ripped "boyfriend" jeans (that had only ever belonged to her, not Raj; Raj did not tolerate ripped anything), and sherpa Birkenstocks. College, but make it chic. The other: a sleeveless Prada shift that nipped at the waist and looked like a Jackson Pollock painting, a riot of squiggles that petered out into a swatch of cream. A different sort of chic. One that required heels. It felt fussy, given that they'd been out all day, it was the height of summer, and she was in her own home with people who'd seen her at her worst—falling-down drunk, death's-door hungover, hair a week unwashed in the midst of midterms and all-nighters.

One was comfortable; the other would pinch and pull. One accepted her as she was; the other demanded she endure discomfort.

One was Hari, and the other was Raj. She might as well admit it, at least to herself.

Oh, Hari. Lovestruck, lead-with-his-heart Hari. What had he expected her to do in the vineyard, fall into his arms? And yet, she almost had, in that split second after he'd said, in so many words, that she didn't have to put up with a husband who belittled her. But Hari didn't understand how hard it was to extricate yourself from a marriage that, for all intents and purposes, was fine. Well, "fine" in the broadest definition of the word. Raj had not made eye contact with or addressed her since the gravel drive of Peninsula. (He had breezed past her in the primary suite, freshly showered and in a hurry to do something or, at the very least, get away from her.)

But the money, but the gifts. But the seven-hundred-something likes on her Money Honeys post from that morning, debuting the Serpenti, and the gushingly jealous comments:

> Girl where did you get that man?? Can you clone him for me!!!

The more hearts they gave her, the worse she felt. It was perverse.

She made a decision. She slipped out of her robe. As she dressed, she told herself that she was going with the most sensible option. That was all there was to it. No need to read more into it than that.

She almost crashed into Ahmad, turning the corner from the foyer into the great room.

"Ahmad, how are you? Thank you so much for coming up to help us with the opening," she said. She had barely seen him since he'd arrived in Napa; she figured that Raj was keeping him busy. In LA,

Ahmad was like a jack-of-all-trades—sous chef, driver, personal assistant, personal trainer, sometimes, when Raj needed a spotter at some ungodly hour.

She asked after his parents back in Pakistan and pressed him about the pickleball league he'd recently joined. Raj had accused her, in the past, of being too friendly with the staff, but Ahmad was practically family. She felt it her duty to treat him as such.

They were talking about a Cantonese noodle shop in Silver Lake that he'd recently discovered when he stopped midsentence, remembering something.

"Apologies," he said. "I realized I never inquired—how was Shenzhen?"

"Shenzhen?" Had she ever been to Shenzhen? Raj had recently gone on business, but she had elected to stay home—not that she had been invited—had planned to take a transcendental meditation workshop, had gotten distracted and rewatched all ten seasons of *Vanderpump Rules*. "You mean Seven Senses?"

Ahmad looked genuinely confused. "You were not at the Upper House? I had packed Sir's bags specifically for a romantic retreat"—she could sense the backpedaling before it began—"but maybe I am mistaken. Maybe I am thinking of Seven Senses, yes, where you went today with Miss Anjali, yes? For a couples treatment? How was the couples treatment?"

"Oh, you know, any excuse to scrub away my sins," she said, which didn't really make sense but lightened the mood enough that she was able to take her leave without Ahmad worrying that the axe was about to drop.

She was glad she'd chosen the way she had. All signs seemed to be pointing in one direction.

12

Friday evening
Kismet Estate, Napa

Silly, the things that winery owners did to try to win him over. He would've been fine riding his bike over to Kismet, ripping down Atlas Peak Road with the wind in his face. His favorite time to ride: dusk, dodging cars, his Creamsicle-colored baseball cap flipped backward, the better to enjoy the view. But Rajan Ranjani—that name, could you get more Bollywood villain?—had insisted on sending his Sprinter and a "welcome basket" that contained a variety of things that Jordan—the Guerrilla Somm's God-given name—had professed to liking and coveting. Sour Patch Kids. Edibles that tasted like Sour Patch Kids but also contained weed. The newest Nintendo Switch.

The harder they tried, the further they fell. Ranjani was a clear mark. The thing was, the thing that any winery owner worth their salt eventually realized, was that Jordan didn't *really* care about wine. He cared about trolling winos, about getting a rise out of the people who prized glorified grape juice wasting away in a bottle. The Guerrilla Somm's social media accounts had been active for all of six months. Bought followers bred genuine ones who asked questions in the comments but didn't care to investigate. Where did this kid come from?

How did he develop this supposedly remarkable palate? What kind of twenty-one-year-old had the wherewithal to buy a bottle of Pétrus?

The kind who graduated from the Rhode Island School of Design and had the backing of Oleg Altsen, the art gallerist most recently famous (or infamous) for staging an exhibition of one-star Amazon reviews printed out, crumpled, and assembled in the shape of the product to which they pertained. Jordan didn't even drink wine, if he could help it. He preferred kombucha.

The agent, though. Jordan felt a bit bad for him. He folded his lanky frame into the side of the Sprinter's first row and gazed out the wide, tinted window, at the trees rushing past in the dwindling light. The agent was an integral piece of the documentary that the gallery was funding; the agent proved that the Guerrilla Somm's influence went beyond Napa, beyond the wine community, that the literati—or at least, the suits who did the literati's deals—were as shallow and social media dazzled as everyone else. The doc would ruin the agent's credibility, maybe tank his career. No one would trust his judgment, once Jordan pulled the wool over his eyes. Unless Jordan took pity on the agent and had him broker a deal for a memoir, or something. Not that Jordan really wanted to write a memoir.

As the Sprinter turned into the estate's long, sloping drive, he clipped his phone into his handheld tripod and started recording. He leaned forward and pointed the camera at the driver.

"Yo, bro, how's the owner of this place? You like working for him?"

Adolfo shrugged and kept his eyes ahead. "Mr. Ranjani? He's fine. They're all fine."

"You can tell me, dude, you won't get fired. I'm not one of them, I'm . . . doing an art project." He felt pretty sure that Adolfo would not pass this message on to Raj; even if he did, no way would Raj believe him.

Adolfo chuckled to himself. "He's just like all the new ones. Looks at this valley and sees green. Hasn't been here long enough to see the other side of it. The drought, the fire. One thing to come to Napa, another to survive."

This wasn't the gossip that Jordan was hoping for, but no matter: video of the estate—a new detail unfolded at every turn; triple-height ceilings, an infinity pool as long as a football field—and his meeting with the agent were what he really came for. What a boon, that they invited him over for dinner. Way better than the agent's original suggestion of Saturday morning at Oxbow Market, a hive of hungover tourists suffering from sensory overload.

The Sprinter came to a stop. Jordan thanked Adolfo, shouldered his backpack, and stepped out. Raj greeted him beneath the pillars of the landing with a magnum of vintage Billecart-Salmon and a one-armed hug.

"Heard the '94 is your fave—may I pour you some?" Raj said. He held what Jordan recognized as a Zalto Universal glass in his other hand. "Know you love a Nalgene"—he forced a laugh as he poured—"but I couldn't get one on short notice, unfortunately. Must be a race or something going on this weekend; the running store downtown was sold out." More forced merriment as he held out the glass.

The guy was like putty, Jordan thought. Almost too easy to manipulate. Hate to see it. Well, *love* to see it, for his purposes, but it reflected poorly on men in general.

"You got any stemless?" Jordan asked. "Actually—a Solo cup would be money, if you have one."

~

"Mushroom cigars," Sammi said, setting a platter on the dining table, which was laden with other snacks: fava-bean hummus, a salad of heirloom radishes, *muhammara* made with walnuts and bell peppers grown in Napa's soil and warmed by its sun. "Phyllo wrapped, stuffed with a mixture of shiitake, portobello, and oyster, and sautéed in"—he smiled at all of them as if about to dispense some delicious secret—"a special ingredient that I don't usually get my hands on—"

"Sustainable avocado oil," Victoria interrupted. She clasped her hands together and beamed at the group. "Gift from the founder of

Lindoviento. He grows avocados on his farm at Costa Cara. Super-limited quantities—he only makes, like, five gallons of oil per year."

"Right," Sammi said, eyeing Victoria. "Well, don't get too full—these are just the apps."

Hari bit into a mushroom cigar. "Damn, these are good," he said.

"Can you grab me one?" David called from the bar. "I'm starving."

One mushroom cigar wouldn't change that. Hari grabbed four and ambled over to where David and Raj had sandwiched the Guerrilla Somm. "Thank you, my man," David said, gratefully accepting the pack.

The track lights were low; the Diptyques were lit; the latest playlist from Hotel Costes, the eminently au courant boutique hotel in Paris (it was on Hari's Paris spreadsheet), tinkled through the sound system. The whole thing felt like the very definition of sophistication, which made the fact that they were drinking out of Solo cups all the more irreverent. Hari had a hard time understanding how the Somm could've developed such opinions about wine and the best way to drink it, given his young age, but he figured it best to play nice. His app would need ambassadors, once it was ready. The Somm could even be a potential investor. Anyone who dropped five grand on a bottle of wine and then used it to tie-dye a sweatshirt had to be made of money. Oodles of it.

"You might be onto something with this plastic thing, Jordan," Hari said.

"For real, it makes your taste buds work harder," said Jordan. "It's like, training in Denver but for your palate." Jordan had set up his camera on the middle tier of the bar, which offered an uninterrupted view of the great room, and asked if it was all right if he filmed. "Gotta feed the beast," he said, referencing, presumably, his social media channels. "Bet," Raj had said, which, from what Hari gathered, was a thing that people of Jordan's generation said to mean yes. "If you could tag Kismet when you post," Raj added, "that would be huge."

Something about Raj's demeanor struck Hari, and it took him a minute to figure out why. Raj was nervous. Hari had never seen Raj nervous.

Now, Raj took a swig from his Solo cup. It looked like he was trying not to wince. He set it down and reached for the decanter on the bar top behind him. "Well, Jordan, if you'll indulge me in glass just this once," he said, tipping the decanter into what Hari now recognized as a Bordeaux Zalto, "I've got something really special I'd love for you to try. Our estate cab."

Hadn't Raj said that Kismet's first vintage wouldn't be drinkable for seven years? "Thought that wasn't ready yet," Hari said.

"You know, plans change," Raj said, shooting daggers at him with his eyes. "I went over to the barrel room earlier, pulled a sample, and decided we're ready. We'll be bottling all night in preparation for tomorrow, but I snuck this one off the line."

"Awesome," Hari said, retrieving his phone from the back pocket of his jeans. "Perfect use case for Wine Spy. Jordan, come here, I want to show you this app."

Raj muttered, "Dude, enough with that app."

"What?" said Hari. He couldn't figure out why Raj had such a problem with the app. Did he feel threatened? Was Raj that insecure? "Might as well try it out. Might not even work, since there's no label and no Kismet in the system to compare it to."

"So the app reads what's in the bottle?" Jordan asked.

"Yep, also tells you the breakdown of grapes and identifies any additives," Hari said. "It's meant to make the wine industry more transparent."

"Kind of like what you're doing, Jordan," David said. "You know, there could be some real synergy here," he added, giving Hari the theatric wink-nod that Hari did when he was trying to dazzle a client while talking out of his ass.

"Oh, absolutely," said Hari. "Tons of synergy. Lots of overlap in that Venn diagram."

"You two"—Raj glanced up at David and Hari as he decanted the estate cabernet into fresh stemware—"are full of shit." Raj distributed the glasses among the four of them. "Your graphics are old-school

Nintendo," Raj said to Hari, "and where did the data you're using even come from? What do you know about wine? Or apps?" He delivered this last part with a laugh while his eyes launched yet another set of daggers in Hari's direction. The dude was like Cutco when it came to eye knives.

"Vivino, *Vinous*, *Wine Spectator*—it crawls every legitimate source on the internet. I know enough that I hired the coders who built Vivino, and, if you haven't noticed, old-school Nintendo graphics are kind of *in* right now." Like a bubble of champagne, a realization fizzed to the top of Hari's mind: he had done something worthy, and Raj couldn't stand it. Jealousy. This was nothing more than good old-fashioned jealousy.

"That's cute, bro," Raj said, lifting his nose from his glass, "but you might want to stay in your lane."

The sound of his own blood rushing drowned out the pleasant playlist.

"What the fuck does that mean?"

"Yo, chill," Raj said, holding up a hand, "we've got company that I actually give a fuck about."

"No, please, go ahead," Jordan said. He was decanting his share of Kismet into his Solo cup.

"You're just jealous," Hari said, taking a step closer to Raj. "You can't stand to see anyone but you succeed."

"Jealous of you?" Raj took one of those teeth sips that made that pretentious sucking sound, the sound that you make when you want the people around you to know that you're a "serious" wine connoisseur. "What's there to be jealous of? Fake vintage T-shirts and all the flight attendants who know how small your dick is?" He turned to Jordan as if he'd just said none of this. "What do you think, my man?"

So Raj thought he could say whatever he wanted and Hari would just take it. Hari would let it slide. Mild-tempered, middle-class Hari, just happy to be part of the gang. Well, Raj was wrong.

"Dude, not gonna lie, this is pretty bad," Jordan was saying. "It's giving . . . chemicals. And feet. Like, athlete's foot."

Hari would remember what followed in fragments. The impact of his fist hitting Raj's cheek. The sound of glass breaking. The contents of the decanter pouring down the shelves of the bar and onto the floor. Raj grabbing the collar of his shirt—vintage Stone Temple Pilots, *genuine*, from 1991—so hard that he tore it. A flash of pain below his left shoulder, white-hot. Blood. David holding him back. Shrill voices, begging them to stop.

Then Rachel was pulling him away and David was saying that he felt sick and Victoria was saying that this wasn't how plant medicine was supposed to work and the Guerrilla Somm was taking it all in, wide-eyed. "Aren't you guys supposed to be friends?"

"It's complicated," Rachel said. Then, to Hari: "Come here, let's get you cleaned up." He saw, to his horror, that he was bleeding on her sherpa Birkenstocks.

"Seriously, Rachel?" Raj said, from the bar. He held the heel of his hand against his cheekbone.

Silence. Even Sammi stopped pretending to busy himself in the kitchen.

"You know what, I don't even care." Raj shrugged dramatically. "Tend to that pussy if it makes you feel worthy. Happy wife, happy fucking life, right?"

Rachel turned to Hari like Raj did not exist. "Let's get you set up at the guesthouse."

~

They had said nothing, climbing over the grassy knoll that led to the guesthouse. Stars twinkled above; the only other light was the beam of Ralph's flash, which fell on them for a moment before Rachel held up a hand, smiled, and nodded into the glare, as if to say that all was okay. As if. She should've sicced Ralph on Raj, although knowing Raj that would've only made him more destructive, more vindictive now, later, maybe both.

Rachel unlocked the door to the guesthouse with a skeleton key and flicked on a light. She saw Hari take it in. Unlike the main house, an ode to a certain kind of Tokyo-Stockholm-Malibu modernism, devoid of genuine warmth, striving to be cool, Rachel had wanted the guesthouse to feel cozy, clubby, like something out of the Scottish countryside. There was a tartan couch and a wood-burning fireplace. An antique bar cart and a forest-green armchair. A kitchenette and one of those old steamer trunks. A ladder staircase led up to a loft.

"Sorry, it's a little cramped in here," she said. "More of a studio than a house."

"It's adorable," Hari said.

"Thanks," Rachel said. "It's the only part of the property I got to design." Partly because Raj had assessed her Pasadena flea market finds and told her that none of it would have a place in any house he owned, and then they'd had a fight, and he'd stormed out and disappeared for two days, and then he'd "given" her the guesthouse, by way of apology, but Hari didn't need to know all that.

She saw Hari glance at the dishcloth he was holding to his shoulder and ran off to find a first aid kit. He eased himself onto the tartan couch.

"I'm so sorry about him," she said, when she returned with a kit and a compress. Neither of them was sure if the cut was an accident or if Raj had purposely come at him with a shard of the decanter, but they each had their theories, and in any case, it was deep enough that more pressure needed to be applied before it could be bandaged. "You shouldn't—this is beyond . . ."

Rachel couldn't find the words to explain Raj's behavior. Yes, Hari threw the first punch, but Raj had been verbally clocking him for days. For years, really, if you thought about it.

Hari gave her a stern look. "Do not," he said. "Do not apologize on his behalf." He lifted the compress from his shoulder to check on the bleeding, then pressed it back down. "Is he like this, normally? This . . . angry?"

Rachel sank her palms into the couch and looked up at the ceiling. She didn't want Hari to feel sorry for her. She didn't want to be the subject of pity. But she also didn't want to spray Febreze on a pile of shit. "Lately, yeah."

"Has he ever hit you?"

"No," she said, quietly.

Hari asked if she was being honest; she said she was. She remembered overhearing a phone call between her mother and her aunt, gossiping about a cousin who'd gotten divorced. "I mean, it's not like he was beating her," her mother had said. The message Rachel received: if the bruises weren't physical, the pain couldn't be that bad.

"Well, it's not fair," Hari said, "that you have to clean up his messes, go along with his whims. Why a winery? Do you even like wine?"

She laughed a little. "If I'm being honest—lately, I prefer tequila."

"Then, let's get us some of that. You got any in here?"

"In fact," she said, moseying over to the antique bar cart before picking up a bottle of Clase Azul and two shot glasses and placing them on the coffee table by the couch.

Hari lifted up the compress again. Rachel peered at the gash and reached into the first aid kit. As she pressed down the sides of the bandage, her hair brushed against his arm. They locked eyes.

"Should we, um, play a drinking game?" Rachel said, straightening up.

"Sure," Hari said. "Never have I ever?"

"Perfect. Never have I ever . . . had sex on a plane." She immediately blushed. In her mind: Why would you bring up sex—are you stupid?

Hari laughed as he poured a shot for himself. "I won't make you suffer through that story. Never have I ever . . . been to Morocco."

She drank.

"Gone scuba diving."

He drank.

"Smoked hookah."

They both drank.

"Wanted you more."

Her head spun. She almost couldn't believe he'd said those words; at the same time, she believed him entirely.

Her mind told her not to. Her rings told her not to. But her heart . . .

Damn her heart.

She dove toward him and the shot glasses clattered to the floor.

13

Friday night
Kismet Estate, Napa

The Diptyques had burned down to their wicks. The spread that Sammi had finished preparing, hurriedly—he seemed to want to get out of there as fast as possible after the fight, and who could blame him—languished under the dim tubes of the modular chandelier. The shawarma that Anjali had looked forward to upon opening the invitation, fine dining but fast-food adjacent, had gone cold, all but untouched. A pity, really. A total mess. The mother in her wanted to make it right and clean it up, make everyone apologize, sit down, and eat their dinner, but the mother in her was also tired. It wasn't her job to make it right. She had enough jobs.

She picked up a piece of the shawarma, dragged it through a bowl of tzatziki so that the cucumber-flecked yogurt hung off the meat in a fat glob, threatening to fall, and folded it into her mouth. It was good. Almost as good as Pita Pit.

Her phone buzzed. The freaking Money Honeys. They posted all day long, about everything under the sun: where to buy Stanley cups and how to deal with lackadaisical home contractors and whether you really *needed* to go to a US board–certified plastic surgeon for a mommy makeover or whether this way cheaper doctor in Tijuana would do.

(They never posted about Peloton). She voyeuristically dipped in and out of these threads, but spurred on by Rachel's comment at the spa, she had also searched for posts about anxiety.

She had not been prepared for the onslaught that came up. Dozens of mothers just like her, analyzing the pros and cons of putting their preteens on Puff, debating whether to do it, wondering if the Pez-colored vapes would become a permanent fixture, reporting erratic behavior in children who were on it, especially the girls. "My Sarah NEVER used to pick up after herself," one mother wrote, "but after six months on Puff, she can't stand the sight of clutter . . . I'm not complaining, but it's also kind of weird?" It was kind of weird, Anjali thought, recalling Lucie's streaks of domesticity, her sporadic fixation with folding her clean clothes into the most compact of squares when she normally let them languish in a laundry basket, as if order in her dresser drawers would breed order in the outside world. But then, she'd also become a biter. The vape quelled one anxiety but spawned new ones, like an anxiety Whac-a-Mole.

Was it worse to be a kid or an adult? To work yourself into a state over evils you can only imagine, or to have lived long enough to know that you couldn't even expect the worst, that you didn't have the mental capacity to conjure how wrong things could possibly go?

Anjali was dragging a second piece of shawarma through the bowl of tzatziki and reading about a mother extolling the virtues of a recently released cotton candy flavor—"acts faster and requires less hits than the others"—when she heard the approach of footsteps.

"How is it?" Raj's voice, flat, came from behind her. He was holding two fresh glasses and a new, intact decanter, one shaped like a fanciful letter U. Red wine sloshed along the curves as he approached. Beneath his left eye, she saw the swell of a burgeoning bruise.

She darkened her phone and shoved the shawarma in her mouth. "Now, this, *this* is worth paying for," she said as she chewed. "Whatever we had yesterday—you should ask for your money back. Report your credit card as stolen."

Raj let out a bitter laugh. "Not a bad idea, honestly."

She had been trying to avoid Raj, as much as you could avoid someone in their own home. She had especially tried to avoid being left alone with him, but this was how the cookie had crumbled. David had gone to bed, nauseated from the mushrooms Victoria had grudgingly admitted to spiking the meal with. "I was just trying to help," Victoria had said, shrugging on a denim trucker jacket, "but y'all might be beyond assistance, at this point." She'd Ubered up to Healdsburg for a party at the Madrona, a hipster-chic bed-and-breakfast where the couple she'd met at Bounty Hunter the previous night was staying. "They're poly, they know how to have a good time." "Bet," Raj had muttered, under his breath.

Sammi and Jordan left soon after Victoria. (Adolfo was scheduled to drive Jordan back to his Airbnb in downtown Napa; Sammi hitched a ride with them and was probably at some sticky-surfaced bar, relaying the events of the night to anyone who would listen.)

Rachel and Hari were, presumably, in the guesthouse on the other side of the pool. You could see, from the part of the great room that looked onto that side of the property, illuminated lights and drawn curtains.

She knew that Raj was in the wrong. She'd heard the crack about the flight attendants. Raj's temper had been legendary, in college. He punched holes through walls and picked fights while waiting in line for a late-night slice. For someone born with a silver spoon in his mouth, he had an enormous chip on his shoulder.

In the years after they graduated, a reason found him: the Ranjani family jet crashed in Costa Rica with his parents and sister aboard. No survivors. Twenty-nine-year-old Raj found himself tasked with running a $500 million commercial real estate firm while grieving the only family he'd ever had.

Besides them. Besides their crew from Cornell. He and Rachel had been on a break; they got back together. Hari and Dev took him to Joshua Tree. He wrote long emails to Anjali, stream-of-consciousness ruminations on time and God and the material world about which she did not tell David. She tried to send thoughtful replies, to hold space.

Maybe that was why she remained downstairs now, even though her rational mind told her that she should excuse herself and go to her room. She felt bad for him. Maybe that, and the fact that she was still hungry. And though it had gone cold, the shawarma was better than what they served at the cart on Fifty-Third Street, and that place was damn good.

And—curse every journalistic fiber of her being for this—curiosity. The stuff that killed the cat. Why was Raj throwing such an over-the-top party if, as he'd claimed the previous night, times were tough? What had he meant when he'd said that all he was really doing was gambling? Had he squandered his father's empire?

Most importantly, what did he want from Anjali that his wife—his pretty, perfect, doe-eyed wife—seemingly could not provide? After all these years, as much as she hated to admit it, it came down to that. There would be a special place in hell for her.

"You should ice that thing," she said now, referring to the bloom beneath his eye, now tinged with purple.

"I'll be fine," he said, slumping into a dining chair and placing the decanter and glasses on the table. "Have some? Opened it earlier to go with the shawarma. Would be a pity to pour ten grand down the drain."

Her brain said no; her body dropped into the seat next to him. "What is it?"

"Raging Sparrow, 2005."

"The year we graduated," Anjali said, dipping her nose into the glass.

"What do you smell?" Raj asked, watching her.

"Mmm." Anjali inhaled again. "Honestly? I smell wine. It smells like wine. Is that stupid to say? I don't get it when people say 'bubble gum' and 'bark' and 'forest floor after the rain,' like they're certified experts on forest floors."

Raj laughed. "Nothing you say is stupid."

Anjali took a sip. It was good wine. She'd give it that. Better than the stuff she'd had on the flight. Was it worth $10,000? Absolutely not. After a certain point, it was all supply and demand and the product of marketing. Raj ought to know that. He'd had good business sense at one time, had built what his father had bequeathed to him into an even bigger company. But there were so many things that could cloud your judgment. Like how she'd put Lucie on Puff. The promise of a solution, a salvation, could make you do strange things.

"So . . . how bad is this situation that you're in?" she ventured.

Raj hung his head. "After today? Horrendous. That somm already uploaded his review." He gave his phone to Anjali; she didn't even need to press Play to know that it was bad. The static image was Jordan holding a bag of ice to his cheek, doing a spit take into a Solo cup. There were words in cartoon bubbles. "Feet." "Battery acid." "Like a hook to your cheek."

"Some people pay good money to get hit in the face," she said, giving the phone back to Raj. Dominatrix logic.

"You always see the bright side," he said, giving her a sad smile. "Unfortunately, we'd have to move as much product as Evian does in a year for me to afford to keep the lights on here, and that's just not going to happen."

"When you say 'keep the lights on' . . . ," Anjali began.

"I mean literally. There's only one way out."

~

The reason that he hadn't chosen Anjali from the start was that she wanted to work. Even then, at eighteen, he could tell—this girl was career oriented. Cared about her grades and going to class, knew words like "kismet," expected other people to know them, too.

His mother, God rest her soul, had not been like that. Catered to his father. Cooked a hot meal three times a day, and not just Indian, either—they'd have Taco Tuesday, Meat Loaf Monday, a "vegetable loaf" for her because she had never eaten meat but loved her omnivorous husband and the American-born children they had bred to the degree that she would form ground lamb into fat patties with her bare hands. The only thing he'd ever seen her read was the *Bhagavad Gita*, a battered edition with gilt-edged pages and a ribbon bookmark sewn into the binding.

Plus, sure, for a guy who grew up on *Saved by the Bell* and *Hey Dude*, Rachel was Kelly Kapowski and the blonde that married Ben Stiller rolled into one. It was impossible not to shoot his shot, to at least *try*. The fact that she liked him back? He felt like the luckiest guy on the planet, for a while.

And if Anjali faulted him for falling in love with her best friend? Well, Anjali had never been a red-blooded American man. Anjali did not know the power of the pussy. Anjali and Raj had hardly done anything besides kiss. Maybe a little over-the-shirt action. Sure, they'd slept next to each other, but he couldn't help where and when he passed out, not back then. She could not expect him to abstain from going after her best friend because they'd shared a few moments, a couple forgettable bottles of wine.

Then they'd graduated. Then he'd realized that, as much as he loved Rachel and saw her as his future wife, he still wanted to have fun, fuck off, be a twentysomething guy with means and the ability to bed women with a credit card paid by the family accountant and a soupçon of charm. Especially once his father let him work from the New York office. There were women practically crawling out of the walls; there was an embarrassment of action to be had, whether that was in a condo in Trump Tower that he owned—*owned*, outright, at a time when most of his peers rented, which was usually enough to get them out of their pants, never mind that the condo was actually in his father's name; they didn't need to know that—or in a hotel room, or the bathroom of a restaurant, or his office, or the fitting room of J.Crew, Bergdorf's, or his favorite, Bloomingdale's (both because of the lighting and the frozen yogurt at Forty Carrots). You did it enough, you stopped worrying about getting caught.

He suspected that his father had engaged in some of the same behavior while married (he refused to wear a ring, said he was so careless that he'd lose it; Raj believed there were other reasons). But his father had grown up in India, in a different time. No one Raj knew got married at twenty-one. He certainly didn't want to. He did, however, want to keep Rachel around, and if that meant feigning support for her "career" in luxury hotel branding, that was fine. She would quit eventually. She lacked Anjali's drive. He had pegged Rachel as a woman who wanted to be taken care of, who would turn on the shine when necessary and fade into the background when not. A trophy wife with an Ivy League degree. It would be best for her to be occupied while he engaged in his extracurriculars. Her business trips—if you could call going to the Maldives a "business" trip—were his opportunities. (Along with, of course, *his* business trips.)

He was never with the same woman twice until Shea. The Nobu hostess who hooked him, who reeled him in like a big, flopping fish. Who got him to pay for a two-year program at the Miami School of Arts and a condo in Biscayne. Who exuded the aura that Rachel had, twenty years prior, the innocence, the wide-eyed enthusiasm for who he was and what he could provide. Whom he'd most recently reunited with at the Upper House, in Hong Kong, where he'd flown her, first class, on Cathay Pacific. She'd come with him to the factory in Shenzhen, but he'd had the driver take her to a space station of a mall while he took the meeting. She didn't need to see him in beast mode, arguing with them about laws and liabilities; you'd think these people would be *happy*, the business he and Sid were bringing to the factory, making the factory the sole manufacturers of the first FDA-approved vape for children, but they had "ethical concerns." Ethics! In a place like that!

Yeah, yeah, he was an asshole, a cheater, all the bad adjectives; throw them at him, fine. Nothing he didn't know. But now he was ready to reform. Put it all in the past. Freshman-year Raj wanted one thing. Forty-year-old Raj wanted another.

"Want to take a walk?" he asked Anjali.

They exited through the sliding glass door and walked toward Kismet Cellars, perched beyond the pool, guesthouse, and vineyard. Spotlights around the base of the winery and tasting room lit up their stone facades, illuminating workers who were setting out high-top tables for the following night. A soft breeze rustled the leaves of the valley oaks. Crickets chirped.

They were past the guesthouse when he spoke again. He'd taken note of the glow in the windows. All the more justification for the plan that had congealed in his mind, redolent as Camembert.

"What if you could blow it all up and start all over?"

Anjali sighed. "I'm too tired for hypotheticals," she said, though her tone suggested she wasn't. He suspected that part of her reveled in the transgressiveness of talking with him like this. A chronic rule abider breaking yet another one.

"Come on. If you could run it back to when we first met. Say Rachel never came into the picture."

Though he could only see her face in profile, he could tell she hadn't expected that.

"I don't know," she said. She sounded less pointed, more open to possibility. "It's impossible to know how things would've turned out. If we would've even ended up together."

"Say we did," he said. "Say we could. Say we could stay up till sunrise. See it for real, this time."

She said nothing. Time to bring out the big guns.

"You know you're the reason for the name of this place," he added.

"You're talking out of your ass," she said, but her voice betrayed her. She was picturing it, he could tell. The kismet-sunrise one-two punch. He was too good. There ought to be an award for this. "In case you've forgotten, I have a husband—"

"*That* loser?" Raj said.

"What about Rachel?"

Raj cocked his head back toward the guesthouse.

"Look, you guys are having issues. It's fine. It's normal. Go to counseling. Save more than you spend. Sell the jet—"

"We don't even *have* a jet anymore, Ji." His tone suggested that he saw the humor in this, but truly, he did not. "We charter through a third party that rents out jets *other* people own when they don't need them. It's like the Southwest of flying private."

"Well, boo-fucking-hoo—you are still the 1 percent, Raj, you . . . talk about things like running for public office like you're debating where to go to dinner. Your dinners cost more than most people's mortgages—more than my mortgage!"

He laughed. "We could change that."

Now she looked at him. "You cannot be serious."

"Look, Anjali, I'm not a bad guy." He turned to her and took her hand, which stayed limp but stayed in his palm, nevertheless. "You know that. You know me better than anyone, better than I even know myself. I screwed up a long time ago, and I don't want to spend the rest of my life knowing that I could have made things right but didn't even try."

He saw it, then, in her eyes: hope. A longing for a second chance, a proverbial hitting of the Reset button, a blowing of the Nintendo cartridge. That told him everything he needed to know. She would be the perfect partner. All he had to do now was execute.

14

Saturday afternoon
Kismet Estate, Napa

She had tried to leave. Had exited the conversation with Raj swiftly after he had picked up her hand, said she needed to go, ignored his entreaties to "calm down," "hear me out," "You wanna smoke? Let's smoke." She had run right upstairs to find David passed out on top of the bed, not even beneath the sheets. In the dark, she'd searched for flights. Didn't matter how expensive. None leaving for hours. What about a room at the Montage in Healdsburg? Sold out. What about Ubering away and waiting it out at SFO?

But then she'd looked over at David's sleeping form, and she wondered if what she was really running from was the fact that maybe she *did* want to start over. She wouldn't trade her children for the world, but her marriage?

She wondered what doctors would pronounce her marriage, were it to arrive in an emergency room. DOA? Did it have a pulse?

She looked back at David. She confirmed that he was out cold. She picked up his phone and typed in his code, went to his messages, and scrolled through name after name that she did not know, so many photos of girls—*girls*—ten years older than Lucie, maybe. Legal but barely. All wanting to break into the industry—as agents, as authors, as assistants to assistants. He had "liked" porny headshots. He had taken video calls. He had written things like "Your energy is really compelling!!!!! [winking emoji]" and "Your go get 'em attitude is exactly what I like to see!!!!! [smiley face with hearts for eyes emoji]."

Did any of this count as cheating? Debatable. Was it legal? Also a gray area. But it was, beyond a shadow of a doubt, creepy, lecherous behavior with which she did not want to be associated. Why had David even made a show of going to therapy if he was just going to keep engaging in conversations like this? Was this not the exact type of "questionable communication" that got him fired from Archetype? Did he really think this qualified as work, as a genuine attempt to get his agency off the ground? Who were these women? Did they really believe that this guy—her husband—was the key to their success?

It was sickening.

She knew that breaking into his phone was a violation of privacy and trust, that even if they were still in counseling she would get flogged for bringing any of this up. It all felt so pointless. Even if he never met any of these women in real life, even if he kept it "professional" (though if this sort of communication was "professional," that was disturbing), even if he never engaged in anything explicitly sexual with them, they would always be out there, in the ether, on his phone and/or on his mind. The pool of potentials only got larger every day, as her own viability waned.

She wanted what they had had in common to be enough. Their courtship had been the stuff of an English major's sun-dappled, nap-on-the-quad dreams. Book launches and *Paris Review* parties and coffee-stained newspapers folded every which way. Friends who were authors and journalists on the rise, everyone, themselves included, brimming with potential. How had they become this cliché of a middle-aged marriage?

Of course Raj had picked up on her dissatisfaction. *Everyone* picked up on her dissatisfaction—from the flight attendant on the way to San Francisco to the Upsilon chef to Victoria. She might as well be walking around with a big, blinking sign around her neck. Probably, she was already wearing it. Probably, people like Victoria called it her aura. A vomit-green glow of discontent that followed her everywhere she went. It made her vulnerable. It made her a target. Raj could see that, clear as day.

He had to bring up that time on the quad. He had to bring up that time fourteen of them—everyone at the estate, plus other assorted friends from college and entry-level drudgery—had gone to Mexico, a sort of spring break for young professionals yearning for the glory days of the very recent past. The time they stayed at a beachfront villa with its own oversized infinity pool (Raj clearly had a type) and a private nightclub in the basement. Before she'd met David, the one time she'd done Molly, when she and Raj had been the last two standing and sat in lounge chairs on the deck, playing backgammon on a set that they'd found in the sprawling indoor-outdoor living room, even though neither of them knew the rules, talking about everything and nothing, watching the Pacific lap against the shore, waiting to watch the sunrise.

The joke was that they were so in the moment, they didn't realize they were facing west until it was too late. For a while afterward, every so often, one of them would text the other, Hey, wanna stay up till sunrise? The recipient would try to think of the most outlandish response possible.

Can't, I'm shorting Kazakhstan.

Would love to, but I'm Diddy's +1 at the Met Gala.

Sorry, meeting Richard Branson about some spaceship.

(You never really knew when Raj was joking and when he wasn't.)

Then Raj's father had summoned him back to LA, Raj had asked Rachel to come with him, and the texts stopped.

Could she be blamed for feeling something for a man who still remembered her as eighteen and full of potential? Full of life? Not like she was going to do anything about it. Did she really have the guts to get divorced? She couldn't be like Victoria, flitting about the world and chronicling her freedom for social media. Co-parenting would be a nightmare. No one ever posted cute, quippy videos about that.

But all his apocalypse talk was weird. His compulsion to blow things up. Why would someone who just bought a multimillion-dollar winery want to start over? Not only had he bought it—he was throwing this blowout celebration presumably to put the place on the map.

She plugged David's phone back into the charger—nothing more to see there—and slumped on the settee by the foot of the bed. It was that time of night when it feels like the sun might never rise again. A notification lit up her phone. Yet another new post in Money Honeys, in one of the many threads about Puff.

Have we seen this?

There was a link to a *Napa Valley Register* story about a recent act of vandalism.

At a winery.

At the estate on the grounds of a winery.

Anjali's heart dropped as she connected the glass-strewn foyer in the picture on her screen with the scene to which she had arrived: the triple-height ceilings, the Craftsman construction, the broken window, the brick.

There was a video from the local ABC News affiliate. She clicked on it.

"Law enforcement sources confirmed that a note was wrapped around the brick thrown through the window of Kismet Estate on Thursday: 'We know who you are, and we're coming for you.' It was signed, 'Napa Valley moms against Puff.' Puff, a new vape-based treatment for anxiety, came on the market . . ."

The sight of those words, Kismet and Puff, so close together, all but stopped her heart. *No. How?* How could Raj possibly be connected to the vape—the drug, really, she might as well call it what it was—that was wreaking havoc in the lives of so many parents and children?

She started thinking. The pieces started coming together.

The man who had come up to their table at Upsilon, who said he just *had* to thank Raj for all the business Raj had brought to his practice.

Raj's aside, in the library, about helping children. His complaints about regulatory oversight. Rachel's mention of him starting a medical business with Sid.

Sid. That fucking creep. Sid would totally make a vape for children.

She caught sight of her face in a mirror on the wall next to her, illuminated by her phone in the inky dark before dawn. She had a vague sense that the earth was quaking, that the tectonic plates of her world had shifted, were continuing to shift.

Why had she been invited? Why was she really here? Had Raj roped her into some kind of sick game? Or had he always been this person, a megalomaniac in a Mercedes-Benz, a wolf in very fine sheep's clothing?

They say that people don't change—the true nature of a person, the elemental thing that makes them tick. She thought back to his first offense. The first time he did her wrong. Leading her on, first semester of freshman year, only to drop her when something prettier and shinier appeared at his feet. What had she been doing, all these years, holding a candle for a cad who had shown his true colors more than twenty years before? Did she think that she could change him? Was she really that naive?

As signs of light streaked across the sky, she called Priya, made sure that her sister knew, in no uncertain terms, that Lucie should never put one of those vapes in her mouth again. "Stomp on it, break it, tell her it's toxic but that she'll be fine." Anjali realized she actually had no idea if Lucie would be fine, and she had to mute her phone for a moment and find a throw pillow into which she released a scream that brought tears to her eyes. "I'll be there as soon as I can," she said.

She was jumping to conclusions, but with her daughter's well-being at stake, how could she not? Journalists had a tendency to do this, to think they knew the story when it was still unfolding all around them. She needed help. She knew one reporter who had the chops. She called Moran, who was in the midst of his morning laps and had a smartwatch that worked underwater.

"You realize you're asking me to spend a Saturday trawling Facebook and cold-calling what few of these Real Housewives deign to respond?"

"*I'm* trawling Facebook. I'm vetting them. I'm giving you their phone numbers to follow up. *You're* trawling FDA records and whatever else privately held pharmaceutical companies need to file to do what they do. *You're* figuring out how this thing got on the market."

"On a Saturday in July?" he went on. "A Saturday in July when I'm at the house in Bridgehampton, if I hadn't already mentioned?" (He had.)

"Consider your word count for the year met," Anjali said. Moran had to file one hundred thousand words per year to receive his staff reporter salary, a four-leaf clover of a rarity in the crumbling world of print media. He had, thus far, filed six thousand.

"Grazie mille," he said. "Back to you soonest."

Several hours and French presses later, she found herself doing her makeup in the vanity of her suite. She hardly knew how to do anything besides apply eyeliner and mascara. Rachel was the expert. Maybe Rachel could fix it.

Her dress: Rent the Runway. Badgley Mischka. A cap-sleeved, black lace sheath with grosgrain ribbon at the waist. It necessitated Spanx. Frankly, everything she owned necessitated Spanx; she just couldn't be bothered to wear them, normally.

There was a knock at the door. She paused, eyeliner in hand, but made no move. David was in the shower. She didn't want to face Raj like this, game face unapplied.

"Anj?" Rachel's voice came through the walnut wood. "You wanted to borrow some heels, right?"

She had almost forgotten. She padded over, her slippers slapping against the soles of her bare feet.

Rachel was in a silk dressing robe the color of rose petals. Yes, roses came in many colors, but something about this shade, a pink the shade of Rachel's cheeks when she blushed, struck Anjali as category defining. She held two pairs of shoes by their ankle straps, hot-pink Valentino stilettos, the ones that she had been wearing the day they all arrived, and black, pointy-toed Gucci kitten heels. Anjali immediately gravitated toward the kitten heel.

"So that would be the obvious choice, right," Rachel said, striding into the suite, "but I feel like the hot pink adds something special, you know? It's unexpected. It's risqué. It's *hot*."

"Let's see how hot I am when I fall down and break my neck."

Rachel laughed. "You'll be fine. Try them both on, see what works."

Rachel seemed remarkably at ease given the events of the previous night. Saturday's agenda had been a choose your own adventure, on account of Raj and Rachel getting ready for the party. Anjali knew, from the group text, that Hari had gone for a long run outdoors, Rachel had gone for a long run indoors, Victoria had returned from the Madrona around noon, in dire need of a nap, and David had gone to Oxbow Market to have a proper meeting with the Guerrilla Somm, whom he was still desperate to sign, and who still wanted to meet with him, despite the disaster that was the previous night. (Well, she knew that last part because David had told her where he was going, while she was curled into the settee of their suite, laptop balanced on thighs, thirteen tabs open, toggling between Moran's reporting and her own conversations with the Money Honey moms.) "Great," she had said, without looking up. Her own marital mess could be dealt with after all of this. That was small potatoes. Fingerling. She had an eight-pound yam to fry.

What weirded her out the most: not only was the combination of drugs in Puff addictive, it also made women who consumed enough of it more servile. More apt to take on chores, to do the things that the people who had power over them—their parents, their teachers—requested. You can imagine how the long-term effects could play out. *Stepford Wives* but with vapes. It disgusted her. She wondered if Raj had endeavored to create a drug that would breed an army of Rachels, without her edges. Without the quirks that made her interesting, that made her human.

Rachel had hired professionals to help her get ready. Her hair betrayed the effects of one of those "undone" yet clearly done blowouts, flaxen locks bent and mussed here and there. Her cheekbones shimmered; her lashes extended far enough that you could be forgiven for thinking they wanted to shake your hand. Any puffiness around her eyes would have been patched, patted, and powdered into oblivion, giving you no indication as to how Rachel really felt, beneath her radiant veneer.

"How are you doing?" Anjali asked. "Given, well, everything."

Rachel blinked as if not understanding, then stretched her mouth into a wide smile. "Oh, I'm *great*, I mean, frazzled. Jany's helper got food poisoning, so I had to handle the caterers and the top of the balloon arch popped and our event planner's asking me if *I* know where to get gold balloons on short notice, as if that's *my* job . . ."

Anjali couldn't help but find joy in her brilliant friend. How resilient she was, how up to the task. Of course she'd find time and space inside her brain to worry about things like a balloon arch. It wouldn't be a party without a balloon arch. And they needed to have a party.

~

You can't, you can't, you can't. The refrain had pounded through her head in time with the balls of her feet on the treadmill. She had thought that Megan's sixty-minute live run that morning—Megan's "60 Saturdays" brought out droves of regulars—would give her a break from spiraling, but it was another encore that had been advertised as live, and Rachel had heard all these aphorisms before. "Be true to you." "Make 'em mad." "Don't settle when you can soar."

Her mind kept replaying the night in the guesthouse. His hunger for her, as palpable as Raj's indifference. She thought she would feel more guilty. She thought she wouldn't be able to go through with it. But she did, *they* did, and then they had ascended the ladder to the loft, lain in bed and talked for hours about things major and meaningless, where they once imagined they would be by forty and what success even meant anymore and the relative miracle of microwaveable popcorn, of which there was plenty in the kitchenette downstairs. It wasn't the content of the conversations that stuck with her. It was the fact that Hari cared. That he wanted to talk. That he wanted to talk to *her*.

She remembered when she and Raj had talked like that. Back in college. Now, their conversations revolved around the admin of life—travel schedules and meetings and commitments, all undercut with an anxiety that despite all that they had, it wasn't enough.

She didn't know when she had fallen asleep. Sometime after dawn she opened her eyes, shot straight up in bed, and hit her head on the slanted ceiling. She had forgotten she was in the loft.

Hari implored her to stay, ice it, sit for a minute, "Let's figure this out." She kept saying, "I can't." There was the laundry list of things she had to oversee for the party. There was hair, makeup. There was *her husband*, the fact that she did not return to *their bed* last night, her mounting fear that, if Raj knew where she'd been, he would kill them both. Certainly, he would kill her. He'd said exactly that, in jest, at various points in their relationship, as if to prove his devotion, but really, as a method of intimidation: "If you ever cheat on me, I will kill you."

Never mind that Raj had cheated on her and remained alive and well. The reason they'd broken up all those years ago: she found an earring in the passenger seat of his Porsche, a cheap, plastic monstrosity that she would never wear, and when confronted, he had said, "If you're going to treat me like a felon for messing up one time, just *once* in all the time we've been together, then you need to think about whether you really want to be with me, because I'm not perfect. No man is."

Of course, she, as his wife, was expected to be perfect. Poised. Happy to swallow indignity, hypocrisy, whatever, really. "You don't know how good you have it." "You would never survive, in the real world."

What did Raj even know about the real world? Who was he to decree what she could handle?

She had run into Anjali in the kitchen, sneaking back into the main house through the sliding doors of the living room. Anjali was making a French press. The sun had not yet revealed itself in full; the birds were chattering to each other at a clip so fervent, you'd think they were on *Fox & Friends*. Anjali asked Rachel if she wanted some coffee. Rachel did. Anjali said she had something—actually, a lot of things—to share with her. They went outside to a part of the property where they were certain no one would overhear or happen upon them unannounced. They talked. They cried. They got into it. Rachel realized that Anjali understood her, understood her central predicament, understood so much more than Rachel had given her credit for.

"I'm not telling you what you should do," Anjali had said. "That's beyond the bounds of our friendship, of any friendship. But I thought you should know what I know, because it's not right that you've been kept in the dark."

Maybe it was a blessing that Megan's Saturday morning run had been a repeat, because the more she thought about it, the more the refrain in her head evolved into something new. Could you? Would you? You . . . *can*?

"Why live small when you can live large?" Megan had asked. "Why compromise your true self when the best version of you is out there, waiting for you to step in?"

Rachel had to get Victoria on board, but that wouldn't be hard. She knew what Victoria wanted, in her heart of hearts, and she had the means to make it happen. Victoria was a hustler. Rachel knew what she was capable of. Sugar babying wasn't it. She and Anjali would be giving her a job worthy of her talents, a chance to step up. And if she said no, and if, by then, she knew too much . . . Rachel dismissed the thought. Victoria would never. Victoria was her sister. Sisters stuck together.

15

Saturday evening
Kismet Cellars, Napa

Tuxedos and cater waiters. The sharp tick of stilettos on sandstone. Buoyant exultations: "Oh, don't you look marvelous," "Well, *you* clean up nice." The unfiltered tangerine light of the sun hovering over the horizon, a grid of leaves and grass. A twelve-foot-tall ice sculpture of Bacchus, sweat dripping from his pecs. A string quartet.

Anjali cast her eyes over the assemblage. About 150 people, easily, many of whom had interpreted the maddeningly vague dress code, "Napa nice," in wild and wonderful ways. By Bacchus: a silver-haired woman in a floor-length gown of burgundy sequins. At the bar: a squat man in a three-piece suit the color of rosé. Beneath an olive tree: a lithe beauty in a silk pajama set printed with cartoonish goblets of wine. She wore Ugg slides like the MILF without borders Anjali had seen on the flight. Seen and judged. Look at her now, two days later, beyond reproach.

"Jordan said he would be here," David murmured to Anjali, scanning the crowd. "He said he'd be ready to sign. Not like he has to sign them in front of me—I sent him the forms hours ago."

"I'm going to get a drink," Anjali said. She could not stomach another word about the Guerrilla Somm. She had looked up the Somm earlier in an over-caffeinated Google blitz. Done a deep dive, figured out who had registered his website, not an elementary internet search but also not that hard. Certainly nothing that David couldn't have done.

Through the magazine she had access to a database that could tell you who owned a website, and she'd shared the login information with David when he'd wanted to get in touch with that tattoo artist who seemed, way back when, like the next Glennon Doyle. (The same tattoo artist who eventually absconded to Bali to "rebalance.") That was how she discovered that Oleg Altsen Galleries Inc. owned GuerrillaSomm.com. She had called the phone number listed on the results page. She had asked the unsuspecting receptionist when the Guerrilla Somm show would be up. It was a lark; she was surprised that anyone even picked up the phone. She half expected the receptionist to hang up, but instead she was connected to a supervisor who interrogated her and then backed off upon hearing who Anjali was and the magazine for which she worked, and finally confided, off the record, that the documentary was scheduled for early the following year. In time for Sundance. The supervisor didn't say the last part, Anjali just figured. It would be *Exit through the Gift Shop* meets *Borat.*

She was sick of it. Sick of having to clean up David's messes, this overgrown third child that she didn't sign up for. Her real problem with him wasn't the DMs, creepy as they were. It was his carelessness, his laziness, his belief that things would just work out because he willed it. His compulsion to fly by the seat of his pants and gamble their livelihood because he was too unformed and confrontation-averse to make tough decisions. The way he allowed his dick to lead when he ought to know better. He had grown up with the inherent privilege of a straight white man, but not all straight white men were stupid. This was something else. She could not be married to someone who could get played, over and over again, and not even realize it.

"Quite a scene, huh?" Hari sidled up to her at the bar. He wore a trim-fitted gray suit and a white button-down. "You think I should've worn a tie?" He rubbed his collarbone, as if adjusting a phantom swath of silk.

"I mean, yes," Anjali said. "Poor Raj is going to have to work to strangle you."

They exchanged a look and laughed. Anjali reached over to retrieve her Setting Sun, a spritz made with an aperitif that tasted just like Aperol but was from Venice and not on the menu of every brunch spot in Midtown East. It was garnished with a half-moon of orange. Hari motioned to the bartender for one more.

"How's your arm?" she asked as they ambled away from the bar.

"Hurts, but not enough to miss this."

"Cost of doing business," she said. This was the problem with being friends with sociopaths.

She panned her gaze over the crowd. She had not seen Raj or Rachel, which made her wonder if they were together, and why wouldn't they be? It would be helpful to keep up appearances. Natural, really. He didn't mean what he had said the previous night. She was too old to go down this road again, to be pitted against her best friend. He's just manipulating you, she told herself. He only wants you for his own gain. Be smart. Don't fall for it. Stick to your guns.

As if she had conjured them, Raj and Rachel materialized on the landing at the top of the stairs, by the entrance to the tasting room. A handful of observers clapped; they waved genially as they made their way down. Raj was wearing a classic tuxedo, sans cummerbund, exuding the vibe of a sixties movie star; Rachel was in a black minidress studded with big red question marks, enamel earring-type things that bounced against her body as she moved. It was not the "casual" gown of emerald-green chiffon, tiered and cut through with gold thread, that she had described to Anjali the day before, nor was it the made-to-order Gucci sheath of chain mail that had been another option. This was from

Moschino's latest collection, a wild card, a dress with character, edge, interest. A dress that, Anjali now recalled Rachel saying, Raj hated.

Rachel's new watch snaked up her wrist; thick, diamond-encrusted loops hung from her earlobes. Her lips were slathered with a cherry-red glaze glossy enough that they could show you your reflection. She looked like one of the women from Robert Palmer's "Addicted to Love" video, a bombshell of a backup dancer who might step on your heart with her stiletto.

"What does it say about us that these are our friends?" Anjali said to Hari, watching their descent. "That this is the company we keep?"

"That we're down with your borderline personality disorder as long as you pick up the check? That we'll suffer through hell to feel like we're twenty-one again?"

That pretty much sums it up, Anjali thought, and was about to say so when Victoria bounded over and cupped her hand over Anjali's shoulder. Victoria was wearing a pale-pink gown with spaghetti straps and a bustier. It made her look like she belonged in the front row of some far-flung fashion week and made Anjali wish that she had never breastfed.

"Did you see who's here?" Victoria's eyes sparkled. She turned and pointed. "I know they teased a special performance on the invite, but I thought they meant, like, a Journey cover band, not Bad-freaking-*Badger*."

Anjali could not believe her eyes. There, coming up the gravel drive, was the Spotify sensation in the flesh, his black-and-white hair combed into a swoop that added six inches to his height. He was trailed by a trio of bodyguards. He was wearing a tracksuit. A Fendi tracksuit, but still, a tracksuit.

He made her think of Lucie. Lucie dancing with her hands in the air. Lucie who ought to be able to dance with her hands in the air without the help of a drug whose dangers were not vetted, were not tested in the way they should have been, which owed its success to the bank account and bribery tactics of a man she could not believe she had kissed. Evil came in so many shapes and sizes, sometimes when you least expected it.

Rachel and Raj had reached the sandstone patio. Raj made a beeline for Bad Badger while Rachel broke off, air-kissing the guests that flocked toward her. Anjali watched as Raj gave him a bro-hug, clapped him on the back, proclaimed, "My man." They talked a few minutes before Raj clapped Bad Badger's back again and drifted over to a man in a baby-blue sports jacket. Anjali felt the vague sense of knowing who this person was, despite the fact that they had never met. Where had she seen him? Why did he ring a bell?

As Raj and the man shook hands, she figured it out. This was the man who'd come up to their table at Upsilon, who said he had to thank Raj for saving his practice.

He had to be a child psychiatrist. It made perfect sense—Raj made the medicine (not covered by insurance, "revolutionary" as it was), this guy prescribed it, they got richer, kids got sicker. He would be an excellent source for Moran. But the rage that burbled within her as she wrapped her head around this felt debilitating. She could not talk to him. Not now. She dug her fingernails into the palm of the hand that wasn't wrapped around the stem of a drink and told herself to get it together.

Rachel's eyes drifted. Anjali followed their gaze. They watched as Hari approached with a flute of Champagne. Rachel fell silent. Her air of irreverence evaporated, a champagne bubble's last gasp.

"Questioning things?" Hari asked Rachel, taking in her dress. His eyes twinkled.

"I mean," she began, and Anjali could practically see the calculus going on in her friend's head as she figured out how honest she could afford to be.

"Who's *not* questioning things, right?" Not honest at all, apparently. "What with global warming, political revolutions, sustainability . . . Jeremy Scott was really onto something with this collection. I wish he was still at Moschino, another topic for another time. I almost forgot, I should check on the spring rolls, make sure there's an option besides Sonoma duck. Excuse me for a sec?"

She dashed off, across the sandstone patio, Hari's eyes trailing in her wake.

"She's just stressed," Anjali said.

"Clearly," Hari said. Anjali heard the longing in his voice.

"Give her time. She's dealing with a lot right now."

He shrugged defeatedly. "I've given it two decades."

"I'd advise you to hold out a little bit longer," she said. "Besides, what else are you going to do? Fall for someone else's wife?"

Hari chuckled. "Touché." He clinked his glass against Anjali's.

~

Anjali had two Dungeness crab spring rolls. She had a talk with V. Nothing in depth—it wouldn't have been wise—but enough to confirm that they were on the same team. She got another drink. She saw Raj in a heated conversation with a wiry guy beneath the balloon arch.

"I know what we talked about," Raj was saying, his voice terse, "but all we've got now are sixteen barrels, and we need some Raging Sparrow–level returns."

"You need a reputation if you want margins like that," the guy said. "And right now . . ." He shook his head. "The best party in the world can't make people drink your wine if it tastes like shit."

Raj gritted his teeth. He locked eyes with Anjali and motioned for her to come over.

"Anjali, meet Jason, owner of Cline's, which used to be my favorite wine bar. Now? I'd love to burn the place to the ground. Or call the health inspector. Either way!"

"Uh, hi . . . ," Anjali began.

"Classy," Jason said as he walked off.

Anjali turned to Raj. "Is it . . . normal to sell off your entire supply before you open? Is that, like, a thing in Napa?"

"This fucking Guerrilla Somm," Raj said, ignoring her question, "he really fucked me." Anjali wanted to point out that perhaps Raj had fucked himself, given that he'd initially said the wine would need seven years to mature, but thought better of it.

"Well, plan B," he said. He moved his head closer to hers and lowered his voice. "Are you in?" She knew he was referring to what they had talked about the night before. Starting over, just the two of them.

"Oh, I'm in."

He smiled slyly and clinked his glass against hers. "Find me during the special performance. Actually—don't worry about it. I'll find you."

~

Rachel was trying to remember the name of the woman who had boxed her into a conversation about demarcating a portion of the estate's land for bluebird nesting when she saw her. It had to be her. The French braids. No one else had French braids like that, cut through with a streak of magenta on the left and violet on the right.

It was dizzying, a wish coming true. It felt like fairy-tale nonsense, like something that couldn't happen in real life.

"I'm sorry, I have to . . ." She didn't finish her sentence, just left the bird woman hanging midsentence and drifted over to Megan, in a daze.

"You *came*," Rachel said, sliding up to her at the bar.

Megan whooped and wrapped her arms around Rachel, and Rachel thought she might burst, the improbability of someone she knew from a screen rendering themselves in 3D and smelling like orange blossom and beaming at her like they were best friends. "I couldn't miss the opportunity to party with RachRunner83," Megan said, when she drew back. "You know you're my number one student? How have you taken seven thousand of my runs, seriously?"

Rachel blushed. "I guess I have a lot of time on my hands." And an apparent need for constant validation, she thought, but didn't say. She knew exactly how many classes of Megan's she'd taken. But hearing

Megan say it made it sound somehow pathetic. As if she'd measured out her life in five-minute warm-ups.

"Girl, if I had a lot of time on my hands and *all of this*"—Megan gestured around the property, lavender in the fading light—"I would not be looking at my face on a treadmill screen, I'm just saying."

"You don't know how captivating you are," Rachel said, with a little laugh.

"Mmm, maybe." Megan took a sip of Champagne. "Or maybe you need to do a li'l audit," Megan said, invoking that aphorism of hers that Rachel had thought of the previous morning, that she knew by heart.

They made small talk for a few minutes, though Rachel had a hard time paying attention. She felt like she was staring into the sun.

People were assembling above them, near the entrance to the tasting room. The event staff was telling guests to make their way upstairs for dinner. Rachel realized she ought to find Raj. But she also felt an urgency to avail herself of any wisdom that Megan could offer, to squeeze her like a tube that promised to make you brighter and better.

Megan was talking about her cold-plunge practice when Rachel interrupted, turning down her mouth in apology. "Can I ask you something personal?"

Megan nodded and arranged her face in a way that said, I'm listening, but I am not your therapist.

"When you quit your job as a lawyer and decided to teach running . . . how did you know that it would work out?"

"Oh, honey. I didn't. I had no idea."

"So you just . . . left it all on the line?" Rachel spied one of the event planner's coordinators beckoning her from the top of the stairs, gave her a forced smile and "one moment" signal.

"Took a leap of faith," Megan said. "It was the only way for me. I mean, look—the life I had wasn't bad by any stretch of the imagination. I was living large, I had my expense account, closet full of power suits, doorman condo in TriBeCa, but if you're dying on the inside? It's not worth it. Get out. Save yourself. Do *you*."

Rachel nodded, though her doubts remained. "And the consequences . . ."

"Everything has consequences," Megan said, brushing away this show of insecurity like an errant fly.

"One thing I've learned," she added, putting her hand on Rachel's arm, "anything can be prison." She twisted the side of her mouth and cast a gaze around the compound, as if understanding Rachel's particular predicament. "Even if other people think it's paradise."

16

Saturday evening
Kismet Cellars, Napa

There were place cards and speeches, bread baskets and enough glassware to make it look like someone had robbed whatever fancy European factory Raj got all his Zaltos from. Uniformed servers danced around the tables, topping up glasses and replacing dropped forks. There were prompts to toast to this, to that, "to a new era for Napa," "an exciting addition to the Atlas Peak AVA." Anjali took it in with a wan smile that belied the pitter-pattering of her heart. She thought about a visualization that Victoria had shared with her earlier in the day: picture a swan, floating atop a pond. "All we see is beauty and grace," V said, "but below the surface of the water? Those feet are getting after it."

Next to her, David sighed. "I don't know what happened to the Somm." He still hadn't shown up. "Really thought I had that one in the bag."

She couldn't take it anymore. "David," she hissed, "that guy is not a somm. He's a performance artist. He's playing you. How did you not know that? How could you fail to research a client before going all in on them *again*?"

"He's . . . what? Are you sure?" It was like he was a child and she'd just told him there was no Santa Claus.

Anjali scooted out her chair so that she could face him. "I can't do this anymore, David," she said. "I can't. You take chances that put our livelihood at risk. You make bad calls. You . . . I don't know, you have some growing up to do, maybe, but I can't hold your hand while you do that, not after what you've done."

David looked crestfallen. "Are you saying . . . Is this because of the messages? I thought we were over the messages."

How could she explain to him that you can't get over someone's fundamental lack of good decision-making? That their history was not enough to keep them going into the future? She loved the idea of him, she loved the person that he had been, but the person that he was now, she could not stand behind.

It was also impossible to be "over" the messages when they kept accruing.

"I need some time, David. I need to think. Think about what's best for us, for me, for the kids."

"But . . . now? You're deciding this *now*?"

The way he phrased it told her everything she needed to know. *You're* deciding this. Not *we*. David had, long ago, let Anjali take the wheel in matters that pertained to them and their family, but the problem with always being in the driver's seat is that eventually the driver gets tired.

"I can't sit here and lie to your face," Anjali said, dropping her hands in her lap. She felt both exasperated and relieved. It was off her chest. She had said the horrible thing. Time hadn't stopped; the world continued to spin. She felt a compassion toward David that she had not in a long time. "I'm sorry to spring this on you now," she said, reaching out to squeeze his shoulder. "I know it must come as a shock, but you can't tell me that you're happy, can you?"

A white-haired woman at the table next to theirs turned around and shushed Anjali. A previous version of Anjali would have felt chastened;

this one made a face. God forbid the crumbling of her marriage interrupt this woman's ability to hear the spiel of whatever self-important wino currently had the mic. Rich people were the worst. The sensation in her bladder: also the worst.

David looked shell-shocked. She apologized again. She said she'd be right back. She got up and strode to the tasting room's vast oak doors.

A left and then a right took her to the women's room, which was preceded by a plush ladies' lounge with no occupants besides herself. She went into a stall, reemerged, and took a good look at herself in the mirror above the sinks as she washed her hands. The reality of what she'd said to David had started to sink in. She felt hot, flustered. She nearly knocked over a basket of neatly rolled hand towels. She found a beige settee in the lounge and sat down.

She told herself that she was capable, she could do this, she could be the hero, she could hold her family together and start anew, and forty was the new twenty, and she *deserved* more, really, didn't she? And if she didn't make a proactive decision to choose herself, then no one would and—

The door to the lounge swung open, revealing Rachel.

"Thank God," Rachel said, plopping down on the settee next to Anjali. "I need a minute." She leaned the back of her head against the stone wall of the lounge and extracted, from her cleavage, a perfectly rolled joint. She opened her clutch purse, a glimmering cube of gold, and took out a lighter.

"You couldn't fit the joint in your purse?" Anjali asked.

"It would make the whole thing smell like weed," Rachel said. "Can't have vintage Chanel smelling like weed." She held the joint out to Anjali. "You want some?"

Anjali shrugged. Why not. It couldn't hurt. It might still her beating heart. She used to think she needed to be sober as a priest to excel, to get straight As in the game of life, but she was increasingly realizing that a little buzz of some kind, something to soften the edges—whether of her, or the world around her—helped. She was better when she was slightly fucked up. Only slightly. She realized that this was a slippery slope.

"Is it terrible that all I can think of is Hari?" Rachel asked.

Anjali thought of all the looks that she had seen them exchange over the years, a sense of yearning and compassion that flowed as easily as water out of a faucet (a good faucet, a Kohler or something fancy, in a place with good water pressure).

"You really love him, don't you?" Anjali said.

Rachel nodded.

~

Prior to her conversations with Anjali and Rachel, Victoria had been hoping to be seated next to someone interesting, someone new. The party at the Madrona had been a bust. The couple who had invited her were San Francisco old money, but they only wanted to watch, not engage, which meant they were not long-term candidates for her portfolio. You didn't get the real money for performing; you got it for the immersive exhibitions, the ones that let the audience participate.

The people who did want to participate were crunchier than a Nature Valley bar. Not at all her vibe.

But now she had a new mission, one she embraced with gusto. She had picked up her place card, which Rachel had asked the party planner to redo at the last minute, never mind that the "cards" were actually cubes of acetate into which names and table numbers had to be hand-carved by a man from Geyserville who was getting paid by the unit, and sashayed over to her new and rightful place next to Sid Gupta, who had also gone to school with them but had always been on the fringe of their circle.

Sid was weird. Like, once-found-a-frog-in-a-gorge-and-tried-to-melt-it-into-DMT weird. Victoria had engaged in a lot of questionable behavior, but something about Sid had always made her uncomfortable. It was the way he looked at people, like specimens, potential pawns for his experiments. You spent enough time with him, you came to suspect that he'd one day be visited by that guy from *Dateline*.

"Sexy lady," Sid said as she sat down. He didn't even bother to avert his eyes from her satin bustier (to be fair, if you're wearing a satin bustier, you have to know that it's going to be hard for certain types of people to maintain eye contact). "How you been?" He inhaled two *gougères*, continuing to keep his eyes on her chest.

Victoria sighed. "Oh, you know, navigating the hellscape that is being newly single at forty," she said.

"Dev done fucked up," Sid said. "What happened to him? Moved to the Bay and grew a vag?"

"Something like that," Victoria said. She slid her quilted YSL purse off her shoulder—well, it was Rachel's quilted YSL purse, but Victoria got the impression that Rachel wasn't going to treat it like a DVD only recently released to Blockbuster. From the purse, she removed her phone, tapped until she reached the voice notes app, and set it, face down, on the table. "People rarely realize that you're recording them," Anjali had said, "even when you tell them that you're recording. They forget. They're generally self-absorbed and thrilled for someone to actually listen to whatever they're saying. No one listens anymore."

Victoria tucked the heel of her hand under her chin and leaned her elbow on the table, which pressed her bicep against her breasts and had the effect of a push-up bra. "How about you?" she asked. "How has life been treating the great Siddarth Gupta?"

"Dude," Sid began. Life had treated him so swimmingly that he had recently bought a compound in Turks and Caicos. "Twelve bedrooms," he said. "Private lagoon. Private dock. Water so clear you can see your toenails. Best part?" He leaned into her and she wasn't sure what was worse: the thought of Sid's toenails, the vague smell of BO, or the crumb of cheese puff that had stuck to his lower lip. "No taxes."

She oohed admiringly, both to keep up the act and because the prospect of no taxes appealed to her as well. "Daddy reeled in a big one."

Sid leaned back and turned his palms up to the air, as if it was all dumb luck. "The lab I founded hit it out of the park," he said. He wiped his mouth. "With our first drug, anyway. Inhalable Ozempic. Weight loss in a vape. Our second one's struggling, but we'll be all right. I keep telling Raj that—it's gonna be *fine*. He's all freaked out. I tried to get the lawyers to hold off on calling him, but lawyers gonna lawyer. Also told him to put his money in the Caymans, but he didn't listen."

"Oh, you're working with Raj? No way." She reached for a gougère and took a nibble. People who peddled in entrapment generally didn't eat while doing it. (Well, that was her working logic. She didn't have a lot of entrapment experience.)

"He gave us the money to make this anti-anxiety vape for kids." Another appreciative ooh from Victoria, set to the tone of "you're so smart." "I said he'd make it back tenfold in a year, huge returns." He pronounced "huge" like Donald Trump. "But fucking regulators, man . . . ," he trailed off.

"What's the problem?"

"Crazy side effects. More addictive than we said it was." He shrugged. "I mean, any parent who puts their kid on a vape has got to know that they're gonna get hooked. It's just science." He readjusted himself in his seat and leaned back into her. "But here's the thing—if you're an adult and you do it for fun, it's a fucking ride. Like sex on Ambien." He tossed another leer in her direction, and she giggled with her hand over her mouth, as if she had never had sex on Ambien.

"You have one on you?"

He pulled out a slim green vape. "Hit it before the special performance and tell me it's not the best high you've ever had."

~

Victoria grabbed her phone, her purse (how easily she came to call it her own), and the vape and marched to the women's restroom, promising Sid that she'd be right back.

She pushed in the door and found Rachel passing a joint to Anjali.

"Sharing is caring," V said.

Anjali handed over the joint. "How'd you do?"

Joint in mouth, V retrieved her phone from the YSL, tapped it until it showed the audio recording.

Anjali nodded approvingly. "You'd make a great reporter. Has anyone ever told you that?"

"I like it better on my side," V said. "More power. More money."

"Spin doctors," Anjali said. "That's what we call people like you, at *Highbrow*."

"Then you're about to watch me do the equivalent of a triple axel," V said, passing the joint to Rachel.

"Are we really doing this?" Rachel asked her friends. The joint had not had the intended effect of tamping down her nerves. "Have we . . . taken all the precautions?"

"Did you give Ralph the heads-up?" Anjali asked. Rachel nodded.

"Did you send me the recording?" Anjali asked. Victoria nodded.

"Then we're good to go," Anjali said. "What could go wrong?"

~

From outside the ladies' lounge, bass began to thump. The special performance. It would be taking place in the grand salon across from the tasting room, a large, open space with high ceilings, Rothko paintings (or very good imitations of them), and Rococo-style couches along the perimeter. (The Rothko paintings and Rococo-style couches, according to Kismet's interior decorator, made the space a "salon" rather than just a "room.")

"I should get out there," Anjali said. She handed the last of the joint to Victoria, who took a toke and pulverized the lit end with her heel.

"We're gonna be okay, right?" Rachel said, looking at Anjali, and then Victoria, and back again. They nodded in assent, even though they had no idea. "Group hug?"

They embraced. "Buckle up, buttercups," said Victoria. "It's going to be a hell of a ride."

The three of them separated as they exited the women's room and marched into the grand salon, three missiles peeling off from their launch point. Rachel went to find Megan. Victoria went to find a human being more physically and spiritually appealing than Sid. Anjali went to find her man. Well, not *her* man. Her assignment. Her target. Raj.

Inside the salon, purple and pink beams of light bounced off the gilded picture frames and antique furniture. Twin strobes revolved around the room, and Bad Badger was in the middle of his latest hit: "Mi Corazón," whose chorus involved him crooning about his thumping heart to the tune of B2K's "Bump, Bump, Bump." To Anjali, it seemed too *untz* for a high-end Napa winery, but what did she know, she was just a mom on a mission to make sure that no child or parent endured the hell that she had been through, to make sure that Raj and Sid—but mainly Raj—never made money like this again. Never made money at all, ideally. If it all went the way she hoped that it would, they would be going to prison for life.

They were as bad as the Sacklers, maybe worse. They fucked with children. They paid off FDA advisers, flew them and their families out to Turks and Caicos for a week in exchange for making sure Puff passed. That's what Anjali surmised, anyway, from Moran's reporting and Sid's Instagram posts. Idiot didn't even have the good sense to make his profile private.

She felt a hand on her shoulder, a hand that she would recognize anywhere.

"Ready?" Raj asked.

"As I'll ever be," Anjali said, smiling at him. His face took on an unholy glow under the purple lights.

"Follow me," he said.

17

Saturday night
Kismet Cellars, Napa

She followed him out of the grand salon, down the stairs, back out to the sandstone patio. “Cold?” he asked, noticing the way she rubbed her arms as the cool night air embraced them.

“Just a little,” she said, “but I’ll be fine.”

He stopped, shrugged off his tuxedo jacket, and draped it over her shoulders. “Please,” he said, “I insist.”

Across from the tasting room was the winery and cellar that, owing to California’s penchant for earthquakes, was not actually underground. It was the kid sister of the main building, a structure made in the same vein but with fewer frills. A path wide enough to fit a truck (or a patrol car) ran between the two buildings, and Anjali observed Ralph and his flashlight, pacing and vaping, close enough to hear commotion in either building, close enough to know if there was a situation in which he ought to intervene. Raj raised his hand up in greeting; Ralph gestured in kind.

(It hadn’t been hard to get Ralph on their team. Raj had underpaid him and refused to honor his requests for lunch and a relief guy. “I’m on two hours of sleep and seven Red Bulls,” he’d told Anjali. “What that guy is doing is inhumane.” She understood his need to vape. She also understood that her indictment of him the other night had everything to do with her ambivalence about putting Lucie on Puff, and given that she'd proceeded to smoke the equivalent of two packs of cigarettes with all of that hookah, she was in no position to judge.)

In front of the winery, Raj reached into the pocket of his trousers and pulled out a skeleton key. He turned it in the lock of the heavy metal door and pushed it in.

Lights came on, motion activated, most likely. Raj held the door open. It was a door that would slam and preclude noise from entering or escaping. A door that would prevent Ralph from knowing if and when anything in which he ought to intervene started within the winery.

"Is it just me, or is it hot in here?" Anjali said, shrugging off Raj's jacket and handing it back to him.

Raj gave her a look. "It's temperature controlled to fifty-five. It's colder in here than it is outside."

"Huh," Anjali said. "Feels like a sauna to me." She wiped her brow as if there were sweat on it. "Do you mind if we prop open the door, get a little air in here?"

Raj gave her another look and said sure. She fetched a loose stone from next to the door that was probably used for that exact purpose and moved it into position. It left the door of the winery open, just a crack, which was enough for someone to hear her voice at an elevated volume, which was all she really cared about.

They walked a few paces and Raj flicked a switch, illuminating the rest of the room. Steel slats ran down the center of the floor, and on either side were eight stainless steel tanks the size of elephants, four against each wall. Piping ran between them and down the corners of the walls, into the earth and parts unknown. It felt damp and smelled like clay. Clay doused in wine.

Beyond the tanks were barrels laid on their side, silicone stoppers pounded into their centers; beyond that, cedar racks stacked with bottles, and finally, a little cave of a cellar guarded by a barred door. Raj homed in on it.

"This calls for something really special," he said, unlocking the barred door, ducking inside, and motioning for Anjali to wait. He emerged with a cobweb-swathed bottle of Peninsula, a wine opener, and two glasses, which he placed on a small table to the side of the stainless steel tanks as the corkscrew went to work. He opened the wine, set the bottle on the table, ducked back into the cellar, and came out with a crystal decanter the size of a house.

"From Zalto's Supremacy collection," he said, following Anjali's gaze. "A beast to maneuver, but it's worth it, for what it does to the wine."

Anjali murmured in a way that said, Okay, dude, whatever you say. Couldn't you just pour wine from a bottle into a glass? Why the fuss with all these decanters?

"I'd like to propose a toast," he said, after he'd sloshed a bit of wine into the glasses.

"What to?"

"Us, Ji," Raj said, handing her a glass. "Us who should've been together from the start."

Anjali laughed softly, as if what he had said pleased her. Before this weekend, maybe it would have. Anjali had thought Rachel had gotten the life that was destined for her. Finery aside, she now knew how bad Rachel had had it. Rachel was a prisoner to what Raj thought a wife should be. A woman dipped in amber at her physical prime and encased for all eternity. Not allowed to evolve, to spread her proverbial wings.

Anjali touched her glass to Raj's and took a sip. "So, where will home base be? Here? New York? LA?"

"Oh, I'm burning this place to the ground," Raj said.

This was news. As if on cue, the motion-activated lights by the door clicked off.

"Why . . . would you do that?"

"Babe"—he laughed mockingly—"the wine is shit. Have you not noticed that you've been drinking Duckhorn all night?"

"Uh . . ." That cavalier use of "babe," another attempt to cut her down. She could tell the difference between Duckhorn and Diet Coke, but between one brand of wine and another brand of wine?

"I thought I could salvage it," Raj said, "but the Guerrilla Somm fucked it all up."

She'd had no idea they hadn't been drinking Kismet. She thought that the Guerrilla Somm's review had been unduly harsh (well, perhaps duly, given the chaos that accompanied the uncorking of the jeroboam the previous night), but she also hadn't had any wine from the jeroboam. Kismet cabernet was what the servers appeared to have poured, whenever someone asked for red.

"So you put Duckhorn in Kismet bottles," she said, trying to understand, "and you're going to scrap all of this . . ."

"Tonight," he said. "Ahmad's going to have a little accident. Spill a little gas, wine, whatever, light a little match."

He was literally going to burn the place to the ground.

"You get the insurance money," she said.

"*We* get the insurance money."

"What if the insurance company doesn't believe you? What if Ahmad gets charged with arson?"

Raj shrugged. "I told him I'd send ten grand to his family in Pakistan. He didn't even counter, the poor motherfucker. What's a guy like that going to do, anyway? Shoot up a grocery store in some jihad?"

Had she ever felt rage like this? No. This was another animal. There were so many degrees of wrong, and Raj bled into several of them. But there was something about this, his willingness to let an innocent man take the fall, that cut Anjali to her core. Maybe it was that on top of everything else. Some people could be rehabilitated, redeemed, but it struck her, in that moment, that Raj was never going to change. Prison would change nothing. He'd scheme and scam his way through that, too. He'd emerge like Jordan Belfort or the Fyre Festival founder or any number of career criminals whose autobiographies and adaptations were gorged upon by people who claimed to be disgusted by the malfeasance of these self-righteous men but couldn't have been *that* turned off, the way they binged and bided their time until another miniseries dropped, until they could feast again. Sometimes, the bad guys won. Often, we let them win. We said that we wanted peace and justice and safety, but we also salivated at the first scent of scandal, of something not quite right.

"The payout will take a minute"—he was still talking, and he reached out to wrap his arm around her waist—"but we can camp out in Turks until that hits. We'll take Lucie and . . . what's his name—Brian?"

The utterance of her daughter's name brought her back to the original plan: to play the voice note, to get on her supposed soapbox, to reveal that her daughter was on this drug that Raj had helped create that was not at all safe, to threaten to publish the voice note on the internet—Reddit would be perfect—if he didn't shut down the medical start-up immediately, if he didn't do something substantial to make amends for the damage he had done. If he threatened her? She'd shout the code word that would prompt Ralph to bust into the winery with backup. No matter what, he would go down.

She could still do that. She could. But what would Raj do, after that? Best-case scenario? Lay low for a while until he could scam again, but make it bigger, badder, "better" in his book but worse beyond measure?

"It's Ryan," she said, pressing her body into his. "But . . . I don't really want to talk about my kids right now."

"Oh?" His face was millimeters from hers.

She had Rachel to think about. But maybe Rachel would be better off this way. Maybe Rachel would finally be free.

"I think we should seal this deal," she said.

"And how would we do that?"

Summon all your courage, she thought.

A gentle shove got him on the floor. The back of his head was on the ground, not far from the table with the glasses, the wine, the heavy-as-a-house decanter.

"Damn, Ji," he said as she tore off his Tom Ford tie and he hoisted up her dress. "I booked a suite at Stanly Ranch, but sure, let's start making up for lost time now."

He reached the bottom of her Spanx and looked up at her, confused. "What are these?"

Of course he had never encountered a woman who wore Spanx. In the world of men like Raj, women were toys that you manipulated to serve your own ends, and when one toy got old, or damaged, or simply required a different level of care than it had before, you discarded it and got a new one.

Raj had had enough toys. Raj had had enough chances. The world, in all its earthly glory and goodness, had had enough of Raj.

"Don't worry about those," she said, nestling her face in the crook of his neck. She remembered this neck. She had once—dare she admit it—loved this neck.

She grabbed the back of his head, as if to bring his lips closer to hers.

She slammed it down.

18

Saturday night
Kismet Cellars, Napa

Sickening, the sound that his head had made, the amount of blood; she had no idea, no idea that the human body even contained this much blood. She had not planned on this, had never gotten into horror movies, true crime; she couldn't even stomach *The Sopranos* even though she knew it was absolutely something she ought to have watched.

"Oh, fuck," she repeated. Several times. A sob escaped from her mouth, involuntarily. She realized her cheeks were wet. She didn't know when she started crying.

She got up. She stepped away from the body (the *body*). In her panic, she thought that mopping up the mess—was it all blood? Was it wine and blood? Did it matter?—would help. But of course there wasn't a mop, or paper towels, or anything remotely practical in the winery. She looked down at her blood-covered hands and dress. Like Lady Macbeth. There would be no getting out these spots. Rent the Runway would have to chalk this up as a loss. They'd probably never let her rent again.

She might be certifiable, she realized, crouching down over the body again (the *body*, the word alone made her skin crawl, the way one could transition from a person to skin and blood and bones, just like that). What kind of person commits a murder and then thinks about renting a dress? The kind of person who goes to jail. The kind of person who becomes a headline for years and years and then gets the Netflix treatment, which they probably don't even know about because they're dead or rotting in jail, and do they get to watch Netflix in jail, probably not, fuck-fuck-fuck, she could not go to jail, she wasn't cool or tough or any of the things you needed to be to survive there, and her *children*, what would become of her children, what with their dirty DMing father and a mother in jail and—

The motion-sensor lights by the door clicked on. The sound of heels against cool cement. She jerked up like a rabbit out of a hat. Someone else was here? Someone had *been* here? To hear and see *that*?

From behind a stainless steel tank, Rachel revealed herself. She held a phone. A phone that appeared to be recording a video.

As Rachel approached, Anjali uttered the names of Rachel and God and several exclamations of utter disbelief. Lots of profanity. Many sorries. Anjali could see the tears streaming soundlessly down Rachel's cheeks, the quiver of her lower lip.

Anjali wondered if Rachel might kill her, might grab her by the hair and slam her into the wall, or the ground, or one of the stainless steel tanks that could surely hide a body and, hell, if Ahmad was setting fire to the place, what did it matter if she went up in flames with it?

What if Rachel was in on it? she wondered now, with sudden horror. What if this had been the plan all along, to get her to commit dalliances with Raj, admit them to Rachel, and then trap her here, to exact revenge on her for being an adulterous bitch now and an envious one before? An envious one all along?

Call it a crime of passion. Rachel would be exonerated. What woman wouldn't side with her? At the very least, she'd have Anjali arrested. Anjali might never hold her children again. Irony of ironies—killing Raj to do right by her daughter and losing her ability to be with her daughter in the process.

Rachel took another step. One more, and she'd close the distance between them.

Anjali panicked. She braced for a blow, a blackout, a bullet train from this world to another. She felt Rachel's hand on her back. She tried to run. Her heel buckled. The goddamn Valentino. This was why she never wore heels. She grabbed a hold of Rachel's waist to keep from falling down.

They stumbled backward, into the puddle, into the side table, the one with the glasses, the wine, the heavy-as-a-house decanter hovering just above Raj's head.

The decanter came crashing down, bouncing off his forehead before erupting on the floor.

If he hadn't been dead before, he sure was now.

"Oh my God," Rachel said. Anjali made a noise like a bird caught by the neck. The next thing she knew, Rachel's arms were around her, and she was sobbing on Rachel's shoulder.

"Don't be sorry," Rachel said. "I heard it all. I would've done the same—well, actually I don't know if I would've had the courage."

"I never . . . I thought . . . I don't know what I was thinking . . . what if he does it again, what if the justice system doesn't do its work . . . what if . . ."

"Honey," Rachel said, pulling back, "with rich people, does the justice system ever do its work?"

Anjali mustered a sound that could be construed as a chuckle. This was so beyond the scope of anything she thought she was capable of.

"When did you come in? I didn't even see you." Anjali tried to conjure their original plan, which now felt as far away as ninth-grade algebra.

"I snuck in before you guys. I don't know . . . I guess . . ." Rachel looked down at the metric ton of wine that had spilled out of the decanter, all over their shoes, mess on top of mess. "Maybe part of me didn't believe what you told me this morning. Didn't want to believe. Not the stuff about Puff—that's incontestable, what with all the evidence you gathered, all the mothers you talked to. But . . . the cheating. Him actively plotting to leave me."

It was Anjali's turn to embrace her friend. She could understand not wanting to believe, the compulsion to sweep under the rug what we did not want to admit to ourselves, let alone the world at large.

The door of the winery opened, reactivating the motion-sensor lights.

"What the," Victoria said, from the landing. "Am I that high, or . . ."

"You're not that high," Anjali said.

Victoria clicked over to them and came to a stop on a part of the floor where blood and wine had not reached. Yet.

"Tell me," she began, "that it was self-defense." (She was not a criminal defense attorney, but she had, in her previous life, as an award-winning crisis communications specialist, worked with them. Many a time. Too many late nights in legal offices to count.)

Anjali sucked air through her teeth. "I mean . . . not self, exactly, but like . . . property? Property defense? Defense of an innocent kid on an O-1 visa who shouldn't be investigated for arson? Is that a thing?" She saw the impatience on Victoria's face and attempted to explain, as sensibly as possible, that Raj was not actively trying to kill her but had plotted to burn Kismet to the ground, make Ahmad take the fall, should there be an investigation, and abscond to Turks and Caicos while he waited for the insurance money to roll in. "Insurance fraud!" Anjali exclaimed, like she was on *Family Feud*. "That's a crime, isn't it?" (For an editor of a prestigious news magazine, she knew surprisingly little about the law.)

"And you have it on tape?"

V had to actively stop herself from smiling as she crunched the numbers of this crisis. She hadn't realized how much she missed using this part of her brain. She had been using her sex appeal as a crutch, a way to feign confidence when she really felt insecure: about her divorce, about her ex-husband getting married again, about hostessing on the side. She had forgotten that she had other talents.

Rachel showed V her phone.

V nodded thoughtfully. "'Desperate Mom Takes Puff Founder into Her Own Hands.' 'Lovesick Mom Avenges Daughter's Drugging.' 'Working Mom Takes On Drug Lord Slash Arson Plotter Slash Insurance Fraudster.' Ooh, I like that last one. We'll workshop it. Of course, the publications will ultimately decide their own headlines, but it doesn't hurt to give these editors options—the less work they have to do, the better. The good news is we've got a lot to work with. The fact that you're a mom? Unbeatable.

"We'll have to edit the video, of course," she added. "Cut to the part where the decanter falls on his head."

"Of course," repeated Anjali. The thought of being search-engine optimized made her feel slightly ill. Or maybe it was the reality that his true cause of death would never be eradicated from her brain, could not be snipped from her memory with the simple slide of a finger.

"You know that Ralph's waiting outside," V went on. "He was wondering what happened."

"Are you saying we should . . . go?" Anjali ventured. "Deal with this later?" As if "this" was a heap of Legos and not a human body that would require a coroner, reams of yellow tape, and a police investigation.

"I'm saying, let's get Ralph in here *now*," V said. She strode off toward the door before waiting for an answer. "Fret not, my loves," she called, over her shoulder. "We're gonna spin this until you two look like saints. Hot saints. Saints that people want to fuck."

"Is that a thing?" Anjali asked Rachel.

Rachel shrugged. "Not that I know of, but there's a Pornhub category for everything these days."

Moments later, Ralph stormed in with Megan, who, prior to Peloton, as a New York–based criminal defense attorney, had occasionally worked with Ralph.

"Oh, oh . . . kay," Megan said as she approached the body.

"Know I'm not supposed to say this," Ralph said, "but he had it coming."

Megan walked in a slow semicircle around the perimeter where the blood had not reached, nodding to herself. Her eyes flicked up at Anjali. "You did this?"

"It was self-defense—sort of—he was plotting to burn down the winery and tasting room and blame it on his assistant. Plus there's everything he's doing with Puff—drugging children, bribery, falsification of, of, medical . . . you know, importance." She was terrible at making her case verbally. This was why she was a writer.

"Plus the decanter," Rachel chimed in. "The thing's as heavy as a house. That falls on you, you're done for."

"Babes," Megan said, touching their shoulders. "It's all good. Ahmad told us." He had approached Ralph, who had been catching up with Megan outside the winery. "He was wondering why 'Sir' hadn't texted," Megan said. "Can't believe that motherfucker made that sweet boy call him 'Sir.'" She stopped abruptly, as if she just remembered who else was in the room. "Sorry, Rachel."

Rachel shrugged once more. "No, he was a motherfucker. Well, I don't think he got that far." The corner of her mouth turned up as she glanced over at Anjali.

"You saw what happened," Anjali said. "He couldn't even wrap his head around a pair of Spanx."

"Men," Megan said, rolling her eyes.

"Maybe I always knew that he would lose interest in me," Rachel said, peering at Raj's head, thoughtfully. "Maybe . . . maybe this was how we were destined to end."

"Might as well look at it like that since it's already happened," said V.

"Awfully fatalistic for a spiritual healer, aren't you?" Rachel said.

"You know, I think the spiritual healing space could do with a dose of realism," V said, "something more concrete than auras and intentions."

"There's this guy I follow that's doing that," Ralph said. He pulled out his phone. "You should check him out."

"Guys, I don't mean to ruin the moment, but can we maybe get a move on?" Anjali said. "Do something with these voice memos? Exonerate the mom? The un-fucked mom?"

Megan laughed. "Honey, with me as your attorney, you're not going to have to worry about a thing."

"Except," Victoria said, "who to give your first interview to." She realized she had been playing small, and like Marianne Williamson said, "Your playing small does not serve the world." Conscious Confidence could encompass crisis PR. Why not? What better way to gain confidence than to put a crisis in your past? There were "Real Housewives" who started multimillion-dollar margarita-mix companies and reality television stars who got wrongfully convicted people out of jail. She didn't have to be one thing. She could be all the things. She still had her contacts. She could still hustle.

Also, if she had another revenue stream, she could stop soliciting tips from her social media followers and glomming on to aging individuals for their money.

"*Today Show*, *GMA*, *60 Minutes*—take your pick."

This was easily the front-runner for Most Feel-Good Murder of the Year. Anjali allowed herself a moment of awe before asking Megan if she did divorces, too.

"You're going back into law?" Rachel asked. Her concern was obvious. "Who's going to teach your classes?"

"I've got someone in mind," Megan said. "I've just gotta ask her."

EPILOGUE

One year later

Friday evening
The Carlyle, New York, NY

The doorman tipped his hat as Hari emerged from the revolving door, and Hari responded in kind. Except that he didn't have a hat, so he felt a little ridiculous. He would never get used to this. His old building, in Williamsburg, hadn't even had a real doorman, just a virtual one. This place had a whole staff of them, besuited men milling about the sidewalk, hands behind their backs, always watching, taking notes.

But he was in no position to complain. He had the most important thing. (He also no longer had a mortgage to pay, a windfall that more than outweighed the occasional feelings of ridiculousness and guilt and, depending on your perspective—not his, of course—might've been the actual most important thing.)

"When's the next trip out West, Mr. V?" the doorman asked genially. Hari had been advising a client in Newport Beach. He would take the 6:00 a.m. from JFK to LAX Monday morning and return home on the 10:30 a.m. out of LAX every Thursday, if he was lucky. (If he was not, it would be an afternoon flight that ate up the opportunity for a nice night out back in New York and forced him to endure murderous traffic on the 405. He tried to avoid it at all costs.)

He'd been doing that commute for two months straight. Until last week. Now, his most frequent commute was between the Carlyle and Fairway, the gourmet grocery store ten blocks north.

"No time soon, Sergio," Hari said. He held up his reusable tote, creased and cracking around the nylon logo. "At the beck and call of the boss upstairs."

Sergio chuckled. "Happy wife, happy life."

Yes, Rachel Ranjani had, at city hall, two months prior, been reintroduced to society as Rachel Venkataraman. Society encompassed Anjali and Victoria; the four of them had gone out for hot pot afterward at a place in Chinatown that Victoria swore by. The bride wore a cornflower-blue slip dress that had been borrowed from Victoria (two birds with one stone), designer unknown; Victoria had scooped it up from What Goes Around Comes Around several years before. Rachel chose it because it alluded to her future without hitting onlookers over the head in the way that something more form-fitting might.

She was pregnant. She and Hari were pregnant. She was six months along when they married. Hari had recently grounded himself to attend to his now-very-pregnant wife's wants and needs. He was, for the foreseeable future, working from home.

People would kill to live here, he reminded himself, as the elevator doors opened on the twentieth floor. After Napa—the news conferences, the press interviews, the seemingly interminable rounds of questioning from the authorities, who, unlike Ralph, did not have a vendetta against the victim—Rachel had planned to sell off every asset that reminded her of Raj. Kismet, for sure. The Trousdale estate, yes. The condo in Trump Tower, definitely. It was a post-college relic that generally went unoccupied, anyway. Or so she had thought. In light of Raj's phone records and credit card statements, a black-light sweep of the surfaces of that home—all their homes—would definitely yield more information than she cared to know. Better to sell it all off. Marie Kondo her marriage, her life. Fresh start, she told herself, new beginnings.

She hired someone to assess the smaller stuff: the Porsches, the Pateks, the Purple Label. Her walk-in closets and their contents.

(She later changed her mind about her walk-in closets and their contents. Would be a shame to effectively toss all that. Plus, what would she wear? It would be bad for the environment, buying new stuff. Better to conserve, in the name of sustainability. She also kind of liked some of the Pateks. They were investment pieces, really.)

Then she'd met with their accountant and the administrator of their trust. Like Ralph and Adolfo, neither of them had been paid in a timely manner. That's when she learned the real reason that Raj bought her a Serpenti.

"He was advised to move funds out of Puff as quickly as possible," the accountant said, "and put them into physical assets that would not be in his name, or on his person." If and when investigators asked how much of a stake he'd had in Puff, he'd be able to say zero. How could he have put hundreds of thousands of dollars into an experimental vape company when he barely had enough money to pay his multitudinous mortgages?

"It was a Hail Mary," the accountant said. "A subpoena would reveal that he'd invested in Puff, but those take time to obtain." Knowing Raj, he probably had some harebrained scheme to deal with that, too.

"What did he buy besides the watch?" Rachel asked.

"Well, there was the party at Kismet. That cost more than a mil," the accountant had said.

"Ice sculptures"—the trust administrator shook his head—"they always get you with the ice sculptures."

"And then," the accountant said, "there was this."

He presented her with a deed to a four-bedroom apartment at the Carlyle. One that went for a "song," which is what you call Upper East Side cloud-line views that cost $44 million. It had originally been listed at $60 million, justified given its location in a hotel whose regular guests included members of various royal families and Lenny Kravitz, but despite its sweeping views and pedigree, it had languished on the market, forcing the price cut.

"It's the interior," the director of sales had said, when Rachel came to New York to check it out. (She flew commercial; Kimberly and the Jet Edge membership were also casualties of the fresh start. First class wasn't so bad. The pods were cute. And you got points. It was kind of like kindergarten with alcohol.) The former owners, safari enthusiasts, had paneled the place in mahogany carved with elephants and other exotica inspired by their adventures.

"It could do with a refresh," the sales director added, when Rachel said nothing. She had paused in front of a picture window that looked out on the Central Park Reservoir.

"Could it?" Rachel replied. She kind of liked how the place felt off-kilter. Like something from another era. Like nothing Raj ever would have stood for.

She had phoned the accountant and trust administrator as she paced through the apartment and asked why Raj had chosen to spend $44 million on this, of all places.

"It's so not his style," she said. She toyed with the links of the Serpenti as she spoke. She had thought about selling it, but then justified keeping it as a kind of insurance policy. That you wore. Daily. It fit with the vibe of the apartment.

"Status," the trust administrator had said. "He said he wanted the status of having a place in the Carlyle."

"And he never stepped foot in it?" she asked. "You're certain?"

"Closed on it sight unseen," the accountant said, "five days before the Kismet opening."

Fresh starts were all well and good, but how better to say fuck you to her philandering, child-endangering, arson-and-insurance-fraud-plotting late husband than to move into his status symbol with the guy who had socked him in the face?

It was also easier. The place was already in her name.

There was a bedroom for Anjali to crash. She got the house, David had a place on the Upper West Side, but their custody agreement stipulated that he come back to the split-level so that the kids didn't have to endure weekends in a barely furnished one-bedroom with a view of a Capital One bank branch. Though she knew that Anjali would never ask, she wanted to be able to offer her friend a place to spend her child-free weekends in peace. Or in party mode, which she was fully entitled to, given that she'd spent her twenties and thirties so pent-up.

When Victoria came to town, there would be a spare room for her, too—she was splitting time between New York and Costa Cara, spinning corporate crises into tales of redemption, and teaching yoga on the beach. (Starting her own crisis communications shop meant she no longer had to hostess at Laffa, which meant she no longer had to live in Silver Lake. Not that she ever *had* to live in Silver Lake; it just seemed like the place for someone like her to be, if she was in LA. But she didn't have to be in LA. She could be in Mexico. Mexico had arguably better beaches than LA. Better backdrops too.)

She called her yoga class Conscious Confidence, but it was a simple Vinyasa flow, nothing more complicated than that. "It's just easier to not peddle bullshit," she'd told Rachel. "I didn't trust that people would come to me for me, but my last two immersions sold out." Some crisis clients even double-dipped. Sammi Ali could now touch his toes.

After years of being sequestered in the Trousdale house, of being another one of Raj Ranjani's closely held properties, Rachel wanted to be surrounded by her friends. They'd still have plenty of room for the baby. Was living in an apartment that her former husband had paid for so bad? He was dead, wasn't he?

Best of all, it was three blocks from Peloton's new studios on the Upper East Side, where Rachel would resume teaching after her maternity leave. Megan had taught her everything she knew, but Rachel had developed her own persona, as all instructors must. Her brand of rah-rah revolved around harnessing your darkness and angst to run farther and faster. "Be monstrous, be messy," she had said during a sixty-minute metal run. "Crush that workout with your bare hands."

~

Anjali slid into her usual seat at the bar at Bemelmans, to the left of the piano, as close to the "Madeline" mural as you could get while still enjoying unfettered access to Roger, her favorite bartender.

"Your usual, Ms. Sharma?" She had reverted back to her maiden name.

"You know it, Roger," she replied. She watched him shake up a dirty martini, Bombay Sapphire, three olives. As he placed it on the bar top, she slid him a ten-dollar bill—a tip, the drink itself would go on the house account. Anjali used to be the type of person who tipped a dollar per drink, if that. She now realized that was no way to move through polite society, to treat the people who sanded down the edges of your life and made it worth living.

She lowered her lips to the glass for the first sip, so as not to spill on her jumpsuit (Prada, borrowed from Rachel, who was weaning her off Rent the Runway and exposing her to what designer clothing looked and felt like when it hadn't been worn by nine hundred different women and dry-cleaned the same number of times).

Why she had denied herself the pleasure of a dirty martini for forty years, she would never understand. Well, she did understand, she only had herself to blame for being that tightly wound, but still. She had a lot of catching up to do.

She and Roger made small talk about the weather, fellow regulars, and the pianist who would begin his set shortly. She allowed the martini to do its work, made it to the halfway mark (though it was always hard to tell what constituted halfway, given the shape of the glass) before she took out her phone and pulled up the Reddit thread. Oh, Reddit. The conspiracy theorist's best friend.

She had received a Google alert when it had been published the night before. "Raj Ranjani murder: Self-defense or premeditated?" It had been started by someone who claimed to have gone to college with "a lot of the people involved" and suspected that Rachel and Anjali had been plotting to "do Raj dirty" all along. "Look who's living in the last place he purchased," another purported user (easily could've been the original poster with a different alias) had said alongside a photo of Anjali, Rachel, and Hari exiting the Carlyle, on the way to city hall. Unfortunate, Anjali thought, zooming in on her dress. Too matronly. Like something fit for the Queen Mum, God rest her soul. She was going to embrace her forties. Live like she was twenty-one. Shop at Forever 21, maybe. Or not, fast-fashion was bad. Bergdorf's. She was supposed to shop at Bergdorf's. Or shop Rachel's closet, anyway.

She pictured Sid Gupta, hunched over a laptop on Turks and Caicos, screen barely visible beneath the blinding light of the equatorial sun. Sad. Sad that you could live in such a beautiful place and fixate on the past.

The case was closed. She couldn't be tried again. Lucie was, thank every god of every religion, fine. Thriving. Priya and Rufus had flown to Napa with Lucie and Ryan when Victoria explained the situation in the calm and organized way that only a crisis communications professional could. Lucie and Ryan had proven essential at the press conferences. No one wanted to see a mom go to jail (well, besides the righteous, women-hating scandal fetishists, of which there were many). Her kids were right there! Look at how cute they were! And while Anjali thought that the separation and divorce would be too much to bear, Lucie's social anxiety had all but evaporated. Maybe it was a phase. Maybe more frequent trips to the city, now that Anjali had a place there, had opened up her world. Maybe she saw that her parents were happier this way and had responded in kind.

David was dating one of the many content creators slash wannabe authors from his DMs. Tale as old as time. Anjali did not begrudge him. David was half-formed, and he ought to be with someone in a similar state. They could form each other. They could turn into a giant blob, for all she cared.

The agency had taken David back when he told them he had signed the Guerrilla Somm. The Somm had come to New York, signed a new "360 deal" with David and Archetype. The Somm had since used the first half of his advance to relocate to the South of France. The memoir was more than six months late.

None of this was Anjali's problem, as long as the child support checks cleared. Her own book, a loosely fictionalized version of that weekend in wine country, had yet to be published but had already started a bidding war in Hollywood. She wanted to adapt the book herself. She might be the one with a place in Beverly Hills, after all was said and done. If she kept her best interests at heart and stayed on top of her game. Once you started pulling in money, once you began building your own empire, your attitude changed. In her nascent view, you had two options once you accrued a measure of success: die and be a hero, or live long enough to see yourself become a villain, a paradox elucidated by both *The Dark Knight* and a Kanye West track in frequent rotation on a playlist she had titled "Bad Bitch O'Clock."

Highbrow's parent company had asked her to take a leave of absence in the immediate aftermath of "the Kismet killing," as the local news stations called it. "I'll do you one better," she had said. "I quit."

It was true that people generally did not have the mental capacity to conjure how wrong things could possibly go. You were lucky if you could see ten feet in front of you, let alone a hundred. But the other side of that coin was that you also couldn't imagine a happy ending. How right you could end up. How your definition of right could change, how what might've seemed like disaster at one point could dissolve into a dream.

She had found her story. She had found her calling. She wanted for naught—well, not *naught*. The list seemed to get longer every day, but now everything felt more attainable than before. A place in Los Angeles. A place in Manhattan for her and the kids. Maybe a membership with one of those private jet companies, if this Hollywood deal came to pass. A second husband? A first wife? Acceptance to that dating service that was like Tinder meets Soho House? Maybe all of the above.

For sure, another martini.

She ordered a second round from Roger and refreshed the Reddit thread. "Mommy murderer looking good." Another photo of her, this time in workout clothes, heading to the studio for one of Rachel's live classes. She smiled to herself and looked at the title of the thread again: "Self-defense or premeditated?" What a simplistic way to put it, ignoring all the shades of gray. As if everything in life fit into one neat category or the other. As if the answers were ever that obvious.

She double-checked which account she was signed into and tapped out a reply.

"Can't it be both?"

ACKNOWLEDGMENTS

Thank you to my agent, Claire Friedman. Thank you to my publishing team, Carmen Johnson, Sangeeta Mehta, and everyone at Amazon Publishing. Thank you to Mindy Kaling for selecting this book for your imprint.

Thank you to my real-life friends in and around Napa: Kim Elwell, Jennifer Chiesa, Christian Navarro, and the many wineries that have opened their doors to me, including Realm, Cardinale, Promontory, Marciano Estate, Mark Herold, Faust, Darioush, Aperture, Ashes & Diamonds, and the Boisset Collection. Thank you especially to Annie Favia-Erickson and Andy Erickson for your hospitality and wine making (and fictional meddling) expertise.

Thank you to my friends in hospitality and real estate, especially Gaggan Anand, Marko Kovac, Alan and Susan Fuerstman, Ben Kephart, Sarah Chabot, Chrissy Bruchey, Tessa Nasso, Lauren Kita, Tracey Manner, Sheila Smith, and Alexander Ali. Thank you to the friends who continually support my work, especially Michelle Lam, Ashley Aull, Aishwarya Iyer, Jen Betts, Ameya Pendse, Zain Ahmad, Laurel Touby, and Jon Fine.

Thank you to Risa Heller for educating me on what a crisis communications professional does, and to Amy Chozick for introducing us.

Thank you to my first readers and friends who provided crucial feedback: Tanvi Patel, Amrutha Jindal, Lina Patton, Ankur Dalal, Colleen McKeegan, Avery Carpenter Forrey, Liz Riggs, and Brittany

Kerfoot. Thank you especially to Diana Myint and Aditya Bhatia for making these characters more realistic and not at all like anyone we know. Thank you to the authors who've given me space to think and plot, especially Caroline Kepnes, Andi Bartz, Kate Myers, Amanda Montell, and Kevin Kwan.

Thank you to the loved ones that gamely helped with research during a 2022 trip to Napa: Ritu Lal, Halsey "Christopher" Harper, Nicole Lal, and Niraj Lal. Thank you to Padma Marikar, Sriram Subramanyam, and the many other members of my family who are perpetually up for a glass.

I owe a debt of gratitude to my friends from Cornell University, and the friends I've met through them: Sukumar Mehta, Sachin and Sapana Kulkarni, Tejas Amin, Anurag and Robin Kumar, Vanisha and Rajan Raval, Ankit Patel, Shiv and Angela Hira, John and Alexa Kranzley, Ritwik Rastogi, Dong Lee, John Kuoy, Naveen Gulati, Matt Van Lewen, Julie Oleskiewicz, Madhu Soma, Aarti Reddy, Stephanie Kwai, Rakhi Garg and Ravi Sutaria, Megha Madhukar, Bansari Modi Shah, Amee Shan, Kanika Mathur and Shalin Patel, and Aemish Shah—thank you.

Thank you, finally, to Nikhil Lal, who introduced me to fine wine and helped sketch out this story over a bottle of something that must've been special. Alas, no evidence of it exists.

ABOUT THE AUTHOR

Photo © Will Tee Yang

Sheila Yasmin Marikar is the author of *The Goddess Effect*. Her work has appeared in the *New Yorker*, the *New York Times*, the *Economist*, *Fortune*, *Bloomberg Businessweek*, *Vogue*, and many other publications. She is a graduate of Cornell University, where she studied history, and lives in Los Angeles with her husband. For more information, visit www.sheilayasminmarikar.com.